R. Rushfort
Blundell's S<
Kent. He has
years, mostly
in the Crime;
Cairo.

He has published poetry in a variety of
magazines, and helps run the *Poetry on
the Lake* festival in Orta, on the Italian Lakes.

The author was awarded an Arts Council Grant to assist the
completion of *The Gift of Honey.*

THE GIFT OF HONEY

R. RUSHFORTH MORLEY

Indigo Dreams Publishing

First Edition: The Gift of Honey

First published in Great Britain in 2012 by:
Indigo Dreams Publishing Ltd
132 Hinckley Road
Stoney Stanton
Leics
LE9 4LN
www.indigodreams.co.uk

R. Rushforth Morley has asserted his/her right under the Copyright, Designs and Patents Act 1988 to be identified as the author of this work.
©2012 R. Rushforth Morley

ISBN 978–1–907401–90–9

British Library Cataloguing in Publication Data. A CIP record for this book can be obtained from the British Library.

Designed and typeset in Minion Pro by Indigo Dreams.

Printed and bound in Great Britain by Imprint Academic, Exeter

Ac yno yd oed udunt lle teg brenhineid uch benn y weilgi, ac yneuad uawr oed, ac y'r neuad y kyrchyssant. A deu drws a welynt yn agoret; y trydyd drws oed y gayat, yr hwnn y tu a Chernyw. 'Weldy racco,' heb y Manawydan, 'y drws ny dylywn ni y agori.'

Mabinogion, Branwen Ferch Lyr

(And there at their disposal was a beautiful kingly palace high above the ocean – and a great hall it was. They went into the hall. They saw two open doors – the third door was closed, and that was the one facing Cornwall. 'Look over there,' said Manawydan, 'the door which must never be opened.')

For Amelia, without whose love and support this book

would never have been written.

ACKNOWLEDGEMENTS

Many people offered their support and encouragement while I was writing this book. I am especially grateful to: my triumvirate of tutors at Bath Spa University for starting me on the road; to Massimo Bocchiola, Isobel Dixon, Sarah Freimuller and Gabriel Griffin for their comments on drafts of the novel at various stages; to Phin Hall, for his bee-lore; and to Alessandra Fuccillo for her photograph. Bless you all.

I am also grateful to the Arts Council, England (South West) for a generous grant that enabled me to complete this novel.

THE GIFT OF HONEY

1846

Dear Miss Sorely,

Your brother would take me for an upstart Joseph were I to parade about his chancel in such a coat as this. Besides, it comes too soon upon our altercation over the Missionary Society, and I dare do nothing that might antagonise him further.

Yet it is exquisite! I cannot thank you enough. For this is just such a priestly vestment as the saintly Froude would have urged upon the clergy of his church. How right you have read my thoughts! And what fine workmanship: such a lovely blue, such warm reds, and all overlaid with a filament of gold!

More the pity, dear Miss Sorely, that I can never wear it. It is the badge of a school of thought that is too progressive for our little town. And for all the show you make of this being a gift from the sewing circle, I know that the idea must have been 'sown' by our fireside chats last winter, and suspect that the workmanship also is entirely your own.

And even you must see that this chasuble would cause tongues to wag if I were to wear it in church. For what would the Miss Whittamores have to say? They would guess its origins straight out, and must take it as a sign of an intimacy between us that goes beyond the simple spirit of Christian charity in which I know that it was given. I trust you to believe me if I say that your gift will be put to good use nonetheless, for I shall wear it in the privacy of my own room to say my morning prayers.

Your grateful friend

Richard Mudge

*(from **The Western Daily Mercury**, February 21ˢᵗ)*

On the evening of Wednesday last, the congregation of St John's, Frome, was addressed by Joseph Cameron, a representative of the London Missionary Society. He engrossed his audience with an account of the progress currently being made among the Hottentot and the Bechuana tribes in the Cape Colony.

Mr Cameron spoke principally of Robert Moffat's work among the natives, and of his valiant efforts to master the Tswana language, so that the Holy Scriptures might be translated into this African tongue. He gave such an account of Moffat's dealings with cannibals and with slave-traders that his listeners were in equal measure horrified and enthralled.

The curate of St John's, the Revd Richard Mudge, brought much colour to the proceedings with a dramatised rendition of the conversion of a Hottentot village. However, the comedy was curtailed after the vicar, the Revd Alfred Sorely, protested over the unseemly attire of the Frome Sewing Circle, who portrayed the village headman's several wives.

The evening raised the sum of three pounds, seven shillings and fourpence, to be donated towards the London Missionary Society's funds.

* * *

Lucy, Mudge's sister, to Arthur Kennington, February

Dear Mr Kennington,

I have read your new catalogue with great interest, and though I am little given to music myself, I can see that such a vast array of instruments would be to those that were.

As to my being at Prompton Lodge when next you come, it is unlikely. Indeed, I hope I shall not be, for it would mean that my sister-in-law were unwell again. Nevertheless, I have taken note of the days that you are to be in Bath, and will try to visit Grace that same week. We must make hay while the sun shines, as my father used to say, and I too have such fond memories of your first visit, as to look forward to a second.

How considerate of you to remember Isobel's birthday! I have refashioned her hair since you knew her, and what with that, and the rate at which children grow, I doubt you would recognise her now. But she is too headstrong, for all her prettiness, and sometimes I wonder how I shall be able to manage such a young woman as she is soon to grow into.

Were it not for my brother, I would say we were faring middling well. But he is always in one scrape or another, and especially with Mister Sorely, the vicar. Now he talks of becoming a missionary and leaving off for Africa, which I cannot see that he is suited for. Why, Richard could hardly cope with Somerset had he not me to fend for him, for all he is the graduate of an Oxford college. And after what we heard recently at a talk on the swarthy tribes of the Cape, I should think my brother need first learn to practise living at peace with his neighbours in a godly society such as this before he traipses off to Africa. Suppose he gets off on as bad a footing with the chief of a band of head-hunters as he has done with Mister Sorely? His prospects do not bear thinking about. I lie awake at nights terrified at the thought of him being broiled in a pot. Besides, the vicar is a patient man, and though Richard means no harm, he is much given to his enthusiasms, which he has in excess.

Yet nor is he safe in Frome, either. For Mister Sorely's sister has stirred late to start her search for a husband, and schemes to be at tea with him every day, either here or at the vicarage. She's quite set her cap at him, and Richard is such an innocent in these matters that he will not see it. It is indecent to see the way she clucks and ogles over a boy like that. He aims at grander things than being a curate in Frome, and though I cannot but wish that he should stay with us, yet would I see him achieve his ambitions, if they are to bring him happiness. Yet to go so far away, and to work in such uncivilised parts – I cannot see that suiting him either. Whether he falls into the clutches of Alice Sorely, or sacrifices his life to the Missionary Society, I cannot see him safe and prospering.

I feel I must thank you once again for your advice. Captain Pelham has written to uphold my late husband's petition, as you assured me he must. Although the pension provides us with but a small income, it is at least secure, which is enough to allay the worst of my anxieties.

I count the days till you next come to Bath.

Lucy

* * *

The Bishop of Bath and Wells to the Revd Mudge, April

Dear Mudge,

I am writing to acknowledge your generous gift, and thought that you may wish to know that I have distributed the twelve pounds of honey as follows: two jars have gone to the deanery, five have been sent out to various almshouses in Taunton and Wells and four have been reserved for our own kitchen. The one remaining jar was offered to Doctor McBride, who is a cousin to my wife. McBride, as I expect you know, is an Edinburgh apiculturist of considerable repute, and his favourable remarks on your 'Somerset Garden Blend', have alerted me to yet another of the talents to be found among the clergymen of this diocese.

Are you sure that such skills as yours would not be wasted among the Hottentots? I have given your wishes to apply to the London Missionary Society considerable attention, and after corresponding with Alfred Sorely on the matter, I cannot but doubt whether your wish to engage in missionary work in

South Africa is not fuelled as much by a desire to escape the restrictions of your present appointment as by any genuine vocation. From the tone of the Reverend Sorely's remarks, and from my own observations during last month's trip to Frome, I have formed the opinion, perhaps erroneously, that there exists at St John's one of those unfortunate incompatibilities of character between a vicar and his curate which, while not necessarily the fault of either, is yet the bane of both.

May I therefore make a counter proposal? The Bishop of Exeter tells me that there is a vacant living at Lancaradoc, in the extreme west of his diocese. The parish is something of an anomaly, and I would be hesitant of offering it to a more conventional candidate than yourself. Lancaradoc has had no incumbent for the past six years, and has in the interim been but fitfully served by a neighbouring clergyman. While Lancaradoc is little in itself, the sea-town of Porthcado lies within the parish, at a few miles distance from the church. The harbour town, however, where it has not forgone those dissolute ways which so marked the Cornishmen of the last century, has quite gone over to Wesley. Moreover, the living is poor – a mere eighty pounds per annum – notwithstanding the grandiose scale of the ancient rectory. In taking on such a parish you could perhaps consider yourself as embarking on missionary work in an area of Great Britain which has been nominally Christian for fifteen centuries, but which – as far as the established church is concerned – remains as pagan as anywhere in the hinterland of Cape Province.

With God's blessing

Michael Pallingham
Lord Bishop of Bath and Wells

* * *

Lucy to Arthur Kennington, June

15

Dear Mr Kennington,

I shall be staying at Prompton Lodge on the Monday and Tuesday of next week, for I have to buy lace to furnish the parlour with new curtains. Anyone hereabouts will tell you that Mateley's on Walcot Street is the only place in Somerset for fabrics, so you needn't flatter yourself that I shall be coming to Bath only for the pleasure of your company! Nonetheless, I hope that the coincidence that brings us both to Bath again is as pleasing to yourself as it is to me.

I am glad that the Wheatstone concertina has, as you put it, caught the public's attention; it is so much smaller than a piano that I cannot see any housewife begrudging it cupboard–space, although to my ear it sounds excessively noisy.

Yes, Richard has left us. We engaged a local man to take his luggage and himself to Bath, and after a night with my sister-in-law he took the post-chaise for Taunton, and thence to Exeter and beyond. The house is empty without him, but at least I have been able to refurnish the parlour. Books do make a room look so cluttered, don't you think?

On the evening before he left, the Vicar and his daughter insisted we go to tea with them. My brother accepted at once, without a thought of our own plans for a final family gathering, nor for the efforts he had seen me going to in the kitchen. I would not have minded so much were it not for my trifle: Sorely's housekeeper hasn't got the first idea of how to make a trifle. Still, the Vicar was uncharacteristically gracious, and I dare say Richard was right to make a show of parting on good terms. Alice, poor thing, looked most dejected.

Write to Prompton Lodge as soon as you reach Bath. If the weather holds, I shall willingly accompany you on a walk in Prior Park.

Lucy

Mudge to Lucy, June

My dearest Lucy,

These last few days I have been skipping like a lamb upon the hills, as happy as a schoolboy at the dawning of his holidays. The house is as old, ample and stately as it was described to me, and the church as picturesque; you cannot imagine what excitements my new living affords me, after all these months of anticipation.

The journey was sorely tedious, however, particularly once we had left Exeter behind us. On reaching Launceston we put up at the White Hart, to sleep on mattresses that were stuffed with meal – I swear it – after being fed a most inedible pie of gristle beef and Swedish root. The following day was the most miserable of my life; we traipsed across a treeless wilderness known as Foweymoor, and did not come down from it till nigh on sunset. But then to catch sight of the pinnacles of my own church in the distance, peeking up above the trees where it nestles in the valley; I confess that my eyes prickled with moisture at the sight, and I began the Lord a hymn of praise in my heart that I am singing still.

I was met by Mrs Tredennick, a dour old matron whose husband is the apothecary in Porthcado. She tells me with great pride that her mother was housekeeper here before her, in the days of Rector Routlidge. It would appear that he died seven years ago last month; that Lancaradoc has been utterly neglected in the meantime was not something that the Bishop saw fit to tell me, and the consequent slide towards Methodism in the parish is, alas, even worse here than is generally the case in these parts. Mrs T has a wart on her chin, and is stouter; otherwise she is the very image of our beloved Dotty.

Although she is most niggardly in her conversation, she

17

had prepared the house as comfortably as I could have hoped for, given its long disuse, and seems a most able and diligent woman. On the first night she made me up a truckle bed in the kitchen, though on the morrow I insisted that she move the bed, together my trunk, upstairs to the large room above the parlour, the weather remaining remarkably clement for the season, so that I shall not be too inconvenienced by the lacunae which afflict the roof. Besides, my first proprietorial act has been to send to Delabole for new slates, and I am assured that they will be delivered to Porthcado when the Bideford packet next puts in.

I have discovered the four vests which you sneaked into my box, and Tendall's water–colours survived the move unharmed. Although I should chastise you for squandering your widow's mite on me in this way, I have not the heart, and instead I thank you, and bless you, for the gift of such fine linen undershirts. These I shall keep for Sundays.

Ditto, darling Isobel's handkerchiefs. How neat her R.L.M. upon them; I never would have believed a babe could do such fine stitch–work, had I not the evidence of it here before my eyes.

I think of you both with the utmost affection, but, needless to say, of the Vicar of St John's with none. Nor the society of the Miss Whittamores' tea dances neither, after such a lucky escape from their clutches! Like the apostles of old, I shake the dust of Frome from my feet, and am happy to start this hermit life in the distant West.

And so, dear Lucy, your brother is Rector of Lancaradoc at last! I shall write a more fulsome letter shortly, but for now, Mrs T has agreed to take this to the village, for a boat leaves for Bristol in the morning, which gives me hope of its reaching you before the month is out.

* * *

Dearest Sister,

I do assure you there is no cause for alarm. I blame myself for even mentioning the roof, which as I write is under repair. I have engaged a Mr William Honeycutt, and his son Simon, for the summer, and am assured that they will not only carry out essential repairs, but restore my new abode to all its historic splendour before the gales of autumn are upon us.

The house, if only you could see it, Lucy, is as handsome as could be wished for, and its present state really not so lamentable as you suppose. The rectory stands upon a natural ledge of ground in the shape of a crescent, between the moor to the north, from which it is separated by a commodious lawn, and a wooded ravine to the south, in which the church is situated. The house is low, consisting of but two storeys, both very low–ceilinged, as was the custom at the time of its original construction. For a century it served as the manor farm to the Fitzpaine family, until they lost their lands in the Civil War. Their arms are still embossed above the porch: a sturdy, square construction with crenellations. Although this too is low, and cannot have served any military purpose, it confers upon the house a most quaint and chivalrous aspect.

On walking through it, a visitor may be forgiven for thinking that the original architect was pisky-led (see, like Moffat, I am become a student of the native tongue!), for they find themselves immediately entering the kitchen. This, after the Cornish fashion, runs the whole length of the house, save for a short connecting corridor at the eastern end, and backs onto another room of similar proportions: a most exquisite apartment, filled with the morning sunlight through three tall windows, that run on to the floor above. Indeed, had the porch been attached here, to what must have made a most impressive manorial hall in the days of the Fitzpaines, I would not hesitate to call this the front of the house. As it is, the rectory is built to such a topsy-turvy design, that I am quite at a loss to know which to call the front, and which the back.

The house has one curious feature which would intrigue young Isobel. In both the kitchen and the hall, which will serve me as a parlour, as upstairs in a corresponding situation, can be seen small doors set in the wooden panelling. Mrs T, on my enquiring of their purpose, mumbled something about their opening onto the 'spirit chimney': for it was the custom in those superstitious days, when the house was laid out, to incorporate a blind vertical passageway, or chimney, for ghosts to walk in, to discourage them from disturbing the other inmates of the house.

With Sunday last, I have now met my congregation at the Communion for the third time: a small band of the faithful, and to call them select would be charitable, but misleading. Of the dozen or so bodies that fill the pews, no more than two or three are counted among the society of the village, the most substantial being Farmer Lobb and Mr Ruan, whose adjacent farms occupy much of the upland portion of the parish. These two gentleman, accompanied by their wives and families, take up opposing seats in the nave and south aisle respectively, and conduct a silent feud of antique origin by glowering and tut-tutting, so that the whole congregation is quite intimidated by them. Of a more friendly disposition is Mr Tredennick, our apothecary, who is as loquacious as his wife is diffident. She, poor woman, has been kept from church these three Sundays running by head pains, which not even her husband's ministrations can cure. Also, there is a Mrs Lorneville, a most charming gentlewoman here from Surrey, along with her daughter Nancy, who will favour us with their society until the autumn.

As to your question concerning the curious dedication of

this church, I have learnt but little myself. St Cadoc appears to have been an abbot from Wales, and both Lancaradoc and Porthcado take their names from this good monk. Were you here, you would find little to marvel over at having such an outlandish and unbiblical saint for a patron, as most of the churches of Cornwall take their names from such figures. Indeed, they say that 'There are more saints in the land of Cornwall than there are in Heaven'. Who such men may have been, and how they lived, poses some intriguing questions, and might provide me with a suitable subject for scholarly research once the long winter nights set in.

As to the impertinence of Revd Sorely, I shall write to him at once to tell him that he shall not have the chasuble back, for it was a gift to myself in person from the sewing circle, and is decidedly not the property of St John's.

1847

My dear sister,

I likewise have had my share of ailments this winter. Most recently a heavy cold, caught while reading a burial service in the rain.

Lancaradoc is proving a grim living, Lucy: never a baptism, never a wedding, but only a succession of dreary funerals! For the Methodists have no burial ground of their own in the parish and I must act as their undertaker. Already this winter I have officiated at six funerals, which is one more than I had in my congregation last Sunday. And it is hard to look into the faces of the mourners at the graveside and see them sullen with resentment, because they are forced to come to me to see their dear ones laid to rest.

The weather continues bleak and stormy. On weekdays I have no company other than that of the censorious Mrs T, and on Sundays but that of a few loons from the village along with the feuding farmers. When I remember our jolly fireside teas in Robins Lane, and Isobel lighting the candles last Christmas eve, such a dull void opens up before me that I am tempted to despair.

Look what my pride has brought upon me: an idle title, an empty edifice, and you, my dears – my only family – so far away. For to be a Rector in this wilderness is a mockery; the petty darts I suffered in Frome were nothing, for all my protestations.

There, it is out! Things are not so bad; it is only the time of year, and a lack of company. To tell you the truth, I am as lonely as a dog. Perhaps this is a just chastisement for my pretensions and my lack of faith. I hope the Spring will bring relief.

I can indeed explain the stain on the chasuble. It was caused by a spadeful of 'mun' – this being the local fertiliser, a fermentation of decaying pilchards – flung at me for risking a procession through the village in honour of the Epiphany, to which certain Dissenters in Porthcado took exception. Should the stain prove resistant to his housekeeper's laundry, then Alfred Sorely may wear it proudly: after all it was gained in the Church's service.

Write to me instead of how you celebrated Isobel's birthday: I cannot believe that she has outstripped the wainscoting in the hall. Will you go with the Kenningtons to Malvern at Easter? How I pray that the coming year may bring some upturn in your fortunes, sister.

*   *   *

Mudge to Lucy, April

Lucy,

You ask for news, and news you shall have – though there is little in the parish that would pass for such in the great world, and even less in the way of events at the rectory to cause any tongues to wag.

My principle excitement recently derives from the bees, for I have had an idea. Suppose it were possible to design a hive in such a way that the Queen Bee were confined to only part of it, while her subjects were encouraged to deposit their nectar in a second, much larger chamber: would it not then be possible to remove this Royal Apartment from the Industrious City when the time came to garner the honey, and thus preserve the court intact? With this in mind I have drawn up two designs, one with the two chambers joined at the shoulder as it were, and the other

23

at the foot, for I am assured both by the scholars I am in correspondence with, and by my own observation of the hives I have split, that the Queen establishes her court in the very centre of the hive and is not much given – unlike our young Victoria – to travelling about her realm. But just think of the advantages of it, Lucy: an enduring hive, from which the honey could be extracted without exterminating its producers. Even in a craft as ancient as mine, there is scope for Science and Ingenuity to beget Innovation and Progress, in this field as in so many others.

But I am indulging my enthusiasm, and have quite exhausted my stock of capitals! You will accuse me of preaching when it is not a Sunday, and conversing on subjects which are scarcely fit for the drawing room.

There was an incident here last week which would amuse you more, and though to report it abroad might be regarded as trading in scandal, I am sure that Frome is a safe distance away, and that by confining this account of it to a letter to yourself, I am doing no more than whisper across the family hearth. Moreover, I regret to have to say that it took place in my own church. Thank heavens that St Cadoc's is such an exclusive club that no breath of what happened here has blown towards the Methodists down the valley. For once, I must be grateful for the prevailing wind, which blows up the valley from Porthcado, but only rarely does the air which blows first over Lancaradoc have any influence on the harbour town.

It concerns those pillars of our Anglican congregation, Dennis Lobb and George Ruan. Both these worthy yeomen hold their tenancies from Sir Harry Plumley, the local magnate, and with Quarter Day nearly upon us, have been treating with Plumley's agent over the next three months' rent. Imagine Ruan's surprise when he offers his customary twenty pound, and the agent sucks in his cheeks and says Sir Harry has in an offer in for twenty-three. But Polgarrick has been farmed by the Ruans since Doomsday, surely Plumley wouldn't take on another tenant? Not generally, no, but with all this new mining money about times are hard even for the squire. There's nothing for Ruan to do but make a counter offer of twenty-five pounds, even though, with another harvest like last year's, it'll mean the end of him.

This much is what Tredennick explains to me in the vestry afterwards. All I know of the matter is that when I begin on the psalm, 'The Lord is my shepherd', which of course is the twenty-third, up speaks a voice in the chancel, saying, 'Here George, why don't you offer to read the Parson psalm twenty-five?' The voice is Farmer Lobb's. By the time I've got to 'He maketh me lie down in green pastures', George Ruan has clambered over the pews, and would have thumped Lobb on the nose if Lobb's boys hadn't restrained him. They have to drag Ruan outside to the porch, where he starts to shout all manner of obscenities after his rival, while I'm doing my best to start the sermon. He must have realised that it was Lobb who put in the counter offer, just to bait him, and there's no quietening him until Mistress Ruan gets up and leads their four daughters out of church behind her, to take him home.

Nor was the farmers' altercation the only instance of strange behaviour I have been subjected to recently. A week ago I was woken in the middle of the night by the most peculiar of antics.

Have you ever had that disagreeable sensation of being dragged from slumber by some untoward disturbance? That was how it started. I could not tell what, or how, but something had caused me to wake with a jolt. I lay under the blankets, puzzled and amazed, for normally I am the soundest of sleepers. Then, beneath the rafters, I heard a scraping and a thud. What was it? Ghosts? For an instant, so disoriented was I, that the notion did

25

entertain my thoughts. Well then, rats? Yet it was too loud a noise, and, as I perceived it, too slow and rhythmical to be the scampering of vermin. I lay upon my back, fully awake now, and gave my ears my whole attention. A minute went by in silence. Then I heard the sound again: a slow scraping and a bumping, concluding with a thud. My best deduction was that it were some form of large bird that had somehow entangled itself with the chimney pots, perhaps a seagull with a length of fishing line about its foot. As I listened again to the scrape, scrape across the tiles, I could imagine the bird dragging itself up across the roof, and launching itself into airy freedom, only to be pulled up short by the length of twine that bound it, and collapsing on the slates with a dull thud. Once I had formed this picture for myself – completely erroneous, as it turned out – I was able to listen to the sound with complete equanimity.

How ingenuous is the human mind: enough that it has an explanation for a phenomenon, and it falls into a false tranquillity! For we humans can bear anything but mystery – and yet it is in mystery that we are forced into the world, and in mystery that we are forced out of it again. Isn't that a fitting theme for a fine sermon, sister?

I was listening to my trapped seagull on the roof, wishing it well in its attempts to gain its freedom, and almost lulled back to sleep by the regularity of the repeated sounds, when I was startled alert once again. For this time the scrape, scrape, thud, was unmistakably accompanied by the sound of a man singing.

There was nothing for it but to pull on some clothes, and light the lamp, for all it was but two in the morning. I took up a stout ash–plant, fought down the fear of what might be awaiting me, and unlatched the kitchen door. Moreover, I did well to resist the terrors of villainy that can assail a man in the dead of night,

26

for as soon as I stepped out into the cabbage patch to get a clear view of the roof, the matter was resolved. For there was the builder, old Mr Honeycutt, perched up upon the gable–end, and he was as drunk as an egg. I told him sharply to get on down, and demanded to know what he thought he was doing. He slithered down the ladder and announced, with much mangled apology, that he'd thought fit to check his handiwork, and professed himself satisfied that his slates were packed down as 'snug tight as the barnacles on Noah's boat'. And now that he knew it, he could sleep soundly, and so could I, and with a 'Goodnight Parson', he was off, meandering through the trees to Porthcado and to bed.

I took his advice, though I scarcely needed it, and slept like a babe. On the morrow, I could not help but be bemused by this eccentric behaviour, which serves to show just how bizarre, and how undisciplined, but also – ultimately – how well-intentioned these Cornish people are.

I have not mentioned that I have discovered another bee-keeper in my parish, a certain Mr Haddon who keeps a cottage in a secluded stretch of woodland further up the valley. Nor, having met him, am I surprised that he lives alone, for his habits are not those that are tolerated in civil society; nay, not even in one as rudimentary as ours. If I might be frank, Lucy, he is given to the vice of frequent expectoration, made freely and noisily, and quite without regard for the company he finds himself in. Also, he speaks with such a thick dialect of these parts that I can scarce tell a third of what he says. However, with the bees he is as knowing as Solomon, and understood my improved design for the hive at once.

But Lucy, I see I have climbed into the saddle of my favourite hobby-horse again, and you would not thank me for riding rough shod into your parlour on it. Perhaps, therefore, it is time for me to bid you a fond adieu.

27

Mudge to Lucy, October

Dear Lucy,

I am fresh back from Truro, much invigorated, and girded for those duties which my calling has imposed upon me. It is a most fine town, whether in respect of its commerce, society or architecture, and to have such a metropolis at the distance of a day's journey is a considerable consolation. The Dangerfields made me most welcome. They have a spacious house on Lemon Street; the most fashionable boulevard in town, and one to match anything that is to be found in Bath.

Above all, I had the good fortune to attend a lecture by Dr David Rees MA, from Pembrokeshire, who, as coincidence would have it, is also a fellow of my old college. The learned scholar is an acknowledged authority on the Welsh saints, and has been travelling our county collecting information for a forthcoming pamphlet on the doings of these Celtic holy men here in Cornwall, the results of which he kindly shared with a small audience of Cornish churchman in Dean Dangerfield's drawing room a week since.

That talk, together with our conversation over supper the following evening, has fired my imagination as little else has done since the Divinity tripos, and as a result I am encouraged to attempt a little research of my own to augment the Doctor's worthy study. For here at last is the beginning of a systematic understanding of those quaint hermits who once peopled this remote peninsular.

Dr Rees categorises the Cornish saints into three waves, three orders, and four major families – categories which overlap, but do not necessarily coincide with each other. The first wave corresponds to those saints of Penwith who crossed over from Ireland to land in the district of the Hayle estuary, where many of them were butchered by the local potentate, a certain King Tewdrig. Thus, in this part of Cornwall we find many martyrs, such as St Erth, St Euny, St Ives and St Anta, all originating in Ireland, and divided equally between the sexes.

A second wave originated in Wales, where they are associated with St Illtud's foundation at Llantwit Major, and these saints settled along the banks of the Camel estuary, where they were more successful in establishing themselves: so much so that their monasteries, such as that of St Petroc in Bodmin, flourished until the Reformation. Such figures – and I am happy to say that our own Cadoc is among their number – were all men, and as orthodox Christians as the Dark Ages would permit of.

A third wave, one of fanatical hermits, with whom all kind of fantastical legends and superstitions are associated, also sullied the shores of Cornwall, alas, bringing with them customs that were more pagan than Christian. Thus one has nonsensical stories of saints who slew dragons, who confounded their enemies with curses, who vied with one another to cross the Bristol Channel employing such unseaworthy means as mill stones, leaves, dolphins, barrels, altar stones, and granite sarcophagi, as well as tales of licentious virgins who were the mothers of other saints, and so on and so forth.

Next, the good Doctor quoted an eighth century Irish author, to the effect that there existed three different 'ordines' styled respectively 'sanctissimus,' 'sanctior,' and 'sanctus', each possessing characteristics of its own, and each gaining ascendancy in the country in three successive periods respectively. The first seems to have observed the rites of the Gallic church, continuing the traditions of Roman Britain. The second, who built their churches in stone rather than wood, and who had learnt to purge their ranks of woman in keeping with the modern practice, seem to have had contact with the churches of Asia Minor, according to an intriguing suggestion offered by Dr Rees – and indeed, there are stories of many of these figures undertaking considerable journeys to Rome and Jerusalem, even, in the case of St Petroc, as far afield as India. The third order were wild hermits, practising asceticisms which rival any extremity to be found in China and Thibet, who followed no episcopal or abbatial authority, and had diverse rules and customs regarding Easter, tonsures, liturgies etc.

Thus clear groupings of the numerous saints of Cornwall can begin to be formulated: we can speak with most certainty, both as historians and as Churchmen, of those associated with St Illtud's school, with which are associated the illustrious names of St David of Wales, St Samson of Dôl, and St Petroc of Bodmin. Then there are those unfortunate Irish missionaries who suffered martyrdom at the hands of King Tewdrig. Beyond this, there is a riot of semi-Druidical figures, which clusters around the names of King Brychan – a mythical Welsh figure who reputedly sired twelve sons and twelve daughters, all of whom are venerated as saints – and King Lud, a native Cornishman whose claim to sainthood was passed down through five successive generations, and whose descendants include St Just, a figure remembered in the popular imagination only for his theft of St Keverne's communion plate!

Lucy, you cannot imagine how this meeting has altered my spirits. Even the approach of winter no longer hangs heavy with me, for it shall not be a repetition of the last. Through the instrument of Dr Rees, I feel that my prayer to be given useful work has been answered, and even – who knows? – my secret wish to undertake literary endeavour may yet be granted. We have arranged that I am to make a study, in the first instance, of Cadoc himself, partly through various medieval lives the Doctor has directed me to, but also by collating any folk memories of the holy monk as can be gleaned in the parish; thereafter I shall be engaged with similar undertakings concerning those members of St Illtud's band as are celebrated in the parishes hereabouts – work, Lucy, which will bolster me against the solitudes and remoteness I am forced to endure.

But to a tale which will be of more immediate interest to you, sister – our jolly farmers. A fortnight before I left for Truro, I determined to take the bull by the horns (if you will forgive such a vulgar, but so apt! an expression) and preached my sermon on the text from chapter five of St Matthew's gospel: 'Therefore if thou bring thy gift to the altar, and there rememberest that thy brother hath ought against thee; Leave there thy gift before the altar; first be reconciled to thy brother, and then come and offer thy gift.' The upshot of this sermon was not quite what I had foreseen, for the next Sunday neither Farmer Lobb nor Mr Ruan were in church, and for congregation I was left only with Mr Tredennick, the supercilious apothecary, together with a few drab stalwarts from the village.

Later, I learnt that the farmers had transferred their allegiances to the Chapel, and learnt it indeed through a visit from the Wesleyan minister himself, a Captain Penworthy. Imagine my surprise when, on the eve of my departure for Truro, Mrs T showed him into the parlour, which at that moment was strewn about with the preparations for the journey. Now the Reverend Penworthy, as he is known in the village, struck me as a most sensible man; and one who performed twenty years' sterling service as captain of the Bideford packet before giving himself over to the Dissenters' cause. Although he refused the sherry I offered him, he accepted a cup of Mrs T's tea and waived aside my apologies for the state of the room. What, if he might discard with the customary introductions, had I said to Messrs Lobb and Ruan to drive them from the Established Church, and into his own fold? Straight out, I told him. I even offered to show him my sermon, for as you know I am most meticulous to keep a copy of whatever I preach. Could he borrow it? Although his request surprised me, I saw no reason not to comply.

Would you credit it, Lucy, but that the Captain preached my self-same sermon from the Methodist pulpit on the Sunday I was in Truro! My very text, repeated word for word. I have heard in the village – indeed, it would be difficult not to, for the talk recently has been of little else – that the two new members of his congregation rose as one, both very choleric in the face, and marched out through the chapel door before the sermon was half read. And that on Sunday last neither they, nor their families, nor their dependants, were seen either here at St Cadoc's, nor among the Wesleyans in Porthcado.

1848

My dearest Lucy,

This is most excellent news, and I am delighted for you both. However, though I do not wish to flatter myself, I must admit that your letter has hardly caused the sensation you imagined, for I had envisaged just such a match months ago. If anything, I had grown impatient for this announcement of an event which, in my mind's eye, had already received heaven's mandate. Nor could you have chosen a better date: there is something quite romantic in marrying on the last day of the year. What a pity I am so far removed from Frome, for I would give my eye teeth to be able to join you. Nonetheless, dear Sister, I urge you to 'go forth unto His temple in joy', for the Lord has seen fit to recompense you for your years of tribulation.

At Lancaradoc things are very middling – no, worse: for your brother is in a nice quandary and no mistake! Just as I was congratulating myself for passing this second winter with such equanimity, the parish has unleashed a storm upon me as wild as anything this exposed peninsular is subject to.

It began quietly enough. I had asked Mr Honeycutt to construct two new hives to set against the north wall, in the expectation that the bees there will feed upon the heather out on the moor, rather than on the woodland flowers as the present ones do. On Thursday last, his son Simon came to install these hives, and with him was Amos Provis, a gross irreligious fellow and a denizen of The Falcon. However, not wishing to be uncharitable, I invited them both for a generous breakfast in the kitchen before they began their work, then retired to my duties. Nor was this approach mistaken, for, on looking up from my work, I could see that Mr Provis was a most dextrous labourer, whatever his habits when his working hours are over, and that the hives had been assembled – and most sturdily set, just as I had instructed – within the hour. Later I went out, thinking to thank them for their efforts, when young Honeycutt touched his cap and asked if, begging my pardon, Mr Provis might have a word with me. It crossed my mind to wonder why Mr Provis could not have asked for himself, for he scarcely seems a timid man, and was indeed fixing me most steadily with his stare while young Simon made his request for him.

I assented, and led him indoors, curious to discover what need such a man should have of his parson.

No sooner were we in the parlour, and I invited him to sit, than he took out a clay and lit it, just as if he were in the snug of The Falcon. The very insolence of it! – obviously the man had not come for confession.

We sat for a while and the brawny fellow eyed me from within his foul cloud of tobacco. I too sat and waited, aware that it would have been beneath my dignity to pre–empt the silence by offering him any small coin of conversation.

Eventually, he took the pipe from between his teeth and spoke: 'There's gentlemen in the parish that has need of the key to your vault.'

What an earth could he mean? At first I found no sense to this at all, although his tone was clearly that of an ultimatum.

The church vault? Of the families entitled to use it, two had died out centuries ago, and the third had left the county. My mind was running on grave–robbers, or as a stow-hole for murdered corpses.

No doubt because he saw my puzzlement was genuine,

the mute labourer was forced to speak again. 'Tis for the *Pydar Rose.*'

The name brought me a glimmer of understanding, for the *Pydar Rose* sails out of Boscastle, and is notorious on this coast for the illicit trade she does with France.

The very idea was preposterous: that I should allow the church vault to be used as a magazine for the storing of contraband! I told Mr Provis so at once.

'Now, Parson, that's no less than the reply I was expecting of 'ee. But will 'ee hear me out?'

I nodded – perhaps none too graciously, for I felt the man was pushing me perilously close to the limits of my Christian duty.

'There's two sides to this business, and I wish to speak plain of them both.' Then he shot me a look which – how can I convey this? – seemed to bring a touch of sincerity to his words. When he started speaking again, it crept upon my consciousness that perhaps the man was less of a blackguard than I'd taken him for. 'First, tisn't anything out of the reg'lar we'm asking of 'ee, sir. All the parsons round abouts give us a hand. Mostly, we've been storing the goods over at Fretton, in the tower there, only the Reverend Finch – well, you know his reputation, sir.'

I did indeed: a monstrous old reprobate. The gossips claim that there's several babes in his parish that have had from him more than their christening, for all he's over seventy, and they say that Bishop Phillpotts hasn't been seen in Fretton since Finch set his hounds on him, some twenty years ago.

'The Excise don't like to interfere with clergymen, but in the case of Parson Finch, we'm afeared that they might make an exception.'

'Which explains your request to me. However, I see no earthly reason – and certainly no heavenly one, either – that

35

would tempt me to comply.' I thought this rather well put.

The man Provis put his hand through his beard – he has a thick black matt of hair about his face – and stroked it. After a while, he said, 'That brings me to my second point, sir,' and went on stroking his beard.

I listened to the clock ticking, and was beginning to wonder if Mrs T had found me a bit of rabbit for my supper, when Provis started again.

'It's easy for wealthy folk like yourself to scorn the *Pydar Rose*. And I dare say her cap'n's a sly old bugger, if you'll forgive the word, Parson. In fact I know he is. And there ain't many of the crew I'd like to meet on a dark night, and certainly not if my coat was decorated with the baubles of Her Majesty's Excise. But 'tisn't of them you should think of giving your assistance to – 'tis the rest of us. There's scarcely a household down about Porthcado that could put meat on the table if it weren't for the *Rose*. What with the barley blight and the pilchards slinking off to the Bay of Bisky we've got to do what we can to scrape by. Truth were told, there's many around as would tell you how Her Majesty levies such extravagant taxes on liquor and baccy a purpose, just to give us Cornish folks a livin. That's because she hasn't forgotten the hand we gave 'em in her great–grandfather's time, when old Ironsides was on the rampage, and we showed her that we Cornish folk be as loyal as any of that fickle lot beyond the Tamar.'

That at least was the drift of Provis's speech, though I must confess to lampooning him somewhat by setting it down thus. Besides, he scarcely uttered two words together. Yet with regard to the families of Porthcado, his words were sincere, and his justifications plausible. I asked if his gentlemen friends would not be as well served by simply forcing the lock and using the vault as the need arose – after all, it was plain that nobody

36

disturbed the place from year to year.

'They could that,' he admitted. 'But in a tight fix, who would speak for 'em?'

So that was it. It was not merely the vault they wanted, but my collusion.

There the matter should have rested – for I dismissed Provis – had I not had occasion to speak to Mr Tredennick after church the following Sunday. He seemed dejected, that I could see: all glum and pucker-mouthed, and quite deprived of his customary jovial salutation. Indeed he would have sloped off, had I not made it my duty to waylay him. I insisted that he accompany me to the rectory for a glass of sherry and a chin-wag. Couldn't prise a word from him. So I led him about the lawn and showed him the wallflowers – only March, mind, and you wouldn't credit the riot of bloom a Cornish garden is capable of even in this early season.

I came out with it plainly: I could see something was troubling him, and I meant to know what it was. What was gnawing at him: was it his wife, his health, his neighbours? No sir, none of these. But he wouldn't tell me. If he wouldn't tell me as his priest, then he should tell me as his friend. I was thanked for my solicitude. We took a turn about the top lawn, having by this time fair worn a furrow in the other. 'Aye, sir, you are right. I should confide in you.' I thought my efforts were about to be rewarded. But no. We tramped on, with Tredennick puffing and fuming like one of Richard Trevithick's contraptions.

To cut it short, the shin of pork I was to lunch on was running the risk of making a Hindu funeral by the time he made his confession. But the tale was this: his shop is short of supplies, and in particular he has no laudanum; this, to ease the last days of those who are beyond recuperation; and there is more than one such case down at Porthcado at the moment. Can't supplies

37

be brought out from Bodmin? I enquired. He looked at me with his cheeks puffed out, and his eyebrows shot up in surprise, like a pair of Norman arches. Bodmin? Who could afford to buy their laudanum from Bodmin? He said that I did not understand at all – the only physic the folk of Porthcado can afford is what gets brought over from France. Nonsense, I said, and berated him for procuring his supplies in such a way, if indeed he did, which I could not believe of him. I told him to get the laudanum in Bodmin and I would make good the difference. His relief was manifest; he pumped my hand and broke out in a rash of smiles. My promise quite restored the man to his customary self. I took him back to the parlour for another glass of sherry to seal the bond. So Mr Tredennick, what will it cost me? Three guineas an ounce, sir – and with just three ounces he thought he could make do. Make do, on nine guineas! I should think he could. More to the point, how was I to 'make do' without them? Nine guineas indeed! But although I thought the man was robbing me, I put a brave face on it, and paid up.

Since then I've made a few discreet enquiries of my own. Laudanum, it seems, is retailed at four guineas an ounce at town prices. But if I was prepared to trust to the free traders – and that is how the deal was expressed to me – it might be had for a mere guinea an ounce.

The information astounded me. Astounding, too, are the dilemmas which this knowledge has brought in its wake. For is my duty to upheld the law, as a functionary of the Established Church, or is it to serve my parishioners, ungrateful as they are?

But on to cheerier news; Lancaradoc is to have a visitor. The learned Dr Rees has written to say that he is contemplating a second tour of the Duchy later in the year, and that I have proved such a competent ally in the cause of the Celtic saints, that he wishes to honour Lancaradoc with his presence for a few days, that we might plan our academic strategy together. As I believe I hinted to you, sister, I have been working at a life of St Cadoc through the winter, and Dr Rees's gracious suggestion of a visit would appear to have been made in response to his reception of my modest treatise. I have done little but collate the two medieval lives of the saint, making what sense of them a modern mind may, but even so humble a task as this, according to the good Doctor Rees, is sufficient.

Trusting more in your sisterly devotion to me, than in any innate curiosity which the holy Cadoc is likely to inspire, I am enclosing some notes made from this work: read them for my sake, Lucy, if for no other.

Notes upon the Life of St Cadoc

The King of Glamorgan 'was given up to carnal allurements, and frequently instigated his guards to robbery and plunder, and lived altogether contrary to what is right, and disgraced his life with crimes' – such is the portrait we have of Wooloo, Cadoc's father.

Cadoc himself took after his mother, St Gladys, and was a reticent and studious boy, who refused to join his school-mates at their games. (*And who would fail to recognise such a type, Lucy? Are our public schools not full of them? The timid sons of swash-buckling colonels away in India, raised by petticoats here at home, then packed off to the bully-yards that go for schools. I have only to think of the interminable afternoons on Erskin's cricket field to feel I know the patron of my church as if he were indeed an elder brother*).

King Wooloo later repented, after seeing a vision of an angel, and built himself a hermitage on a hilltop, in a location revealed to him by a white ox.

In adult life, Cadoc is remembered as an inveterate

traveller, and as a founder of many religious houses. The earliest written account we have of him, that by the twelfth century monk Lifris, tells us how at Llancarfan, his chief foundation, St Cadoc 'fed daily a hundred clergymen, a hundred soldiers, and a hundred workmen, and a hundred poor persons, with the same number of widows, and many guests besides.'

Among his many journeys, Cadoc visited Scotland, Wales, Brittany and Cornwall (*mandatory destinations for any Celtic Holy Man, no doubt akin to the Grand Tour so popular in our grandfather's day*); but more unusually Greece, and Rome and on several occasions, Jerusalem.

Lifris records how in Cornwall, tired after a day's trek on his return from St Michael's Mount, Cadoc struck the ground with his staff, Moses–fashion, thus originating the Holy Well near Harlyn Bay, which bears his name. On a later occasion, after a trip to the Holy Land, St Cadoc poured a bottle of water taken from the River Jordan into the well, thus increasing its curative properties a hundred-fold. To this day, the waters of Cadoc's well are deemed efficacious against disturbances of the bowels and of the belly, and are particularly recommended in the treatment of worms. (*Though one has to hold one's nose to drink it.*)

Lifris shows a detailed grasp of the topography of our county, which is quite remarkable in a Life of this kind, and which adds a certain authenticity to his treatment of Cadoc's sojourn here. Moreover, this life is rare in devoting equal space to those incidents set in Wales, and to his doings in Cornwall and Brittany. Generally those sons of Wales whose fame stems from their exploits across the St George or English Channels – Petroc, or Samson, for instance – received scant attention in their native land. This is hardly surprising, if one reflects that a man who does great work in a colony and becomes famous there is often

40

hardly remembered in the mother country which he left as a child. *(Indeed, who here remembers Robert Moffat?)* Yet Cadoc is the exception to such a rule; in Wales at least twenty–five churches and chapels are known to have been dedicated to him – and only St David can claim more.

The other extant 'Life', by a Breton monk, is more prosaic in tone, and differs in the lists of monasteries founded and journeys undertaken. Otherwise, the two works would appear to share a common source, since lost. *(Pious they may have been, these medieval monks, at least in the choir stall, yet once at their desks they became inveterate cribbers.)*

The greatest discrepancy between them lies in their treatment of the Translation. For medieval legend has it that at the end of his days, St Cadoc was translated to Beneventum, near Naples, where he became known as St Sophias – the church there having deteriorated both materially and spiritually, and being in great need of a good bishop. Yet whereas Lifris has Cadoc being taken up in a cloud from Wales at the climax of his Palm Sunday sermon and meeting a martyr's death when the Italian peninsular was ransacked by Goths, the Breton monk has no more imagination that to have him walk to Naples, and to die in the peaceful sanctity of his bed.

No doubt the story of his Translation is a late accretion, and may have arisen (and here I am following a suggestion of Dr. Rees's) through confusion in the medieval mind between Bannium, that is to say Benevento, and Gobannium, which was the Roman name for Abergavenny. That a Welsh saint retired to the misty hills surrounding Abergavenny is plausible: that he was enveloped in cloud and born away to sunny Italy, may be deemed less so.

(Lucy, you cannot imagine the delight these arcane studies bring me, for to draw out such reasonable conclusions from a hive

41

of superstition is sweet work.)

But I am sure I must have taxed you by writing at such length. I leave you therefore with God's blessing, my tenderest thoughts, and with my heartiest congratulations on your engagement. Please extend the same to Mr Kennington.

*   *   *

Lucy to Mudge, May

Dear Richard,

What tales you have to tell! You paint just such a picture of Cornwall as to confirm the worst of its dreadful reputation. Have you seen any more of Provis? I implore you not to give him the key. I cannot believe that you would contemplate conniving with such outlaws. Nor does your friend the apothecary sound any better. Surely, from what you say, you must suspect that they are in this together?

Richard, take a sister's advice and stick to your books. Your studies may be dry, but they are harmless, whereas these barbarous parishioners are like to embroil you in all sorts of mischief. I urge you to confide in Dr Rees when you next see him. After all, as they say, two heads are better than one, and he too is a man of the cloth.

I have had my own tribulations. I have always known that Isobel had a headstrong character and feared that when she was of an age she would cause me problems. Alas, that age has come upon us sooner than I feared. You would think, at scarcely sixteen, that your niece was still but at an innocent babe. But, no, she has struck up a liaison. She has a young officer in the dragoons quite infatuated with her, and she, the little minx, does all she can to encourage him. I have read the letters that prove it. It is a most unsuitable attachment: the young man in question is so far above our own station that, if left unchecked, this will end in nothing but tears and scandal. Isobel is still too much of a child to understand as much. All her life I have tried to instil in her the lesson that unless the heart is yoked to a cool head, it will inevitably lead her astray. And if she has not the good sense to govern her feelings, then it is my duty to see that they are governed for her. I have undertaken to write to the boy's father, begging him to speak to his son – not that the boy is to blame, but to save the reputation of my child, who is the daughter of a fellow officer. Meanwhile I have forbidden Isobel to leave the house.

Arthur, of course, agrees with the course I have taken, but has been at pains to point out that these measures must appear to come from myself alone: he is too new to this family to perform the role of father yet. Oh, but why are such trials sent to worry a poor mother?

Remember, Richard, that at the end of the day we must act on principle: one has a certain standing to protect. No amount of good will or romanticising must be allowed to obscure our plain duty from us.

Your loving sister,

Lucy

* * *

Mudge to Lucy, September

Lucy,

You write with such reasonable advice that I feel I am bound to disappoint you. Life goes very quietly with me, despite the excitements of the spring.

Poor Isobel! You must not be too harsh on her. The passions of youth are like kindling: they may flare up with a great roar and high flames but, unless there is solid fuel to hand, they are apt to burn themselves out soon enough; parental opposition must be applied with utmost tact in such cases, lest it prove the slow combustible.

We have enjoyed a long, still summer, which is only now showing any sign of ending: the lanes hereabouts are a wealth of blackberries, which, inexplicably, go unharvested.

I have given up the key to the vault, but it is of no great consequence. By Easter I had made my decision, and let it be known to the landlord of The Falcon that I wished to speak with Amos Provis, whenever he should return from Redruth, where he had gone to seek employment. For a month, nothing. Then – it would have been one Thursday morning at the beginning of June, for Thursday is the day I devote entirely to the bees – and I had just come into the kitchen with my face still enveiled in muslin, when Mrs T announced a visitor. It was Provis. I went through into the parlour to shake his hand, and straight out again, to ascend to my study to fetch the key. When I returned to offer it to him, he took it gravely, put in his pocket, then – much to my consternation – he put his arms around me and hugged me to him, in what I supposed was a gesture of gratitude. There was a strong smell of beer upon his breath, for all it's being but ten o'clock. And all this in a mummer's pantomime, for not a word was exchanged between us, and I still in my hiving helmet!

The outcome of this little ceremony has been a long period of anticlimax. I suppose I must have been expecting to be immediately caught up in a tale of smugglers' brawls, and moonlit visitors, and to receive suspicious delegations from the Excise, or I know not what. Instead, the handing over of the key has been quite without issue. However, I am content to think that I have acted from Christian charity, and, like all those who break the law with impunity, the lack of consequence is teaching me to live in peace with my criminality. Occasionally I check the gate to the vault, but it remains undisturbed. And the whole summer has passed without any mention of the *Pydar Rose* – her

44

landings anywhere along the coast usually proving a vivid enough topic of conversation to reach even the isolated rectory of Lancaradoc.

Nor is this the only respect in which I have been left becalmed. For I have received a letter from Dr Rees regretting that he is unable to visit Lancaradoc next month after all, but has had to postpone his journey into Cornwall till next Easter at the earliest. I am disappointed, especially as I have been employing two lads from village to prepare the garden for his visit. Yet if Dr Rees is delayed, the lapse will but serve to enhance the preparations for his eventual arrival. For I am determined to present him with a bolder work than the one he asked of me: some tales of the saints hot from the kiln of the imagination, and more suitable for the modern age.

For you are right, Lucy: Clio alone is a supplier of thin gruel, and if we are to interest the public in our research, then her sister muses must be invoked to add seasoning and sustenance. The work I have in mind will be a novelistic treatment of St Cadoc's life, aimed at appealing to a larger readership. For if the medieval clerics, on whom we are forced to rely for our knowledge of the Celtic hermits, were not averse to decorating their histories with a few literary flourishes, then why should we not attempt the same today, to render our subject matter more palatable to a modern public? What I am aiming at is less a work of scholarship than a 'midrash', to use the Hebraic terminology: for I have heard that it is the custom among the Jews for their Rabbis to write the scriptures anew for each generation, so that the old stories should not lose their heat, but blaze forth with contemporary meaning.

1849

Lucy,

Of course Isobel shall come. Already I have written to the bishop and spoken to Mrs T, so consider it settled.

We have decided that Isobel is to have the west bedroom, above the kitchen, which has a large fireplace and a fine view of the moor. I have asked Mrs T to plan new furnishings, a task for which she has shown uncharacteristic enthusiasm.

I am sure that Mr Kennington's reasons are sound, however harsh they must seem to a mother's instincts. Isobel cannot stay in Frome, whereas your duties, in the first instance, must be to your new husband.

I need scarcely mention my own happiness at having dear Isobel with me for the summer: suffice it to say, she shall have everything which Lancaradoc and a doting uncle can provide.

Trust me, Lucy. Isobel shall return to you in the pink of health, and I am not so wrapped up in my solitude and my antiquaries that I cannot act when action is called for.

*   *   *

Mudge to Lucy, March

Dearest sister,

I am delighted to show you part of my work, and have chosen an extract which gave particular offence to Dr Rees. For yes, that man has been to Lancaradoc, and – for which I am more grateful still – he has gone away again.

A more curmudgeonly and less appreciative guest could not be imagined, Lucy. Even Mrs T was glad to see the back of him, after he complained that she had oversalted his broth and mutilated the mutton. His bed was too soft, the sea air gave him migraine, and the rooks were too noisy – the complaints of that fastidious man were endless.

As for our work together, he treated me with all the condescension one might expect him to show a half-wit. His role was to hand out the word from on high, and mine but to listen: and whether he discoursed on the broadest historical platitudes, or the most arcane of hagiographical niceties, I was treated to such a feast of the Doctor's wisdom that I could barely edge a word in past him. For three mornings we were cooped up over our books, and the Doctor held forth indefatigably. Moreover, the pleasure he took in quoting from his medieval texts in their original Latin was commensurate to his discovery of my near–ignorance of that tongue: I found myself reduced to the status of a trembling school-boy who has but half-learnt his lesson. To be thus humbled in one's own study is no holiday, I can tell you, sister.

All the while I was wanting to raise the subject of the Life of Cadoc I had prepared for him, but he never gave me an opportunity to speak of it. Eventually I left an excerpt from my manuscript on his commode, and crept off to bed.

'Is this a joke, Mudge?' were his first words when I joined him at breakfast the next morning. My mouth fell open. 'Well, is it?'

'By no means,' I found the wit to retort, as I reached for the kidneys.

'Then you must explain what you meant by it, sir.'

'I meant – and still mean – to write something that may be of interest to a wider public. After all, the Celtic saints belong to the church. They cannot remain the property of a mere coterie, however learned. I thought I had adumbrated as much in

47

my letters.'

'Adumbrated, Mudge? You may 'adumbrate' as much as you wish. That hardly gives you the right to insult me with such piffle.'

I reacted to his insult in the only way I saw open to me – by making a dignified retreat. That is, I left the room. I carried it off rather well, I believe: my only regret was for Mrs T's kidneys, which became the innocent victims of this altercation. Once in the hall, I lent my head against the wainscoting and considered my next move. Would the Doctor be waiting for me in the study once again, and if so should I attempt a justification of my work? Or would it be better to ignore the manuscript entirely, along with the discussion it had given rise to? I pictured that book–lined room upstairs, until I could see Rees sitting in the chair at my desk, just as he had been sitting there for the last three days. I shut my eyes, and prayed for the strength to go upstairs and face him again, in a spirit of Christian charity. But only for a moment. Then, I turned upon my heel, and walked out through the kitchen and into the sunshine. Besides, it was Thursday, and I knew that the bees would settle my nerves.

For all his great learning in matters relating to ecclesiastical history, Dr Rees shows a remarkable ignorance of the natural world. Even if he was unaware that black affects bees in much the same way as red affects bulls, one would have thought it only common sense not to approach a simmering bee-hive when it has its lid removed.

But that is precisely what he did. About an hour after we parted, he came out onto the lawn in his black cassock, flapping his arms around to attract my attention, and walking straight towards the hive I was scraping. Had it not been for the gauze of my helmet I might have seen him in time to prevent the ensuing accident. As it was, he brought the whole hive about his

48

shoulders, and fled out onto the moor. By the time we recovered him, he had received more than a score of stings to his neck and head, and nearly the same number again to his hands – a total of fifty-three in all. And that was but half the damage. Once he had been led indoors and given a glass of brandy, I left him to Mrs T while I went out to salvage what I could from the hive; for there is a great danger that bees that have suffered an attack in this way will refuse to settle back. Anyway, one would have thought that as a country woman, and the wife of an apothecary at that; she would have known to treat bee stings with ammonia, and that vinegar is for wasps. And that by dousing the poor man with vinegar she was compounding his agony. Worse, it turns out that Dr Rees has an allergy to vinegar. He was abed three days. At first his eyelids were so swollen, that he was afraid for his sight, and could take nothing but milk, through a glass straw, because of the swelling to his lips. In all, Rees was forced to prolong his stay with us by nearly a week, sister – and I have rarely known a week to pass more slowly.

He is a great scholar, granted, and I a mere neophyte: but to find a noble mind allied to so few of the Christian virtues is disconcerting.

He departed on the Wednesday. His last words to me, after he had been helped into the Launceston coach, were that we should forget the temporary vicissitudes of his visit, but remember our common calling to scholarship. He enjoined upon me to set aside my 'tendency to romancing' – those were his words – and concentrate on certain documents he has left in my keeping. I suppose I shall oblige: to do less would be to betray the trust he has placed in me. More mule work of the type I performed in relation to the life of Cadoc can be offered him, with respect of Samson, Petroc and the others. But what can be ground from the mill of such drudgery? The dubious 'facts' of medieval clerics, dry husks, a systematic winnowing of chaff – in short, a flat pattercake.

St Teilo's talent

The rift between the Christian saints of Wales and the maverick saints of the West Country might have widened benignly, like one of those cracks in an old oak – which provide such habitable nooks for owls to nest in – had it not been for St Teilo.

St Teilo was an outstanding preacher, a capable organiser and the possessor of a singular talent. In Jerusalem, the Arch Patriarch himself was so moved when he heard Teilo preach, that he awarded him an antique bell, encrusted with jewels and occult powers. In Wales, Teilo laid the foundations of more monasteries than any of his compatriots, except perhaps for David the Waterman. But it was in Cornwall that Teilo's especial gift was made manifest.

On their return from the Holy Land, when St David went back to Wales, and St Padern set off for Brittany, Teilo accepted an invitation from King Gerrant to settle at the Cornish court.

Cornwall, in the reign of King Gerrant, was as peaceful and as prosperous a country as at any time in its history, and as benign a corner of the world as the benighted years of the Dark Ages would allow for. Across Europe, hordes of Huns and Visigoths were dyeing their cloaks in the blood of the corpse of Rome. Yet beyond the Tamar, crops were sown and harvested, a generation of saints stalked wisdom, each in their own quiet way, and even the seasons seemed to respond to Gerrant's good governance. Every spring, Easter was celebrated in the Cornish fashion, when, with the first fair seas after winter, ships sailed in from the Levant, bringing their cargo of saffron to Cornish harbours. Ovens were lit anew after the Lenten fast, and the smell of golden saffron cakes, stuffed full of moist, contented currants, wafted from homestead to homestead, and from bay to bay.

So why did St Teilo hate it all so much? Or, if he did not hate it, what were the motives that led him to unleash such destruction upon this peaceful land? Was he homesick? Was he jealous? Did he detest the saints of Cornwall for seeking their sanctity each after the dictates of their own heart? Did he hope to force them to submit to a common rule?

And why, on that fateful Easter morning in the year of our Lord 547, did Teilo refuse to leave off his fasting, or to come out of his hut and accept the Easter cake which St Allen and St Cadoc had trekked through the woods to bring him?

At first his visitors feared that he might have died from the rigours of his Lenten penance. But no, they heard a stir and a shuffle within. 'The Lord is risen, Teilo. We bring you an Easter blessing!' they called. There was no answer. They banged on the door. 'Leave me in peace,' croaked the voice within. 'Be off with you'.

There was nothing for it but to prop the saffron cake upon the window sill and leave.

It was St Mabyn who first noted the thin trickle of yellow smoke that rose from the chimney of Teilo's hut, and hung in wisps above the trees in the damp March air. She sent word to her neighbours, St Cadoc and St Allen. On the Monday afternoon, the three of them stood together on the crest of the hill behind St Mabyn's chapel, from where they had a clear view of the valley.

'Tain't natural,' concluded St Allen, and speaking for the three of them. 'Never seen no smoke that colour before!'

'Maybe he's burning saffron,' ventured St Mabyn.

St Cadoc sniffed the air. 'Can't smell no saffron.'

'Reckon he's fumigating mackerel?'

'This far inland? Besides, bain't the right time o'year.'

51

'Best we ask out,' said St Cadoc. 'There must be someone wise enough to know what he'm up to.'

However, by Tuesday morning there was such a thick column of yellow smoke over the valley that the three saints didn't need to ask out to anyone; it was visible from everywhere in the Hundred of Trigg, from Wadebridge to Stratton. Moreover, the air was tinged with an unmistakable whiff of sulphur.

All that week the smoke poured out of the chimney of St Teilo's hut. It billowed out into a thick toadstool of malodorous vapour. Sometimes, in the morning sun, the yellow cloud looked like a marvellous sculpture. At night, lit by the moon, it was almost more tangible than visible, and seemed to be brooding malevolently above the Cornish hills. Then, on the following Sunday, the stream of smoke was suddenly cut off. St Teilo's chimney fell silent: the crooked funnel of bricks now looked so small that St Cadoc, who had spent the week watching it, let out a nervous laugh.

For another week the cloud tottered in the air, uncannily intact. Those who saw it were inclined to hold their breath, either for fear that this miracle would collapse with the slightest stirring of a breeze, or from an instinctive fear of what they might breathe in.

Slowly, slowly, the pillar of smoke began to change shape. From its base, a miasma of yellow mist began to creep out along the ground, following the valley bottoms before crawling up over the hillsides. Overhead, the great yellow cupola began to shrink. St Teilo's cloud had begun to unravel, collapsing like a schoolboy's sock.

Then the rumours started. Two of St Endellion's cows were possessed by a violent demon. There were reports of sheep sick upon the moor. A school of whales ran aground on

52

Perransands, and died there, their rotting corpses causing a most unholy stench. Out at Davidstowe, the son of a shepherd had fallen into a coma after straying into a bank of Teilo's yellow fog.

In the plague that followed, half of the current generation of saints were harvested home to heaven.

St Teath, a daughter of King Brychan, died; St Docco, whose monastery was a byword for iniquity, died; St Clether, a son of Brychan, died; St Wenna, the wise virgin, died – along with three of her sons; St Brewerd, who could not pray upon an empty stomach, died; St Minver, who once threw her comb at the Devil, died; St Kerry, who could not abide the wind, died. St Teilo, along with many others, fled into Brittany.

There he took refuge with St Samson, at Dôl, and devoted himself to laying out the monastery's extensive apple orchards.

At the end of seven years, St Teilo had a dream concerning his former patron, King Gerrant, and in consequence of this dream he went to speak to St Samson. 'Brother Samson,' he said, 'it is time for me to return to Cornwall. I have worked for you for seven years, and I have given you the finest orchard in all of Brittany. Relieve me of my duties, but let me stay here until the spring. Before I leave, I want to work in your mason's yard. Oh, and I need a block of your best Caen marble – about so big.' And he traced out a rectangle on the ground, about the size of a bed.

Now, King Gerrant had ruled with humility and wisdom in the intervening years. In truth, since the Yellow plague, he had been a broken man, for not only had the disease weakened his once prosperous kingdom, but it had carried off his wife, Queen Enid, whom Gerrant had dearly loved. The king had become like one of those old ash–trees, stricken and shriven by a bolt of lightning, which nonetheless continue to put out a few fresh leaves each spring–time, and provide a favourite shade for cattle to rest under.

But when the news was brought to him that a holy man had been seen sailing into the cove beneath Dingerrin Castle in a stone boat, and later, that the blessed hermit was none other than St Teilo, and that his vessel was a marble sarcophagous, with King Gerrant's name chisselled upon its prow, the king took to his bed; and within a week he was dead. For St Teilo was blessed with the ability of his Celtic forefathers, and could unleash a curse of unstoppable fury.

*　　*　　*

Mudge to Lucy, April

Dearest Lucy,

The room is ready, Mrs T has scrubbed the house from stem to stern, and we have laid in enough provisions to withstand a siege. Trust me, Lucy: Isobel's arrival could not have been better prepared for.

Moreover, I have been in contact with a family who are everything you would have wished for. Isobel's coming will be a boon to us, and I am counting on her company to lift me out of the state of dejection that Rees's visit has engendered in me.

Indeed, I have now broken with the scholar from Wales, for despite all the evidence I have supplied him with, he still insists on his distinction between St Illtud's monks – all, in his opinion fine orthodox churchmen, and, coincidentally, all Welshmen too – and the *hoi polloi* of legendary figures who are remembered here in Cornwall.

For last month Dean Dangerfield lent me a Life of St Keyne, the *De Sancta Keyna*, which originates in the Welsh Abbey of Margam. Imagine my consternation when I came across the following: 'Saint Cadoc, visiting St Michael's Mount on a pilgrimage, found his aunt Saint Keyna there'. This had me doubly confounded. First, because such a juxtaposition of saintly names is shocking in itself: St Keyne is a daughter of King Brychan, and has not our learned preceptor declared that a net distinction between the dubious brood of Brychan, and the Welsh saints of the monastic tradition, is the very cornerstone on which our studies rest? But more alarming still, I wonder that Dr Rees should not have read this in the De Sancta Keyna himself. For mark this, we have here the assertion not merely that they met, the fabulous, spurious hermitess, and the historical Cadoc – but that she was his aunt? And how can Dr Rees have overlooked this text? How can he explain it away? I confess that after shouldering this conundrum for a week, and carrying it about on my walks across the cliffs, I could restrain myself no longer, and wrote all my thoughts out in a letter. Howsoever I worded it, I fear that this letter will be read as an indictment of Dr Rees's scholarship.

Indeed, my secret conviction is that the man's a fraud. There, Lucy, I have said it. So much 'scholarship' and academic niceties piled up like an antique cairn, and all in the cause of a patriot's prejudice. It is only because his chosen field is so barren, and of so little profit to the great estate of scientific knowledge, that all the world accepts his proofs and theories unquestioningly.

But what am to do? I have not the reputation – the doctorates and the Oxford gown – to unmask him. Moreover, I haven't even the stomach for his game, for I see no use in rattling around among the arid bones of history. What a dance he's led me these last few years! So you will hear no more of the Cornish saints from me, for all that my studies have given me some respite from the woes of this remote and dismal parish. Here I am in the wilderness of Cornwall, a dupe to Rees, and a dupe to the village, and all my work has come to nothing.

Yet despite my history–making coming to such a sorry

end, my story-telling has met with more success than Rees would allow for. Not only have I your husband's enthusiasm – for which you must thank him – but Dean Dangerfield writes to say that he was amused by the tale. It is small reward for so many hours of scholarship, but at least it's something, I suppose.

*   *   *

Isobel to Percy Wattling, May

Dear Mr Wattling,

It was most kind of you to send me the plates of the Paris fashions, although I am alarmed to see the coming season makes such use of lilac. It is not a shade which flatters all complexions, and I fear it does little for mine.

I was right to come by sea: the post-chaise would have taken forever. Moreover, I discover myself to be in possession of a dexterous pair of sea legs, and though the waves upset several of the men aboard, they did not unsettle me. We put in at Bideford, an elegant town set on a wide estuary, and then again at Bude, where we had our first taste of Cornwall's wildness. The cliffs on either side the town have been wrenched and contorted by the Creator into the most fantastical lunar shapes, and beyond it, we passed several wide and barren beaches, so pummelled by the surf, that I could imagine myself in distant Bermuda. Both landscapes were a delight to draw.

Thereafter the coastline settles into a monotony of black crags until one comes to a single solitary valley, like a gash scored across these bleak buffs. In its hollow lies a little fishing town, and this is Porthcado. It is only a jumble of tumble-down cottages clinging to the steep hillsides and, as we approached, I imagined it as the last town before the world's edge: beyond here there is nothing but the lonely ocean and America.

But I fear I have not the skill to conjure up with words what I am more able to render with a stick of charcoal or a few dabs of pastel. I have arrived safely, my days here are comfortable but dull, and I am grateful to you for this reminder of the wider world.

Isobel

*   *   *

Mudge to Lucy, May

Now Lucy, have no fears for Isobel – she eats well, sleeps well, and is most serene. By heavens! I would go further: to my eyes she seems quite radiant.

Mrs T adores her. I have never known the old dragon so docile. She clucks and fusses over her like a mother hen, and has transformed the kitchen into a wizard's cave of savoury broths and cream puddings. This afternoon, while I was working on my sermon, I heard such peels of laughter from the parlour, that I got up from my chair and resolved to join them. But as I reached the top of the stair better sense prevailed, for surely they would be talking on matters pertaining to the gentler sex, and I felt it was hardly fitting for me to intrude.

Isobel has already made quite a hit in the neighbourhood. We are even planning to hold a dinner party in the rectory. Mrs Lorneville has graciously accepted my invitation and is to bring her daughter, who is Isobel's age, and will, I hope, provide her with companionship. We are also to have the local miller with his wife and sister, as well as one of the more respectable fishing families from the village.

You may remember my mentioning Mrs Lorneville, from Goddalming, who was in the parish several summers ago. I was delighted to see her in church once again on Sunday. It would appear that Nancy, her daughter, is engaged to a deacon at St Nicolas's, Guildford, and presuming on this connection with the cloth, Mrs Lorneville detained me in the porch and was most insistent that I visit her should I find myself in Porthcado in the week. Naturally, I explained that as it was the principle settlement in the parish, it was my habit to pass through the village three or four times in the week, for although I have little to do there, I consider it my duty to show them my cassock. She gave me tea on Tuesday afternoon, which will explain my returning her invitation yesterday.

She is a most intelligent listener, and, besides being curious to see over the rectory, showed an appreciative grasp of the improvements I am experimenting with for the bees. Thinking that it would be of interest to her, I also introduced her to some of the curious figures who embellish the ecclesiastical history of this part of the country, and must have mentioned – for it appears that her daughter's birthday is the fourteenth of February, the day before Isobel's – that here we even have our own patron of sweethearts, St Advent, and that Valentine is quite unknown in the county.

Imagine my surprise, then, after I had shown Mrs Lorneville to the door, when I turned to find Mrs Tredennick standing behind me in the kitchen, and bent double with laughter just like a school girl. I asked if I might be permitted to share in the joke.

'Aye, you'll have to pardon me,' she said. 'But twas hearing you explaining away our Adwen to the lady when I was bringing in the heavy cake. Sweethearts, parson? Now, tain't just sweethearts – 'tis fornicators and adulterers that she sees right.'

What do you make of that? I confess, that on the spot, it struck me as a most vulgar and tactless remark to make with Isobel in the house, but later, when I was alone with a glass of Madeira after dinner, it made me ponder the pagan nature of these Celtic people; for below their Methody, there lies a thick stratum of superstition which we English can scarcely begin to comprehend. And besides, what can my housekeeper have meant by this? Can it really be that a saint should be venerated for conniving with sinners, or that something as harmless and engaging as the feast of St Valentine, should here be substituted by something so lewd?

I have taken Isobel to witness a most quaint festival. Last Friday was the day when Porthcado goes fishing for pilchards, and the village marks the day with all the pomp and ceremony it can master. The band leads off from Top Town, and the little seine fleet is then towed by donkeys down the hill towards the harbour. The boats are crewed by Porthcado's children, who scatter petals in their wake, while the fisherfolk fall in behind and add to the festivities with their songs. One or two of these were in the old tongue, which is the first time I have heard it, and others were so scurrilous that it is just as well they are couched in a dialect broad enough to be barely comprehensible. Last year was a wet day and the parade was a shambles, but this year we had splendid weather. Isobel confessed to being delighted with our outing; she has done some very pretty sketches, which I am sure she will show you in due course.

Though pilchards form the town's chief catch, fishing for them involves but three boats, which sit out in the bay from dawn till sunset each day, and will remain at their stations from now until the onset of winter, working two immense nets between them; they are directed in their movements by a huer, who signals instructions to them from the cliff. When the pilchards are to reach Cornish waters, and where their shoals will run in first, is the cause of much anxiety and debate, and is all the town's talk in the summer months. It is Mr Veen – he who is to be our dinner guest – who manages the seiving fleet, which at Porthcado belongs to the community of fishermen, and is not privately owned, as are the pilchard boats in the larger towns along the coast.

I hope, Lucy, that what I say is enough to reassure you regarding Isobel's health and happiness. You will see that we can put up enough dash and excitement to content the exigencies of youth when the need arises, although in the main we live as quietly as Isobel's condition requires. I am sure her own letter will paint an equally propitious picture of her sojourn at Lancaradoc.

* * *

Isobel to Edward, June

My darling Edward,

No, no and a thousand times no! We have been over and over this ground before – rid it rough shod, and combed it painstakingly, like the widow gleaning through the stubble for any grain of wheat that might have been missed. I shall not return to Frome before you leave, and we shall not meet again.

Accept this commission. It is what your family expect of you, and – much more than that – it is your duty to yourself.

Do you think I do not know how noble you are? I do not mean by birth, or in the eyes of the world, but you, Edward. After your madcap coming, after you risked everything for me, after such a week – believe me, I am as convinced as you are that our souls belong to one another's.

But – at least in this world – we must be content with what has passed between us. There will be no more. I am not so selfish that I could allow you to sacrifice yourself for me. Accept the rank and position which are rightfully yours: use them, as I know you must, to make your mark upon the world.

Yes, the news you have had from the Reverend Sorely is essentially true. I am convalescing. The climate is mild, and the air is wholesome. If you could but see the colour in my cheeks, Edward, you would not fret for my health. Why, I do believe that you would want to kiss them!

60

I shall not be back before the autumn, and by then your regiment will have sailed for Africa. So go, my gallant Captain, and prove yourself your father's son. And remember that whenever the North Hampshires' valiant exploits are reported in the broadsheets, somewhere, by whatever humble hearth I find myself, your Isobel will be reading them, and her ardent heart will glow with the love she bears you.

Your devoted Isobel.

* * *

Isobel to Lucy, July

Chère Maman,

Of course I am well. Bored, indignant, sometimes indisposed, but incorrigibly well! I have respected your wishes – or those of Mr Kennington – and accept this dismal banishment, but, please Mother, let there be no pretence between us: I am an embarrassment to you, and my removal from Frome is proving most convenient. For my part, I am almost glad to spend the summer here.

Lancaradoc is quaint for all its backwardness, and Uncle could not be kinder, nor more attentive. Indeed, he is so lonely in this remote district that I believe my sojourn with him serves some useful purpose other than my own.

Last Sunday he came back from church visibly distressed. The reason, it seems, was that there was no one there! I asked why he hadn't come back the sooner, but he says that it is his habit on such occasions, which – especially in the winter months – can be as frequent as one Sunday in three, to conduct the service in exactly the same fashion as if he had a congregation before him. I suggested that he skip the sermon at least, and put it away to save him the pains of writing a fresh one for the following week, but Uncle wouldn't hear of it. We dispatched the goose in complete silence. By the time Mrs Tredennick brought

61

in the flummery I could bear it no longer – poor Uncle looked near to tears. I put down my spoon, determined to give him the chance to air his distress.

'I'm sorry Uncle, I should have come.' I had not been nearly as incapacitated as I made out: it was more for the luxury of eating Mrs Tredennick's breakfast in a warm bed that I had kept away from church in the morning.

Uncle waved his hand: 'No child. It is not the one or two faces that make a difference. It is that Porthcado scorns me.' Quizzing him further I discovered that when he was first here there had been quite a posse of the local farming community who regularly attended communion. However, Uncle tried to intervene in a feud between them but his actions caused offence. Thereafter they stopped coming, and took their dependents away with them.

So now it seems he has only Tredennick for his congregation, and even the apothecary makes the excuse of having his patients to attend to as often as not. Mrs T says she has Uncle's Sunday fowl to put on the table. Thinking how much it would help Uncle if at least she could be relied upon to put it an appearance, I stole into the kitchen while she was washing the pots. 'Mrs Tredennick', said I, beginning as tactfully as I could: 'I don't suppose you could do the Parson the kindness of joining him in church on Sunday mornings? I'm sure a cook as skilled as you could leave the range for an hour, and you would only have to step across the lawn.' 'Lordy be!' was her reply: 'I could never do that. If I took my communion from the parson after I've been washing his smalls all week, 'twould turn me proper heathen.' The excuse was ridiculous, but there was a look in her eyes like a cornered cat's. Besides, we both knew that I had deserted him myself that morning, so I did not insist.

I have been much in the company of Uncle's housekeeper

this last fortnight, and little by little she has taken me into her confidence. She is quite unlike the formidable woman she would have us believe – and as Uncle still most emphatically does: beneath her blunt exterior there is much of the timorous girl who, it seems, was deplorably misused. The other afternoon, while I was helping her with the week's baking, she confessed her history to me: when she was just fifteen she was taken advantage of by one of the fisherman, then thrown out onto the street by her mother when she was found to be with child. It was then that the apothecary took her in and offered to marry her. And though she did not love him she accepted him, for what else was she to do? She still yearned for the callous fellow who had spurned her. And as if these misfortunes weren't enough, her pregnancy did not reach full term, but ended in a miscarriage.

I do not know why Mrs Lorneville was not in church. She normally attends: no doubt because she needs somewhere to show off her hats. Indeed, I do believe that Uncle has an admirer, although he fails to notice it. We have twice had Mrs Lorneville to tea, but he is as immune to female charms as an old bull is to horse flies, and to watch her making eyes at him, and hanging upon his every word, and he so oblivious to her game, is quite comic.

Now she has imposed upon Uncle to hold a dinner party at the rectory. This he has never done before, but he is fortunate to have the doughty Mrs Tredennick to think of everything. Everything but the guest list, that is, and here Uncle is like the host who must scour the hedge-rows to fill the places at his table; we are to have a motley selection of the local big–wigs, and I only hope that the evening's tedium might be relieved by Mrs Lorneville's daughter, who has just joined us from Surrey. She, at least, is near to me in age, and I hope to goodness that I shall find her someone to confide in in this dreary place.

Yet I would not want to give you the impression that I am despondent. Far from it – I have even found a project that should amuse me! When we were returning from our walk the other afternoon, Uncle took me into the church to show me a most curious feature: there is a secret hidey–hole built into the North wall, which can be reached from a flight of stairs going up onto the rood screen. It is known as the Pope's Chamber, and is so cunningly constructed as to be quite invisible to the casual eye, even though it has a window, which is hidden from without by the buttresses. The room's purpose seems to have been for the harbouring of catholic priests in the days of the Reformation. I have persuaded Uncle to let me restore it to its former glory as a secret den, for it is currently no more than a junk room. We are to make a start tomorrow.

Your devoted daughter,

Isobel

*   *   *

Isobel to Percy Wattling, July

Dear Mr Wattling,

I did not expect such a speedy reply to my letter, and am most grateful for it.

Rest, and the attentions of my uncle, are what my delicate constitution have need of, and when I do return to Somerset, I believe you will be surprised at the benefits my convalescence has worked upon me. If nothing else, Uncle, who enjoys the pleasures of the table, is served by a devoted and very capable housekeeper, and even I have been tempted by the quality of the cream and the butter, not to mention the cakes and pies of this county, which I believe have no equal.

We live doubly secluded from the world, both because the rectory is three miles from the village, and because these Cornish folk have no need of either an English parson nor his church. Moreover, my uncle is suited by neither class, nor race, nor temperament to live among them. He is one of nature's originals, and beneath his bearish exterior he is as kind as butter. We spend our days sauntering through the woods and along the perilous cliff tops, and pass our evenings in talking books. Uncle has quaint notions concerning the coming of Christianity to these parts, and I do my best to humour him.

You are right concerning the society here, or rather the lack of it. Our principal company is that of a Mr and Mrs Lawson, and his spinster sister, who run a mill in the neighbouring valley. Their kindnesses extend to euchre evenings once a week – a local variation of whist, but so engrossing that I would adore to introduce it to Frome – and more recently, to luncheon parties. Twice now, thanks to the clement weather, we have been able to lunch *en plein aire*. Jemma Lawson, the miller's sister, has made me quite her confident!

As to your comments regarding your commercial concerns, I have caught your drift quite plainly. Yet whereas it is flattering for any girl to have a gentleman explain his position in the world so candidly, I must beg you not to insist on making such disclosures; neither our brief acquaintanceship, nor my own intercourse with you, have given you ground to assume such intimacy.

Nevertheless, I am happy that you business dealings will be bringing you back to Frome this winter, and you may rest assured that both my mother and myself will be most flattered should you choose to accept our humble hospitality and continue to call on us for tea, whenever your engagements permit it of you.

Till then, may God's hand guide you to prosperity.

Faithfully yours,

Isobel

*   *   *

Mother dearest,

I have not been over-exerting myself, I assure you. Rather, I believe that the balmy sea-air and the cheerful footpaths hereabouts are having a most beneficial effect on my health. But if it will set your mind at rest, you might like to know that I am now walking less than formerly, but spend most of my afternoons in the garden, reading in the shade of a giant cedar tree. The lawn is quite yellow, much to Uncle's consternation, but the fields are flourishing, and they say that this summer promises a harvest to compare with any in living memory.

The dinner party was a qualified success. Mrs T did us proud, and the guests rose to the occasion. To judge by dress, or manners, or menu – to judge, that is, by appearance – Lancaradoc Rectory may claim to have put on a fair showing. Neither the Lawsons nor the Veens would have disgraced even a fashionable soiree in Bath. There was wit – more, there was affability, a quality which can be sadly lacking at far grander gatherings than ours.

Yet for all that there were undercurrents of unease around the dinner table, like an autumn draught that chills the feet, but whose source eludes detection. Perhaps it was because the Lornevilles are strangers to the parish, or because the Lawsons have their private tribulations, or because Uncle introduced a topic of conversation which quite upset Mr Veen. I failed to catch what he said, but it was something about one of those obscure hermits of his, the which Mr Veen seemed to take as a veritable insult.

I was troubled to see the Lawsons so preoccupied, for Jemma hardly said a word all evening and although her brother was as engaging and as seemingly carefree as ever, I could see that Beth was oozing with worry. I managed to catch Jemma for a *tête-a-tête* before they left, and implored her, as my friend, to tell me what was amiss. It was nothing, she said, looking for all the world as though it were something very large indeed. But when she eventually confided in me I was inclined to agree that the Lawsons' problems are small enough – merely that the miller has been accused of giving short measure by a local gossip.

My restoration of the Pope's Chamber is now complete. Once cleared, and thoroughly cleaned out, I gave the walls a coat of whitewash, and enlisted Mrs T's help in polishing the floor. She, in turn, pointed out the deplorable state of the boards in one corner, which I had overlooked, and was good enough to arrange for her husband to come and replace them. Next, I brought out some furniture from the house and *voilà*, I have created a snug apartment. Uncle now has a desk to write at, an armchair, and two portraits on the wall. These I found in the attic. We have no idea who they are portraits of, but they are tolerably well executed: one figures a debonair gentleman in a feathered hat and gauntlets; his partner is a dusky coquette, who we have decided must be his mistress. I also found a carpet, very threadbare, that nonetheless brings a note of comfort to the chamber. When I showed Uncle my handiwork he said little, but I know he is delighted with it, for he has twice gone off there with his pens and ledgers. What a shame the chamber has no fireplace, as he will be forced to abandon it when winter comes.

Yet even in wintertime, he will derive some benefit from my exertions, for I have supplied him with a congregation! There was a great deal of lumber to remove before we could restore the priest hole to its former glory, and we spent an afternoon carrying it out to the porch. While we were thus engaged I hit upon the idea of using some of the boards that I found there to paint caricatures of the apostate farmers. Uncle proclaimed himself well pleased with the likenesses, even though

I have seen my subjects only once, on the day of the pilchard fair. We have hidden them behind a curtain in the ringing chamber, and it is Uncle's intention to drag them out and preach his sermon to them on those Sundays when the rest of the congregation have deserted him!

This summer has crept by. To be cooped up here in winter storms, as poor Uncle will be, does not bear contemplation. I have ached for the society of a town, and fretted, and born the days as best I must, but at least my banishment is coming to an end.

Incidentally, Nancy proved a disappointment, and I will make no friend there. As her only topic of conversation seems to be the preparations for her forthcoming wedding, and as marriage was given little space in the general discussion, she was as mute as the vinegar cruet. Besides, she hides so much behind her mother's fortune and her fiancé's opinions that her own personality has quite disappeared from view.

Another month, and we shall both be back in Frome again. But tell me, how was the house in Malvern? And Mr Kennington's sisters? Have you found the curtains for my room?

*   *   *

Mudge to Lucy, August

Dearest Lucy,

I am delighted that Mr Kennington's sisters proved such genial company, and that your summer in Malvern has been so restful.

Lancaradoc, under Isobel's influence, has shrugged off its customary reticence and on the night of our dinner party the house was ablaze with candles and gleaming silverware. Mrs Lorneville was good enough to pronounce herself quite enchanted by the evening.

Our entertainment also provided me with a chance to interview the Lawsons, and arrangements have now been thoroughly discussed and concluded to the mutual satisfaction of all parties. You would be delighted with the family, I am sure, and Jemma's friendship adds a bond of affection which is of inestimable value. Lately she has being calling on the rectory almost every afternoon, and Isobel is teaching her to draw.

Beth Lawson was in a most agitated frame of mind, and at first I believed that she was showing less enthusiasm than previously. However, she assured me that was not the case, but rather that they had worries of quite another sort. It transpires that they have had a run-in with the parish witch, an old crone by the name of Hannah Hawke. She is a wizened, sorry–looking thing who calls at the rectory from time to time, and Mrs T kits her out with rags and something from the pantry. So notorious is this half–crazed woman in the district that little credence is likely to be given to the rumours she is spreading, yet it is not for any damage she may do to their reputation that the Lawsons are discouraged, but rather that they fear her, for all I could see, for her 'Evil Eye'. Nor is this the first time I have heard of the old witch's proclivity for malice: there's a story about that forty years ago she had her own brother–in–law hanged by turning king's evidence against him, and all over the robbery of a trifling amount of contraband tobacco.

In short, the Lawsons are inexplicably consternated to have made such an enemy. Normally the miller is not easily ruffled, but beneath his ebullient exterior, I could see that even he was as anxious as his wife.

As chance would have it, superstition proved to be the topic of our conversation for much of the evening. Veen sustained that the notorious reputation of the Cornish as a superstitious people was not due to their being backward, but rather derived from their having to earn their living by such hazardous means. Whether in the mines, or on the sea, the

Cornishman is constantly forced to put his life at risk to earn his daily crust. This much I conceded him, for in my experience, though they want much in the way of instruction, Cornish folk are well-endowed with native wit. What, asked Mrs Lorneville, were the typical beliefs of our fishermen? Why, to begin with, that any four-legged creature brings ill-luck to a boat. Veen recounted the rumpus that ensued in his father's day after the drawing of a cat was discovered chalked upon the prow of a half-built skiff. No doubt it was just some boyish prank, but when word of it got round they insisted on taking the boat apart plank by plank, and the building of it was begun again from scratch. Women, too, were a bad omen: not only must none come aboard, but some of the 'touchier' crew turn back if they meet a woman in the lanes on their way to the harbour, and refuse to put out to sea on such a day. 'Then I thank you,' replied Mrs Lorneville, 'for you have furnished me with an excuse to keep to my bed in the mornings.' Mrs Veen put the custom down to laziness rather than cowardice, and cited a remark she'd heard from a Newlyn jouster: 'When there's a wind they wussn't go, and when there's a calm they cussn't go.'

Veen also told me an intriguing story about St Selevan – how the good hermit miraculously caught two fish on a single hook – and he confirmed that Selevan's name is much invoked among the fishing community along this stretch of the coast. I was intrigued to learn as much, and as he had been so good to raise the subject, might I ask him if he could help me with certain other queries I had regarding Cornwall's saints? He would be pleased to help. Had he heard of St Advent, or Adwen as she is locally known? Was he aware of her reputation as the patron of sweethearts? 'Adwen?' says he, colouring up as bright as one of his own lobsters – and I noticed that his wife also seemed to have been put to some embarrassment by my enquiry. 'What are you implying, Parson?' Veen happened to be peeling a pear at the time, and he pointed the blade of his fruit knife at me in a most piratical fashion! 'My dear Mr Veen, I am implying nothing – nothing at all. I merely wish to ascertain in what esteem this saint is held. From all accounts she sounds a most colourful character.'

'Now Parson,' the miller interrupted with a lewd wink, 'You don't want to go quizzing good married folk with Adwen, though I dare say Jemma here has lit her a candle or two.' And in the ensuing merriment, any embarrassment my remarks may have caused was swept away.

My interrogation may have caused a momentary hiatus at the table, but secretly I thought such a response was most fortuitous: it fully justifies my formulations with regard to the role she plays in the Cornish imagination.

Finally, Lucy, I must inform you that Isobel confronts her predicament with great fortitude. We are all in a state of readiness and anticipation, and there is nothing to suppose that all shall not go well.

*   *   *

Mudge to Lucy, September

Dear Lucy,

No doubt you are enjoying Isobel's sunny company just as Lancaradoc suffers the lack of it. The rectory is very large without her, and Mrs T and I are finding it difficult to return to our former habits.

As to all the unanswered questions concerning Isobel's crisis, despite all my attempts to draw her out, I have learnt nothing. Nothing! She has been as discreet as a terrapin, wearing the armour of her charm upon her back, and ready to dive into an ocean of reticence at the first hint of intrusion.

She was given a good send off. There was such a gaggle of well-wishers come to say goodbye, that they blocked the entrance to the jetty. Miss Purvey brought her class, most prettily arrayed in their Sunday frocks. Mrs Veen came with the twins and enough provisions to equip Isobel for a voyage to the Antipodes, let alone Bristol. The twins overcame their girlish timidity and were most animated; they even sang for Isobel before the boat left. Yet only Jemma came from the mill: I would have thought to have seen Beth and the baby, but Isobel did not appear surprised to find only her friend at the quay. They must have come to some understanding between themselves that I knew nothing of.

When all was ready and the sailors about to cast off, Isobel bade them wait and called to me to come aboard. She thanked me most prettily and presented me with a portrait as her parting gift. I had to struggle to keep my composure before such a crowd. I had no idea that she was drawing me – it is a very good likeness indeed. I left as soon as the boat was past the breakwater. I could not bear to watch it dwindle to the horizon.

On my way home I was overtaken by Sir Plumley's carriage. Normally I would have declined his offer to ride with him, but I was so ponderously glum after saying farewell to Isobel that I had not the wit to refuse. His lordship was in a most contrary mood, and the interior of the cab reeked of cognac. He evidently knew that I had just come from seeing my niece set sail, and began singing her praises. Indeed, he insisted on so many compliments of her 'spirited character' and 'tidy young figure' that I was dreading him saying something untoward.

Then he noticed the portrait: the thin quadrilangular parcel balanced between my knees could scarce be mistaken for anything but a painting, despite the sack it was in for its protection.

'That's her parting gift?' Then he chuckled and said, more to himself than to me, 'Doubtless in a gilt frame to assuage her guilt.' His eyes closed and his thin lips settled into a sleeper's smile. I thought I was to be spared further conversation. But no, suddenly his eyes shot open and he lunged forward to grasp my portrait along its furthest edge. 'Something she did herself? The pretty filly paints, does she, Mudge? Show me.'

My first instinct was to resist – I had no wish to watch those bloodshot eyes flickering over Isobel's work, nor to see his yellow tongue poke its way out between his lips prior to uttering a disdainful judgement. Yet what would I have gained from struggling against this wilful grandee in the confines of his own carriage? So I tipped the painting upright upon my knees, holding it firm with one hand, and used the other to coax down its sackcloth wrapping.

Plumley sat forwards, his little eyes lit up like a pig's when it has scented truffles, and scrutinised the work. The light was poor inside the carriage and constantly wavering, and I had a job to keep the picture still: he peered at the work for what seemed a long minute, before speaking: 'Well, well! So she's done you a picture of Amos Provis.'

'Don't be ridiculous! You can see it's my own likeness.' I made to cover the painting again, but Plumley put his hand on my knee to restrain me. Indeed, he gripped my leg like a vice. 'Don't you see it? Look, Mudge: shave off his beard, give the man a decent set of clothes, and – *cum grano salis* – the two of you are veritable twins. Surely someone must have commented on the resemblance before now?'

I admitted that Mrs Tredennick had mentioned something of the sort.

'How funny – our pious parson being a ringer for the town's leading free trader. If he exists, this God you preach, he's the most implacable ironist. Wouldn't you agree, Mudge!'

I made no reply, being loathe to enter into a discussion of

my beliefs with such a man.

'Though you are friends, are you not? I hear that you have offered to assist the *Pydar Rose*.'

'I believe I have acted in the interests of the village.'

Plumley received this politic but frank reply with a contemptuous snort.

'Don't look so shocked, Parson. It would seem she's working in the interests of most people hereabouts. She's certainly working in mine – *sub rosa*, she pays me six percent. No doubt that ship serves us all. And anyone who has sunk as much money into the Rose as I have is entitled to know her dealings. But her captain is certainly no philanthropist, nor your friend Provis, either. You've heard what happened to the sexton at Fretton, I suppose?' I shook my head. 'You should ask Provis: he's got quite a way with those that blab.'

We had by this time come to the crest of the hill, and although the lane meets the rectory drive a mile on, I asked Plumley to set me down at once. I had had enough: a mile's walk across the fields was infinitely preferable to that fetid coach.

Plumley leaned out of the window as the coach pulled away (I was by then atop the stile) and his voice boomed back at me: 'Don't run away from us, Parson. I'm sure it's just a touch of *post festum pestum*. And remember: we damned sinners have more need of a priest than those who find their way to church of a Sunday!'

Yet is was less the words that impressed me, than the strange strangled laugh that accompanied them: I do not know if he was mocking me or in earnest.

*   *   *

Mudge to Lucy and Isobel, October

My dearest sister and my dearest niece,

I dare say, as I pen you this, that you are sitting down to read my

74

last letter by the kitchen lamp. Yet the man of whom I wrote is already dead. On Tuesday I walked to Fretton to attend his burial.

It is a commonplace to see such coincidences as God's dexterous fingers at work, kneading the world for some fabulous pastry we know not of – yet in this case, one suspects the cook to be some bungling demiurge.

Porthcado is in a state of shock, for we have lost a figure who was assumed to be a pillar of the modest firmament under which we live.

The enclosed article appeared in yesterday's paper.

A blessing to you both, from your brother and uncle,

Richard Lancelot Mudge

* * *

*(from **The Western Daily Mercury** October 6th)*

Following the death last Thursday of Sir Henry Plumley of Fretton Hall, Fretton, in the County of Cornwall, his will was made public on Wednesday last, at the offices of Poldean and Judd, attorneys of law, whose premises are situated at Mount Folly, Bodmin.

The will's stipulations have been the cause of much comment and no little consternation, largely because they reveal qualities of generosity in a man whose reputation was that of a hard–living county squire of yesteryear rather than a modern–day philanthropist.

Although most of his fortune is to be spent in paying off his manifold debts, the residuary assets of the estate, estimated at £7,000, are to be put into a trust for the maintenance and re-education of disadvantaged ladies in the port of Plymouth, with the further £1,000 likely to accrue from the auctioning of the contents of Fretton Hall left for the refurbishment of Fretton church.

Yet the most controversial clause of the will provides for the surprise endowment of the house itself, which has been bequeathed to an order of Catholic nuns, who lost their previous habitation near Caens as a result of the anticlerical policies pursued by the present French government.

Although the coroner's report denies any such suggestion, Sir Henry Plumley is rumoured to have died by his own hand, and the unexpected generosity of his legacies have gone some way to mitigate the revulsion felt at so unnatural a death.

* * *

Lucy to Mudge, October

Dear Richard,

I was surprised to read the report of your neighbour's death. Do you not think that with so much money to spend on his church, the Vicar of Fretton might consider having an organ made for it, and were he to do so, perhaps you could suggest my husband's name as the perfect agent for overseeing such an improvement?

Can it really be that Sir Plumley died by his own hand? I find it hard to credit such a deed in a nice gentleman who had everything to live for. But perhaps there is more to this tragic tale than The Western Daily Mercury reports?

I have other news. Isobel is to be married. Mister Percy Wattling spoke to Arthur and myself last Thursday evening after the bridge party, requesting our permission to ask her for her hand. I cannot tell you how anxiously I awaited her reply; even more than her suitor, I should say, for I know Isobel as only a mother can and I know how flighty she is, and – for her all her grace and cleverness – how little endowed with good plain sense. And he is such a sound prospect. I have even heard him say that if his business in Salisbury continues to flourish, he has plans to open a second shop in Chichester. We were delighted by the proposal and immediately urged Isobel to accept, which I am glad to say she has had the good sense to do.

*　　*　　*

Darling Isobel,

This is indeed good news – and of course I am delighted for you.

They say that Salisbury is a most civil town, and the cathedral quite a monument of grace. How is the road from there to Frome? Where will you be living after your remove? And as to Percy Wattling, I wish to know everything: your mother, with her eye to practicalities as ever, writes only to confirm that he is a prosperous draper, but as to character, or the circumstances of your courting, not a word.

It has been unseasonably warm in Lancaradoc this past week, such that my rambles through the fields have brought back all the memories of last summer, and of your stay. You are still talked of with affection in the village, and Miss Purvey, likewise the Veens, Amy Towan, and even Old Jarvis, have begged me to include their greetings when I write.

But to my main news. The Lawsons brought the babe to church on Sunday, and he was baptised in true Cornish fashion, with candles, and the north door wide open – which they say is to give the Devil his exit! Jemma Lawson took the godmother's vows, myself and Mr Tredennick those of the godfather. Richard Edward Jonathan were the names bestowed on him, and he hollered lustily throughout, which is as it should be. Then, during the Christening tea, not a peep from him: so perhaps his future is marked out as a diplomat in Her Majesty's Colonial Service!

And goodness me, Isobel, you would not recognise the Rectory were you to approach it now – such grand airs has it

77

assumed since the division of Sir Henry Plumley's estate. You will have read, where the article I sent you speaks of the will, that those items superfluous to the house in its new role were to be sold off by auction. I made it my business to attend, chiefly to form an idea of what the library contained, but found nothing to grace a respectable household. However I did come home with a fetching view of Porthcado jetty executed in oil, circa 1785, which now adorns the wall above Mrs T's chair, and – would you believe – two splendid white peacocks, which can be seen strutting about the Rectory lawn.

They too require christening, but neither Mrs T nor myself have hit upon anything to suit. Perhaps, Isobel, your sharp wit will furnish us with something appropriate?

* * *

Mudge to Lucy, December

Lucy, dearest,

It is decided – Fretton church is to be fitted with an organ. These musical contraptions seem to be all the rage! Certainly I should be delighted to entertain your husband when he comes to Cornwall – but are you sure that you will not be able to travel with him? I could scarcely sleep last night for the thought that I might persuade my dear sister to come and see how we live here in West Barbary!

I beg you to consider this opportunity: till I hear of your final decision my nerves shall be all a-jangle. Still, whether Arthur Kennington is to come alone, or to bring you with him, and whether he is to come in April, or at the end of the summer, you must rest assured that I shall put myself completely at his disposal. Nay, you may tell this organ–making husband of yours that the Rector of Lancaradoc undertakes to 'pull out all the stops' on his behalf!

Since I last wrote, there has occurred one of the most

extraordinary Sundays that I have witnessed since I took the cloth. Immediately on letting myself into the vestry for the nine o'clock service, I perceived that something unusual was afoot, although as I donned my robes, I was quite at a loss to account for what it was. I felt a sensation akin to that when a high tide is running in coincidence with a gale, when the murmur of heaven's fury is in the air. Yes, that was it, I decided – a curious murmuring in the air. No sooner had I thought so, than I moved to the door, and pushed it open a crack. And would you believe what I saw? Not the usual two or three gathered in His name at all, but a solid mass of folk squeezed into the pews. All the labourers and fishermen of the parish in new–polished boots, and their women in white shawls. There were even people standing at the back, under the bell tower, for want of somewhere to sit.

I was seized by a momentary panic, I will confess, but thought that I must carry on as though this crowd were an apparition. I forced myself to remember the empty vistas I was used to, and called up the weary faces of my regular congregation, all of which helped me get through the hour with my customary dignity, but even so I stuttered shamefully on the sermon. Nonetheless, I was listened to respectfully enough, and afterwards, what hymns were sung in St Cadoc's! – why it was such a music that the Methodists must have heard it in their chapel down the valley.

Afterwards I pushed my way through the tumult to the porch, and what should I find upon the slate bench there but a half-anker of the best French brandy, topped by a long–stemmed yellow rose. At once the meaning of these extraordinary crowds became clear: here was my thanks for the tacit assistance I have been rendering the parish since last year, through the agency of Mr Provis! The congregation began to file out, and in the next ten minutes every face I recognised from Porthcado, and quite a few besides, passed before me, with so many nods and smiles that I had to pretend a cold, and extract one of Isobel's kerchiefs from the sleeve of my surplice. My hand was pumped till it was quite sore. Finally, in the rearguard of this throng came Tredennick, with a wink upon his sly old face that would have shamed the Devil himself.

Last Sunday I was back to a congregation of three, but for all that my involvement with the *Pydar Rose* has put me on a new standing with my parish. Whether this is because the unredeemed world recognises me as one of its own, or rather because I am perceived as playing a useful function in the affairs of the village at last, I have been unable to decide. What would be your opinion, sister?

As for the scandal which has brought our secluded corner of the world to public notoriety, I do indeed know more than has been written in *The Western Daily Mercury*, for Porthcado is abuzz with the talk of it. I have even spoken to one of the men who found the body and helped to cut it down. It seems that the under-gardener was alerted by the whining of one of his mastiffs, which was down in the cellar with him, and must have been a witness to his end. It took three men to beat the creature off with sticks, which they were loathe to do, as the dog showed more love for Plumley than any Christian had ever done. They had to chain it in the yard before they could cut his master down from the beam.

It is true what you read: the estate was plagued by debt, but how the debt was come by – that has not found its way into print. Yet the how, in the main, is no secret, and tongues down on the quayside are awag with it. Plumley was a gaming man. I've heard it said abroad that there was a regular gambling syndicate he played with, over in Callington, and that it contained at least one mine owner as well as a Plymouth shipbuilder. With purses as big as that to play against, it's no wonder he soon ran through the pockets of country squire.

So much for the public scandal, which has been compounded by the reading of the will. The lands have gone, and these so-called friends of Plumley's have been the beneficiaries thereby; what Plumley has done with the house, however, and the numerous bequests he made with the remaining monies have astounded the neighbourhood. Who would have predicted that such a scoundrel would have played the benefactor at the end?

But it does not end there, Lucy, for I've heard whisperings over this affair that have had me down on my knees at night. It has to do with a parlour maid at the house, Roslyn Cridden – her father is a Porthcado fisherman – who died last winter under the surgeon's irons. She was operated on for a burst appendix, by a Doctor Killigrew, and was barely fifteen.

What the housekeeper says is that Roslyn was a silly goose, and forward, and no doubt too young to know the danger she was in, and that she died not from her appendix but for an intervention which Killigrew will have to answer for on Judgement Day. That Plumley must have footed the expense, and that Killigrew is a doctor at the Callington mines, is what gives the story credence. Moreover, they are saying that it was remorse for the girl, rather than his debts, that drove Plumley to put the noose about his neck, and that by doing so he did no more than save the cost of the Bodmin hangman; for to use the girl in such a way, and then to pay a saw-bones for his butchery, is a hanging crime, and would have damned Plumley as a murderer, should it ever have come to light. But Mrs T has a long tongue on her, and maybe this is no more than wicked prattle. And yet she says that her husband was called in at the very end to try to save the girl, in which case her story comes straight from the horse's mouth.

As for the will, I don't know what to make of it. Of course, the world at large is up in arms: they regard a shipload of French nuns as an affront to every decency that England stands for. Yet the law upholds Plumley's right to leave the manor house to whomever he likes, and the nuns are to take up residence sooner than was expected. Moreover, it seems that they are not abroad at all, but already in Norfolk. Plumley's executors have received a letter asking him to have the house ready by August.

A band of fishermen – Methodist stalwarts all – marched through the town last Thursday and left their banners on the Pratt; from their violent slogans, you would think Napoleon had joined forces with the anti–Christ and hatched a plan to billet his hussars up at Fretton! Mrs T tells me that some of these same Porthcado lads have been prowling round Plumley's house at night, and are responsible for lobbing bricks through the casement. From the way she spoke, I gather she was not entirely unsympathetic to these ruffians, either.

Yet I go against the common view: it is time for the breaches of the past to be healed. One must welcome a manifestation of religion in any form, and this Romish convent will at least provide a counterweight to Methody. The nuns are the neighbours that Finch deserves: indeed, his vicarage abuts their orchard wall. Let us hope that if the Pope is to make converts in this part of the world, they shall be from Finch's congregation, for he is as likely to lead the people of Fretton to the very Devil. And who knows but that an act such as this – reverting to the Papist sympathies that still smoulder in the old Cornish gentry – should not augur well for Plumley's soul. Besides, it is the very nature of a closed order that they keep themselves to themselves. When the fuss dies down I don't suppose we will even notice that they are there.

I know that you will berate me for my High Church

sympathies, Lucy, but I shall bear your taunts with pride. And imagine the coincidence – which I will claim as an honour! – when I tell you that I have received a letter from a former champion of our party in person: for Bishop Newman has written to me, requesting additional information about King Gerrant. It seems that he is a friend of Dangerfield's, who showed him my story concerning St Teilo. The dean tells me that Newman was touched by the scene of the good king awaiting his death, and is considering it as a suitable subject for a poem.

1850

Mudge to Isobel, January

Isobel, my angel,

What a wicked suggestion – no sooner had I read your letter than the peacocks were christened at once! For though not even Mrs T will hear them from my lips, I cannot look at the bedraggled fowl without your names for them springing to mind. If the truth were told, they have not proved the addition to Lancaradoc Rectory I had envisaged: for they dirty the lawn more than they adorn it, and put up a most raucous din from dawn till sunset. No one may approach the house, but that they hiss malevolently – I had not known that peacocks were such a belligerent species, and scarcely provide an appropriate welcome to a Christian home. Moreover, even their proverbial vanity fails to redeem them, as one is losing the feathers from its chest – whether from mange or mere antipathy to his new surroundings I cannot tell – and flaunts pink sores that would shame a scrag-chicken. But I am grateful to you, Isobel, that the genius of your wit has gone a little way to reverse my misgivings, for I have only to remember your suggestion and the folly of my acquiring them is offset by a smile.

But were these birds my only anxiety at the moment! There is worse. Porthcado suffered a shipping accident last month such as all in these parts go in constant fear of. Five men drowned, and all leaving families behind them, who face the workhouse but for our attempts to start a public subscription. What with the burying of them, and letters to write, I've had no time for anything else these past few weeks. How it happened remains a mystery – in a calm sea, off Crad Head, the men having set out early to check their pots for lobsters. I had news of it at once, having gone to Porthcado to buy ink from Miss Tingham, and being on the quayside at about ten o'clock when Sam Shepherd, the village natural, came running down the hill, shouting for help. He was at work on a wall over towards Cadoc's Zawn and had been the first to see the capsized boat. At once a rescuing party was got up, and two boats went out. They were back within the hour with sorry news: they brought four corpses with them, and there was much talk, after, of the misfortune of it, for the men could not have been in the water above a couple of hours, in clement conditions, and they were no more than half a mile from shore. If only they had been able to swim, they would still be alive. The last body was washed ashore at the cove some five days later. It was John Veen's.

On a cheerier note, I had occasion to visit the Lawsons last week and see the boy. How he prattles now! I hinted that he was old enough to be brought to church of a Sunday, but Beth Lawson would hear none of it, saying that so much of their business was with chapel folk, that to do so would be to steal the bread from their own table. Reluctantly, I gave over insisting, for I can see the truth of it. Still, I wish I could see more of my godson, for I have little occasion to get out to Winnard's Mill.

*   *   *

Mudge to Lucy, May

Really Lucy, there is no need to apologise again. I quite understand how busy you have been with the preparations for Isobel's wedding. Indeed, it was tactless of me to insist, and not to have realised your predicament for myself.

It is unfortunate that Mr Kennington should be coming when our little world is in such turmoil, except for one thing: Plumley's bequest ensures that Fretton can have the finest organ that money can buy, and your husband will be delighted to find his hands are not to be tied by any financial constraints.

*   *   *

Dearest Lucy,

No doubt your husband will be sharing his impressions of his visit with you, rendering this missive superfluous. Yet I cannot shake off the habit of correspondence, even though it is a habit born of loneliness: though for the duration of his stay I have been far from lonely. Indeed, I would go so far as to claim that if he came to my house as a brother, he shall be leaving it also as a friend.

Besides, I find your husband's company so congenial that I am almost tempted to say that I am glad he came alone. He and I share the same tastes exactly, and on the days he has no business over in Fretton we have taken to meeting at half–past twelve for one of Mrs T's lunches. Contrary to my usual custom, we permit ourselves a bottle of Muscadet with lunch, and what seemed an extravagance on the day of your husband's arrival has, through repetition, already established itself as a necessary custom! Our afternoons are spent walking, and in the evening, before dinner, your husband entertains me to a half–hour of music. Why! you never told me he had such a talent for the violin, and were he here for a little longer I do believe I would beg him to accept me as one of his pupils.

On Wednesday he invited me to walk over to Fretton church with him to see his work for myself, for he said it was one thing to see his drawings in my own study, but quite another to appreciate them *in situ*. Despite some initial reluctance to go where I might meet as obstreperous a colleague as Finch, I allowed him to convince me, and I must say that the outing was a great success: there is a pathway up Fretton Hill which offers such an excellent view not only of Lancaradoc tower, but also, due to the way the valley falls off sharply at that point, as far off as Porthcado harbour, with a glimpse of the glittering sea, and the rugged cliffs of The Pinnacles beyond, that I feel it is a shame that I do not go that way more often. Consequently, we had just debouched into the lane above, when I let out a hallelujah of satisfaction: 'So Kennington's to bring the bellow's breath to birdsong's temple!'

Naturally, your husband was at a loss to comprehend me. 'Don't you see, sir, you are the bringer of organ music, which is bellow's breath, and birdsong's temple is Finch's church. It's a kenning, which is a figure of speech employing a figurative circumlocution in place of a common noun. A kenning for Mr Kennington!'

Your husband did not appear to appreciate my jest. Not immediately, at least. We reached Fretton, just as the first drops of a shower began to splatter on the flagstones of the churchyard path. It was a typically Cornish shower, by which I mean we had been able to watch it blow in from the sea, the one black cloud shepherded inland among a flock of many white ones, and just as we had been able to watch its arrival with the calm assurance that it would not reach us till we had gained the protection of the church, so were we persuaded of its rapid passing with equal equanimity. All we had to do was to prolong our visit to the church by a little more than was necessary for your husband to take the measurements he had come for, which gave me ample time to peruse the windows. Some of the glass is medieval, and I was able to make out several of the saints, including one I took to be St Cadoc, for it shows a torrent of water springing up between the hills, where a cowled figure stands, striking the ground with his staff.

Alas, however, our sensible arrangement was confounded by the arrival of Fretton's vicar. He rushed into the church in a hunting jacket, and scarcely grunted a greeting to your husband. He just charged through to his vestry, then shot out again clutching two bottles of wine in his fist, as unceremoniously as if he were visiting his cellar. Luckily, I was half hidden behind a pillar when he came in, and had the wit to remain there, so that he failed to see me.

After Finch had gone, slamming the door behind him, I moved over to where your husband was crouching in a corner of the north transept, jotting down the last of his measurements in his pocket book. He looked up at me with a grin: 'It seems that the songbird is stealing his sun's blood from the Son's house.' And although I thought this was a rather feeble attempt at a kenning, it was a kenning nonetheless, and I was delighted that he should have risen to the game.

Since then our jests have been coming thick and fast. Thus, at table, I ask Kennington for the *crystals of woe*, and he passes me the salt; *the snake-charmer's limp* was your husband's reference to pepper corns. Indeed, the little game that we have invented is proving a useful code in Mrs T's presence, as well as affording us both much amusement. My housekeeper has ears everywhere. Moreover, and much to my consternation, she appears to have developed an antipathy for your husband which borders on outright rudeness. I fail to understand why.

For example, at lunch yesterday, after the conversation had turned to the late Sir Henry Plumley and the circumstances of his demise, your husband alluded to the unfortunate stories he has heard concerning Roslyn Cridden. Of course, Kennington could not have been spared such tattle, even if he had wanted to, for the village is still awash with the sorry saga of Fretton Hall. Was it true, he asked, that the maid had been expecting Plumley's child? Just then, Mrs T entered, bearing a tureen of mulligatawny soup. It was clear that she must have heard his question, and were I not to answer, it would be all too obvious that her entrance was the reason why. So I offered the best circumlocution I could muster: 'There's many a spring flower,' I proffered, 'who'll open her petals to a hoary sun, though the reasons for it may beggar belief.' By the rules of our game, this was a weak retort indeed, for it was but the feeblest figure of speech, containing no true kenning at all – and yet I believe it was enough to give your husband his answer, and to save face before the housekeeper.

But the morning grows late, and I must leave you now if I am to carry out my plan of secreting this letter in his luggage, along with a small gift from the kitchen, for I would not wish to encumber Arthur with a protracted leave–taking, nor do I trust myself to carry one off. I have engaged a carter for half–past two and your husband's bags are already in the hall. For the love I bear him, and you, my good sister, I shall endeavour to make our last meal together as jovial an occasion as those that have gone before, although in truth his departure fills me with a sadness that verges on despair.

* * *

Mudge to Lucy, August

Dear Lucy,

Mrs T says to tell you that the trick of a heavy cake is to roll the dough out flat and to bake it in a quick oven. I have made enquiries of my own regarding the name, which is not, as it would appear to be, a slander against this most toothsome and digestible currant bread. Rather, 'heavy' is here a corruption of the Cornish word 'hevva', which is to say, a shoal of fish. The fishermen's wives make the cake in summer time, when the pilchards are sighted, to provide something to eat during the hectic days when they and their children are engaged in stacking and salting the pilchards, and for weeks at a time are too busy to bake bread.

This afternoon I have received a visit from Jack Purvey, the carter from the parish of St Breward, up on the moors, which has re-awoken my interest in Cornwall's saints, as well as supplying me with yet more proof that Rees's distinction is unsustainable.

Admittedly, Mr Purvey is a rough-looking fellow, a former sailor, with a complexion as dusky as any Spaniard's, and a furry birthmark upon his neck, such that Mrs T was loathe to show him into the parlour, fearing as she does for the antimacassars.

But bless my soul, if he didn't tell me the most intriguing tale about St Barry of Fowey! Excusing, as one must, the accretion of quaint superstition which these tales invariably acquire when passed down from generation to generation as local folk-lore, one point of the tale struck me with such force that I was inclined to clap the fellow upon his back, for it demonstrates that Barry, or Fimbarrus, one of the sons of King Brychan, had dealings with St Illtud's school at Llantwit Major, which exactly confirms my suspicions.

So when Carter Purvey had delivered himself of his tale, I was as eager as a school boy to put it down on paper, and sent him to Mrs Tredennick's kitchen for a cup of tea.

Here is the tale, which I set down at once, lest any detail be lost. This may excuse the lack of polish about the draft; but to place a son of Brychan's with St Illtud, thereby reopening the vexed question of a net divide between true saints and false, is one of those advances which are the culminating joys of the scholar's efforts.

How a son of Brychan came to Llantwit Major

King Brychan had so many children that he couldn't even count them, let alone remember their names. Among the boys there was Nectan, of course, his first born, and Clether and Issey, but it was the girls he chiefly recognised – after all, anyone who has fathered fourteen – or twenty-four, or sixty-four – children is bound to be something of ladies' man.

Barry was one of the boys he had quite forgotten. Born to an Irish slave-girl, who left the world in bringing her love-child into it, Barry was taken by his sister, Endellion, to Cornwall, when she went to join her brother Nectan there, and given to a tanner's daughter to suckle, in exchange for a bag of barley.

Yet saintly blood will out, and as soon as he could walk, Barry attached himself to St Hydroc and tended his pigs.

Now Hydroc was a tepid saint. On high days and holy days he felt called to a hermit's life up on the moor, but for the rest he liked the beech wood valleys, and was too fond of a leg of pork and a jug of ale with his neighbours to change his ways. It was these mingling currents of hot and cold that rendered Hydroc lukewarm. His brother, St Madron, thought him affable but uninspired; only Barry knew the alternating warmth of his affection with the chill of censorship. Hydroc would beat the boy, and curse him, and chase him away when the moods of God were on him, but cram him with solicitude and acorn fritters six days out of seven.

Neither treatment was satisfactory to Barry. He was a quiet boy, but stubborn and proud, who used his hands in the service of Hydroc's pigs, while his heart was set on emulating his more fortunate brothers. However, a saint needs a good education, and that costs money: the years of his boyhood were slipping by, and Barry – forgotten by his family – was little more than a swineherd and a servant to Hydroc.

So when it become known that St Illtud was offering a scholarship to study at his school at Llantwit Major, and that this would be awarded for the best essay, in Latin, on the subject of living arrangements aboard Noah's Ark, Barry went down on his knees between the pig troughs, and praised God for answering his prayers.

No matter that his dog-Latin would shame a hedge-priest, or that the pages of his spidery scrawl resembled leaf-mould in a state of advanced decomposition – Barry would take his essay to Bodmin Priory and ask the monks there to make a fair copy for him.

And it was only when his essay was wrapped in oilskins and safe in St Goran's scrip, and the scrip was about Goran's holy neck, and St Goran was in his coracle, paddling down the Camel towards the sea and to Wales – only then – that Barry dared approach his master in confession and tell him what he had done.

Hydroc was furious. He beat Barry so hard that the old man couldn't lift up a candle-stick for a week. Moreover, even when his anger abated, he couldn't resign himself to what Barry had done. How had he done it? Where had he got the money from to pay the monks at Bodmin?

'From my sister,' admitted Barry. 'Do you remember the day I asked to take the pigs as far as Killibury? On the way back I called in to see St Mabyn. I was hoping she could help me with my Latin.'

'And did she?'

'No, but she gave me three groats, though. It was money she was saving for a cow.'

'So you robbed the blessed Mabyn of her cow?' Hydroc reached for his belt again. But this time the strokes were so feeble that it took Barry all his sense to keep a grin off his face.

Hydroc was still bemused. Only three groats? That would hardly recompense the Bodmin scribes. After compline he put his hand on the boy's shoulder, determined to quiz him further. 'So tell me, Barry, what's the going rate for a page of fairest Latin?'

Barry's eyes flicked nervously about the corners of the chapel before he answered. 'A groat, Father.'

'But you had only three, you say?'

'Exactly. I asked the monks to do the first page, and the last – and one chosen at random from the middle. The rest I left to God.'

When the old saint saw the limitlessness of Barry's faith, he relented. 'Good lad,' said Hydroc. 'You had better have my cloak. And be sure to wake me before you leave in the morning: I wouldn't want you to sail without my blessing.'

Alas, Lucy, I am cast down, and justly rebuked for my hubris of yester-eve.

I had not a half–hour finished my writing, and picked up a volume of Bishop Taylor's sermons to wile away the time until supper, when we were disturbed by a most unseemly commotion on the lawn.

Lobb and Ruan were hissing and squawking like the geese upon the Roman Capitaline, all but drowning out the sound of shouting.

It was that man Purvey come back. He had evidently spent the intervening hours availing himself of Landlord Barret's hospitality down at the Falcon, for he was as boisterous as a miner on Mazey Monday. Lifting the corner of a curtain to espy the lawn – for in such a situation I felt the most prudent course would be to ascertain his request in this tangential manner, before opening the front door to him – I could see him swaying upon the lawn like a scatter-crow before a gale. The peacocks had hold of a trouser leg apiece, as valiant as any bull-terriers, but the man was not affrighted. He was cupping both hands to his mouth and hollering the most vile insults. I was heralded as a 'fat black beetle' and worse, but the drift of the message was that he had traipsed all day across the moor, and 'where was that b....'s silver shilling to?'

It is true, that often in exchange for such information I reward the teller with a coin from my waistcoat pocket, but yesterday I had evidently overlooked my customary habit, being so eager to have at my desk. That he should come back to claim his shilling as though it were a 'wage' struck me as the height of impudence, but nonetheless, to calm the fellow's nerves, and for the sake of the peacocks, I instructed Mrs Tredennick to set a lamp and take the carter his coin.

This morning I awoke with a most foul suspicion. If the word has got out that Parson Mudge is prepared to pay a shilling for items of folk–lore treating of Cornwall's forgotten holy men, do you think that a merely mercenary incentive might not encourage the less scrupulous to embellish their tales somewhat, and that my generosity is having the unforeseen effect of tainting the font at which my scholarship is watered?

But this realisation, far from plunging me into one of the moods of despair which I am prone to, fills me with a curious elation. I have a strange sensation – call it an intuition if you like – that such setbacks are but the prelude to a great work, a new work, that I am called to. What it is to be I do not know exactly, but the clue lies somewhere with St Adwen and the extraordinary reactions her name provoked both from Mrs Tredennick and the Veens. My vocation is to uncover a new meaning in the lives of Cornwall's saints – for if they are to serve us still, then they must do so as a living witness, as resurrected figures, and not as Rees would have them: mere cadavers on the antiquarian's dissecting table. Perhaps I have been brought to Lancaradoc for a great purpose, and begin to envisage God's plan for me. The time has come to work on, as the Carthusians would recommend, in exile, in silence, and in cunning.

* * *

Dearest Isobel,

Your letter brings such happy tidings! I would that I could kiss you on the cheek, and shake Mr Wattling by the hand! If it's a boy and he is one wit as clever as his mother, or a girl who is one jot as pretty, the child shall be fortunate indeed! And what of your mother? I expect she plans to come to Salisbury for the lying in.

For my part, I am similarly in a position to cosset my godson, for I am preparing a fine gift for him. Do you remember that gully that lies half-way between Crad Head and The Pinnacles? I was out for a walk there, last Friday morn, on the first calm day after a week of gales, when my curiosity was aroused by an object among the rocks. It was something red and white. On clambering down I discovered that it was a rocking horse! Perhaps it was part of the cargo of the *Tracey Vine*, which went down off Pentire last month – but that is only a conjecture. However, despite its ordeal among the breakers – one white horse among others you might say! – it was remarkably well-preserved. Apart from a few knocks to the paint on one of its forelegs, it is only the red velveteen saddle which needs repair, and Mrs T has agreed to undertake that for me. Hoiking it back to Lancaradoc, however, called for quite an exertion, I can tell you, but it will be worth it just to see the delight on Dickie's face. Besides, to come home with my sea booty made me feel a proper Cornishman!

I have had a curious introduction, of which I shall write more below, but my main news – that which treats of those you know – is sober, if not unexpected. A week ago I buried Alice Veen. She was ninety-three and passed away peacefully. To bury a righteous woman like that, surrounded by her family, in the fullness of her years and on a placid spring morning, makes if not for a happy end – for there are none – then at least for a fitting one. Were it not for her funeral coming so soon upon that of her grandson, there would have been little to grieve. As it is, Matthew Veen is distraught enough to talk of selling up and trying his luck in New South Wales.

Surely not? said I. We were on the rectory lawn, Veen having come to discuss his mother's headstone. Well he didn't see much hope for the twins in Porthcado; the fish were too fickle to offer any of them a future.

I had heard that last year's fishing brought in a record catch. It had. But with pilchards in Plymouth fetching as little as threepence a hogshead, and all the profits of the continental trade going to middle men, the seine fleet had barely met its overheads. And was there no money in the Italian trade? Aye there was, but that was all going to the merchants in Falmouth and Bristol, and not to the fishermen. But what if the seine fleet were to sell to Italy direct? Were there no boats in our harbour that could make the voyage out to Leghorn, or Porthcado mariners experienced enough to sail them? Veen agreed, in a lacklustre way, that there might be. The problem was how to manage such a venture. For who would they sell to, and how would they go about finding a merchant in Genoa or Naples with any command of English? Why not try Latin? said I – after all, they were the Pope's own people, and the Italian dialects were descended from the Latin tongue. Suddenly Veen looked up, his eye a–twinkle. 'By Jove, Mudge, I think you've got it!' and before I knew it, we had gone indoors and Veen was dictating a veritable commercial treaty for me to translate. We closeted ourselves away in the study, and as we worked I was toasted with a bottle of my own brandy, and extolled as the saviour of Porthcado's fisher fleet.

The euphoria was short-lived. It was not simply that I may have taken a glass more brandy that I've a head for, but that when, on the morrow, I read over those eight close-packed pages that Veen had made me write out, what with their lading charges, and freight charges, and points of exchange pertaining to aforesaids and heretofores and I know not what – I could scarce understand a word of it. And if I were not able to follow their import, how on earth was I supposed to translate them into Latin, a tongue I have never had much skill of?

I had all but chewed my way through three quills when I was bit by a crafty idea. Surely those French nuns who have hidden themselves away in Plumley's great house would speak Latin like they were born to it? What else did they spend their days at, but gabbling away at a Latin psalter while clicking their worry beads? For an hour I put the idea from me: it was hardly seemly that I intrude upon them, least of all to beg the translation of a letter of commerce. But when I had struggled with the letter some more, and admitted that my task was hopeless, the notion of introducing myself to the convent increasingly presented itself as a courteous and neighbourly one. Surely they would accept the letter as my pretext for disturbing their solitude? So I set aside my reluctance, put on my coat, and set out for Fretton.

The reception they gave me was most cordial, although for a moment, as I stood before the great iron gates and pulled at the bell rope, I imagined myself to be some antique Greek on the threshold of Hades. For there I stood, with the Cornish sun upon my shoulders, clutching the gift I'd brought, a three-pound jar of moorland honey, and waited to be led into the bowels of that dark house. Soon, a silent black-clothed wraith slipped out by the main door, and glided down the gravel path to meet me. Moreover, she unchained the gates and bid me follow her without a word – whether because of her order's strict rule of silence, or because she spoke no English, I have no idea.

Yet the moment I stepped across the threshold my forebodings were dispelled. There was something reassuring in the beeswax odour of the polished floors, and in the fragrances emanating from the kitchen, something in the warm gleam of polished brass that met the eye. Although the house had been grand enough in Plumley's day, then its dim interiors had spoken of dinginess, but now there was an aura of decorum and comfort which struck a new note, and which I had not been expecting. The silent sister glided up the stairs before me. I followed. She knocked on the door that had once been Plumley's bedroom, but which was now a handsome study. Within, I was greeted by Mère Agathe, the mother superior. She stood between the casement windows, a tiny woman, in a black habit like the nun's, but without the wimple. She took my hand in both of hers and smiled, saying, before I had a chance to introduce myself, 'Ah this must be Parson Mudge. And you have brought us some of your famous honey. How kind!'

I was offered tea – a pale, tepid brew, when it came, soured with a rind of lemon – yet that hardly mattered. We began by talking of the clement weather, which Mère Agathe said she was delighted with. Before she came, she had been most fearful of the English climate, which apparently is much maligned in France. I replied that such a mild winter as this was quite an anomaly, and that I had even spotted some leaf bud on the hawthorn as I was coming up Fretton Hill. Was not the absence of frost a good omen for the bees?, she asked. I replied that it was. These French ladies have such courtly manners. Would I like to see the improvements to the grounds? The house, as she was sure I would understand, could not be viewed, but she would gladly give me a tour of the garden. I went out without my coat; nor did I feel the lack of it. She showed me the orchard wall, where the nuns have planted a row of pear trees, mere seedlings as yet, and have installed an ingenious system of wires to train them to grow flat against the bricks. From thence the good mother superior led me to the gate, and I realised that she meant to take her leave of me. I'd left my coat in her study, I explained. And besides, there was something I meant to ask her. We went inside again. Seated at her desk, I took out Veen's letter and told her my hopes of finding a translator.

Mon Père Mudge, of course it could be done. But why Latin? One of her nuns was from Nice, and of mixed parentage: surely it would be more useful to have these letters rendered directly into Italian? I could not believe such fortune. Soeur Madeleine was sent for – a swarthy girl, and most timid – or perhaps she was shy of English, for she answered Mère Agathe rapidly enough in French, and I could see from her nods and smiles that she would accept the work, and with enthusiasm also.

When the Italian nun had left us, Mère Agathe invited me to look over their new chapel, which had been constructed in the north wing by converting Plumley's billiard room, as well as the servants' rooms above it. She was particularly proud of the ceiling, which had only just been completed. I was surprised to learn that she had engaged two plasterers who came all the way from Antwerp to do the work. I replied that I would be intrigued to see it.

Then the doubt struck me – and I felt confident enough in Mère Agathe's company to ask at once: in a houseful of nuns, who said their mass for them? Why their priest of course: Father Benedict. And did he live with them? That would be hardly fitting, would it, for all that he was in his seventies? And as she spoke, Mère Agathe tossed back her head and laughed. No, he had taken rooms next door, with Parson Finch. With Finch? I could scarcely conceal my surprise. That Finch was in cahoots with the convent, even to the extent of having their priest lodge with him, seemed most incongruous. However I was unable to enquire further. Just at that moment – we were at the foot of the stairs – one of her nuns – I believe it was the one who had met me at the gate, though I could not be sure – came scampering up and begin addressing my hostess excitedly. I could see at once from the mother superior's face that something untoward had occurred. And indeed, as soon as they had finished, Mère Agathe turned to me with a distracted air, proffering her hand. She was extremely sorry, but her presence was required immediately in the scullery. One of the sisters had sliced off her the top of her thumb while dicing turnips. Would I mind letting myself out? No of course not. But first I must take a look at their chapel. Yes, yes, I said I would. I stammered my concern – as well as gratitude – by way of leave–taking, but already my remarks were addressed to her retreating back.

The ceiling was indeed quite remarkable. It is decorated like a cave of ice, in which are set three octagonal paintings. I could not help but feel that such an ornate roof must be a distraction from prayer, as well as an invitation to cricked necks and stumbling feet. But what a blaze of colour! Of blue and golds! I had never before thought that the tone of a Roman church would be so different from our own, nor how our notions of the Divine could be so moulded by the plastic arts. Moreover, here the focus is all upon a little chamber above the altar, where they keep the host. Rather than the cross, one's attention – when it is not wrenched upwards by the figures overhead – goes to this little cupboard, which sits above the altar like a pixie's den.

My musings were interrupted by the realisation that I was not alone. Along the back of the chapel runs a gallery, which is fronted by a heavy grill: this presumably is to screen the nuns from the common gaze. And some of the nuns were up there now. I do believe that the noise that drew my attention to them was a kind of tittering. I do not know what they found for their amusement, but it was a most unsettling incongruity to hear nuns giggling, and in their own church. Then a voice spoke, most clearly, which seemed to be Soeur Madeleine's: 'Regardez là. Le voilà notre cornichon.'

Now I am no linguist, Isobel, but this much I could understand. I thought to reply, and to tell them that they were mistaken: for I am no Cornishman, and that to be an Englishman in this strange land made me as much a foreigner as they. But I kept my tongue – it is strange how self-conscious one grows in the presence of other people's laughter.

1851

Oh Isobel,

I have written you a letter – and such a letter – but more fool I am for that, for who is there to take it hence? Isobel, I wrote to tell you that Dicky, dear Dicky, is dead. The Lawsons are all dead, all except Jemma, and she lies in a corner of our hospital now, and I fear it is but a question of time for her too.

We are besieged, marooned, forgotten. Truly the dead have been left to bury their dead, and as rector of this parish it falls upon me to wield the shovel. How is it possible that we have been so utterly abandoned? Even the sails have disappeared from our horizon. But such thoughts are the results of the fever.

When I woke this morning and saw the letter I had written to you lying on the table, I resolved I would begin again and set everything down, from the first hint of our disaster until today, in the hope that one day this account might reach you, and you might know how it had gone with the child, and with your uncle.

Possibly, I was the last person in the parish to hear of it. Mrs T had just taken away the supper plates – this was on a Tuesday, for I distinctly remember it was mutton broth – and had snuffed the candles, and turned up the lamp by the reading desk, when she made her extraordinary request. Might she and her husband have the use of the spare room for a while, beginning that very night? I looked up in surprise. 'We've visitors – a cousin from Plymouth and all her family. They came on us of a sudden, or I would have able to make other arrangements.'

What a bizarre request: the apothecary sleeping under the roof of my own house! Of course, from time to time Mrs T sleeps over – she even keeps a bed made up for herself in that small chamber on the stairs – as housekeeper, her duties occasionally oblige her to. But to have the both of them, man and wife, moving in as though the rectory were an hotel! I didn't know how to answer. Or better, I did – that this was most irregular. Whatever could have made Mrs T countenance such a notion?

Yet that was not my answer. Looking back, it is as though a sixth sense alerted me that some much larger drama was afoot. I don't think I believed her story for a minute, although I made a pretence of doing so.

'Mrs T,' I replied: 'I am sure I can rely on you to see that I am not inconvenienced in any way by this arrangement.'

'Oh thank you, sir.' And she said it with such a rush of emotion, that when she left the room I sat staring at the study wall for nigh on ten minutes, wondering what could be at the bottom of it. Then I was aroused by the noise of his arrival at the kitchen door. He must have been loitering in the outhouses, anticipating my acceptance of his wife's request. Not that they made much noise, of course. He crept in, and up the back stairs, like a thief in the night. I confess: I strained to hear as much as I could; I even went to the foot of the stairs when they were on the floor above, in the hope that a word or two of their conversation might enlighten me as to what was going on. But I heard nothing.

I arose the next morning in a belligerent frame of mind, for as you can imagine, I had slept fitfully enough. So when Mrs T began to bring me my breakfast in the parlour, as she is wont to do of a Sunday – for all that this was a Wednesday morning – and I knew that the man was enjoying the warmth of my own kitchen range, I couldn't resist a barb.

'What, has Mr Tredennick caught some infectious disease, that he is not able join company for breakfast?'

And never did barb strike home more deeply. Mrs T dropped the tea-pot. You may remember the one, Isobel: the four-cup pot, in the form of a Java pineapple. It has always been a favourite of mine.

'Infectious disease, Mr Mudge? Then you have heard?'

It was my turn for surprise. 'Heard, Mrs T? I have heard nothing. Although there is evidently something to hear. Tell me, what is passing for news at the fish stalls of Porthcado?'

But the good Mrs T refused to respond. 'Nothing that I know of, sir,' she said, and went out for the mop. The tea was made afresh. Mr Tredennick declined the invitation to join me. I heard no more of him – neither mouth–speech nor footfall – yet he stayed in the house, I am sure of it. All morning I was listening for the sound of the gate, but it never came. Strange that he should not be off to his shop, I thought: but it was no business of mine.

I spent the morning in the study, to work on a story I have been writing about St Selevan. Then, at lunch, Mrs T again put me in the parlour, treating me like a lonely potentate. I went back up to the study after I had despatched a turbot, and finished a dish of Mrs T's excellent Queen's pudding, but I could not settle to my work. So I forsake my desk for the armchair and took down my copy of 'Tales from Shakespeare'. However I could not even manage that gentle task of self–improvement, and I was itching to get out for a walk, only the morning's fret had changed to drizzle, which seemed set to worsen into rain, when – and this must have been at about half-past two – I definitely did hear the gate, and the peacocks too. A visitor! I went to the window, and stooped down to try and make out who it was, but the pane was so misted over and runnelled with rain, that I could make out no more than that it was a man in a cape and sou'wester: yet I could see both from the cane he was carrying, and from his bearing, that this was a gentleman, and not one of the Porthcado fishermen. So I changed my shoes, and waiting for Mrs T to announce him.

It was the Methodist, Reverend Penworthy, and I could tell at a glance that he was in a most agitated state of mind. Yet I have always been well-disposed towards Penworthy, and remembering his former visit here, when I was still quite green in the parish, I offered him a cup of tea.

'Tea, sir! At a time like this?'

'Granted, it is a good while before the customary hour, but on such an afternoon as this...'

'Fool!' he shouted. I must say, I was quite taken aback. My look of puzzlement – indeed, it must have been a wounded look, for that is what I felt – could not have gone unnoticed, because Penworthy was obliged to explain himself: 'Damn it all Mudge, you must either be a buffoon, or a hypocrite, carrying on as if we were paying social calls at a time like this, and keeping the apothocary locked up here in your fine old country house when Porthcado has never had such need of him.'

'Tredennick? Locked up?'

'Yes, sir. You want to lord it over the teapot in this safe retreat, having engaged the only man with any medical experience as though he were your private physician, while the cholera carries off those souls that parliament, and our taxes, have put into your care.'

'Did you say cholera?'

It was Penworthy's turn to look perplexed. 'Good God, Mudge, you really haven't heard, have you?'

I got my coat at once. Penworthy gave an account of the

victims. The first had been Arnie Cridden, a fisherman in Dolphin Street, and already half the houses in that tight–packed slum up against the harbour where rife with the affliction.

'Good God in Heaven!' I stuttered as we stood together in the porch. 'What can I do? What should we do for them?' For I was anxious that I, who lived among them as a man of God, might be of some comfort to them in the hour of reckoning. I handed Penworthy the spare umbrella.

'Do, Mudge? There's not a lot of doing left. That was for Tredennick, but he bolted at the first hurdle. All we can do is walk among them and offer the consolation of our faith to whoever is prepared to accept it.'

'I suppose you are right, sir. And if you've no objection, we'll make our visits together. This is no time to stand upon squabbles of doctrine, and if I were to go alone there's many a family in Porthcado who'd give me a friendly wink in the ally, but who would thing twice before having me in their parlour.'

Penworthy gave his consent most willingly, and even urged me to fetch my stole, observing that besides bringing comfort to those who were inclined towards popery, it would certainly brighten up our appearance, for in our black cassocks we resembled a couple of carrion crows.

It is hard to describe my thoughts as we trod the familiar path along the stream towards Porthcado: fear for what I would meet there, certainly, and a prayer that I might be of some use, but beyond that a withering numbness, an inability to think, which descends upon us when faced with calamity, and which is as much a blessing as an affliction in moments of crisis. Porthcado high street was ghostly quiet. We trudged down it and straight towards the jumble of fisherman's cottages that lie at the bottom of the hill. Imagine, the second of the houses we visited was deserted, empty – one of the children had already been carried away for burial, along with their mother, and Tom Badding, their father, had disappeared along with the eldest girl. Later we discovered them at his wife's sister's, he with the blueness already on his lips and his daughter in good health, but shocked – she did not acknowledge our presence, and sat in a corner of the room, hugging her knees and rocking herself, staring fixedly at the wall opposite. Penworthy laid his hand upon her head and blessed her with such fervour that it was a most moving sight, though I fear I was touched less by his show of faith, and more by the seeming ineffectiveness of the gesture upon the girl, and by the pity that such a scene evoked.

We toured the fisherman's hovels till well into the night, and in cottage after cottage we met with the same terrible absences: of those who had been carried away by the epidemic, and – which was worse – the vacancy in those who were left alive. The disease's progress is dramatic, and though I would have wished it otherwise, I am now well acquainted with its stages. It begins, like many a minor indisposition, with a headache and vomiting; then precedes to a chronic loosening of the bowels. At this stage there is no telling whether these initial symptoms are all the infected person will suffer, or whether the disease is to run its full course. If the latter, this is usually signalled by perturbations to the victim's mental state: he or she will begin to garble and is given to anxiety-ridden hallucinations: I saw one man tear off his shoes and throw them in the stove, for he was convinced that they had come to eat him – and those who ministered to him had to come into the room barefoot until the end. Once such raving begins, it is but a short time before the critical phase is reached – a terrible coma in which the victim's whole face appears to shrivel and wither, as though it were some head-hunter's trophy. The lips turn blue and the tongue exudes a coat of white slime. Yet the most alarming system, and the one most indicative of the outcome of the coma, is to be seen in the whites of the eyes; most of those who fall into a coma have demonstrated such a yellowing of the eyes that I can tell at once that I shall soon be reciting the prayers for the departed.

When we had visited all the houses in Low Town we decided to return to those which were worst afflicted. Although whether our presence there brought them any consolation I could not say. I doubt it.

By ten o'clock we adjudged that we had done as much as we could for one day, and Penworthy invited me to join him for a bite of supper before I walked the three mile home to Lancaradoc. Indeed, he urged me to consider his invitation for my health's sake, for the cholera is more a prey on man's good sense – or rather, lack of sense – as an indiscriminate pestilence. If a man takes care of himself, rests, eats, keeps his person and his household clean, and above all, if he looks the disease straight in the eye, without succumbing to his fear of it – why, I do believe that such a man will no more die of the cholera than a shepherd is likely to drown at sea. In short, Penworthy would not have me walk the road home on an empty stomach, and I was glad of his company.

However, I was shocked by the modesty of his household. He has one of the new cottages upon the cliff; from without it is remarkable for its tidiness, and the neatness of his patch of garden, but within – why the house was as bare as a herring–bone. He offered me some wizened cheese and a piece of bread that was none too fresh, and I would have enjoyed this meagre fare more willingly had he produced a bottle of claret, or even some ale, or the cider that the labourers use, except I dare not ask for any liquor, knowing how dear the temperance cause lies with the Wesleyans. It was a dismal meal after such a harrowing day, and though the minister offered me a bed for the night, for it was nigh on midnight by the time we'd supped, and I would have to be in the village again on the morrow, I refused. Indeed, I fair fled that cheerless house. The day's experience had taught me one thing: in the face of death I have found that I am a braver man than I would have given myself credit for, but before an empty pantry I am reduced to whimpering cowardice!

It was when I was crossing Long Meadow – for the moon was up, and I know that path so well that I have no need to take the road even by night – that I remembered the Lawsons. Oh Isobel, forgive me – but such had been the shock of the day that I had not given Dicky one thought till then! Who knew how they were faring at Winnard's Mill? Not that there was much that I could do at that hour, but I resolved to walk over there as soon as it was light, despite my promise to Penworthy to return to Porthcado early next morning.

And another thing troubled me as I walked through the wood, now grey and ghostly, towards the rectory. What would I say to the Tredennicks? Such a pair of conniving cowards they had turned out to be, Isobel, and how disgracefully the apothecary had abandoned his calling. I am not comfortable in the robes of the stern admonitor, but this was an occasion when it was my clear duty to don them. I would have to have words – that I knew – but which words? For all my years of experience in the pulpit had not prepared me for the homily I was called upon to give that night, by my own fireside, to my housekeeper and her poltroon of a husband.

I was still turning the matter over in my head, and was no nearer to satisfying myself on how to begin, when I came up through the field that adjoins the bottom lawn. How odd, it struck me, that there should not be a lamp in the house. Even if they were abed, it was most unlike Mrs T not to leave a light for me. I reached the porch, and tugged at the bell-pull – for in my haste to leave the house with Mr Penworthy, I had forgotten my latch key. There was no reply. It was only when I pulled on the bell a second time that the truth began to dawn on me: they had done a flit, my housekeeper and her husband. Their cowardice had found them out, and the shame of it was too much for them. I pushed against the door, and found it open. Then, on going in, I wandered from room to room, for while my mind had understood at once that they had clearly fled, my heart was unable to reconcile itself so easily to such a loss. Indeed, they have not been seen in the parish since, and although I have made enquiries, I have come by no news of them. A pity, for I counted Tredennick as a friend of mine and his wife has served me devotedly for the last five years. Despite their desertion, I cannot find it in my heart to wish them harm, and would be right comforted by the news that they are well.

And so, as the great diarist said, to bed. I slept in my clothes and without a fire, for I was exhausted. I woke the next morning with a raging headache, but had the sense to see at once that this was the result of yesterday's exertion, and of the tension that my nerves had been exposed to – I am sanguine enough not to have been to duped into the suspicion that this was an early symptom of the cholera. Breakfast, alas, was little better than the last night's supper, for Mrs T had abandoned her duties in the pantry: I found some bread and enough milk in a jug for half a glass. I drank it off, although it already had a whiff of cheese about it.

Thence to Winnard's Mill. As I approached, the scene looked reassuringly familiar: the three goats were tethered to the hawthorn bush in the meadow as you come out of the wood, the geese were kicking up a rumpus as I crossed the stream – the which brought Michael to the upstairs window. In other circumstances his 'Halt, who goes there?' would have seemed an uncivil greeting, but under the circumstances it was prudent enough. When I showed myself and explained that I merely wished to ascertain that they were well, Mike Lawson relaxed somewhat, and called upon Jemma to come to the window. They were all well, thank the Lord, and were determined to live in quarantine until the epidemic had passed. Was there anything I could bring them? No, they were well supplied. Then little Dicky was lifted to the window and piped up for a pound of 'nicies'. I was about to say I would see what I could do, when his father clipped him round the ear for his impudence in addressing the parson in such a way, a rebuke which the little fellow took in good humour. And with that I left them, promising to return in a day or two with the news from Porthcado.

A pound of nicies, indeed! If I had known then what was to befall them at the mill, I would have hot–footed it to Exeter to buy up all the nicies in the diocese. As it was, I took the lane out through Polgarrick with a light heart and came round to the sea town by the cliff path.

Penworthy was already out visiting along Fore Street when I arrived. Although the casualties there were not as grim as in the squalid quarters we had visited the day before, we were to assist at one scene which ended tragically. You will remember Miss Purvey who keeps the school? However, I don't recall if you knew of her father, who, alas for the good woman, is as monstrous an old rogue as any in these parts. He works, when he's fit to, as a carter out towards St Breward, and only makes demands on his daughter's society when, after some high-jinx or other, he can no longer show his face abroad, or when he's gone through his money. It is Miss Purvey's ill-fortune that he should have chosen this month for an extended visit – and more than once I have met the good schoolmistress in the village of late and observed her looking most pitifully careworn.

With the scare of the epidemic she had thought to lock her father in the attic to keep him out of the beer dens he is all too fond of. But the old scoundrel had succeeded in climbing out onto the roof and was yelling every obscenity he could muster. Then some wag among the crowd that had gathered on the hillside to witness this entertainment attempted to arm him with a firkin of cider. A rope was thrown, which Jack Purvey managed to catch and secure around the chimney with impressive dexterity. The cider was duly dispatched – first to him, then by him – and we were all treated to a concert the like of which has never been heard outside the meanest kiddleywink. Penworthy implored him to desist, and had a slate thrown at him for his pains. Then, the firkin empty, and Eliza Purvey adamant that she wouldn't unlock the attic till her father was sober, the old reprobate got it into his head to climb down by the rope. No doubt his years at sea would have equipped him for such a stunt, except that the chimney collapsed under his weight, and left him dangling from the guttering. A ladder was fetched, and Dennis Lobb's two boys rushed in to the rescue with great pluck.

I cannot be sure exactly what ensued, even though I was witness to it. It seems that the guttering gave way just as John Lobb reached him. We saw the edge of the rusted gutter give the lad such a blow to the side of his face that both he and Purvey swung out, desperately trying to straighten their teetering perch, then collapse onto Will Lobb, who was trying to steady the ladder from below. The upshot of all this is that John will be lucky not to lose his left eye and Will has three cracked ribs, whereas Purvey got up and dusted himself off without a scratch, but hollering for another drink to calm his nerves.

It never ceases to amaze me that a weasel of a man like Dennis Lobb should be blessed with two such outstanding sons. I have seen them both since the accident, and can only remark on their fortitude, and the charity with which they speak of Purvey, while their father huffed and puffed about the farmyard, and would scarce thank me for taking the trouble to visit them. It seems that far from the sins of the father being visited on the sons, Dennis Lobb has such boys that a king would be proud of, while many a more worthy man raises a brood of wastrels and scoundrels.

But to return to the epidemic. On the Friday afternoon, Penworthy and I again made another round of Low Town, where there were fresh cases in almost every house. We were most insistent that the windows were thrown open, for the sake of those as yet safe from infection, yet the villagers were loathe to take even this most elementary precaution.

It was about 4 o'clock when Amos Provis came running up to us in Dolphin Street to say that Old Jarvis had shown symptoms of the disease and that his neighbours insisted that his daughter put him out of doors. We were dumbfounded. This was the first instance of contamination among the big-wigs who live along Top Town, which was discouraging enough, but that the people of Porthcado should turn against their neighbours in such a fashion betrayed a disease of the spirit just as alarming as the physical affliction which blighted us.

Penworthy and I agreed to go with Provis at once. As we laboured up Harbour Hill, I was berating the denizens of Top Town for their coldness of heart. 'You know, Mudge, they may not be entirely wrong,' Penworthy replied. 'Heartless enough, I grant you, but it has always been the habit of the healthy to protect themselves by sending the afflicted away. Just think of the leper colonies of medieval times. The trouble is, Porthcado is such a small place, and so close–packed, that there is nowhere to send them to.' It was at these very words, and we were standing in the shade of that young ash tree, where the road widens, above

Dilley's Cottage – surely you remember the spot I mean, Isobel, for it is impossible to walk up that steep hill without pausing to rest, and this point, just clear of the jumbled roof–tops, offers such an enticing view – when I had an experience which I can only compare to the one which bandy–legged Saul was granted on the road to Damascus. When the idea first struck me, I hardly dare speak for the excitement of it. Nor, indeed, for the audacity of what I was about to offer.

I clutched Penworthy by the elbow. 'Then send them to the rectory. Surely Lancaradoc is remote enough.'

'Good God, man...' Penworthy was beginning to grasp the enormity of what I was proposing.

'We can use the church, too.'

And so it was done. I committed myself to living in daily contact with the disease until either I succumbed, or it receded. I, who have always been incapable of preparing even my own breakfast, and stay abed a week with a cold, was offering to run a hospital! In any other circumstances I would have been laughed at for the buffoon I no doubt am – yet with the threat of the sick contaminating the hale, and the anarchy that would ensue when people started pushing their ailing relatives out of doors, I dare say even Parson Mudge seemed a suitable guardian. Penworthy suggested that he ask for volunteers to share the burden of the quarantine with me, but I would not hear of it. Rather, I said, I would need supplies, in the way of bedding and victuals. For, in the sudden state of euphoria in which I found myself, I was as yet scarce able to focus realistically on the myriad practical difficulties which lay ahead.

When we reached the top of the hill it was agreed that Provis would harness his donkey to the cart, and he and I should begin our rounds at once, asking in every house for whatever bedding they could spare. At about seven o'clock we returned to the harbour, and I was surprised that the poorer homes should have shown themselves so much the more generous. 'Aye. Well they would have more beds to spare,' was Provis's terse reply: 'Like as how there's no one left to fill 'em.'

It was dusk when we set out for home. I do not often travel round by the lane, for the woodland path is more direct, as well as a more picturesque route. Yet there I was perched up on a dozen mattresses, atop of Provis's cart, for all the world like some Ottoman satrap, and high enough to see over the hedges. What a vantage point! It may seem whimsical to remark upon it, and whimsical to have noticed it – but was it not whimsical of the Omnipotent to have thus ordered it? – for the evening was as serene, and the setting sun as beautiful, as any I can remember. For all the exertions of the day, and the evils of the present hour, I fell into a trance which was as near to an intimation of the Lord's presence as I have known for many a year. Even Provis, who usually terrifies me with his rough manners, was changed in an eye. I felt myself in the company of someone strong and peaceful, one of God's own primitives, such as the disciples were, and wished to stretch out and clasp him by the shoulder and would have done so, but for the restraints of my natural reticence.

We unloaded the mattresses by the light of a lamp. Provis carried them into the parlour while I removed the room's furniture, and struggled with it up the stairs. Then together we took up the carpet. It was exhausting work, but by ten o'clock we had set the parlour up as a most creditable hospital ward, with six beds along each side, and a disposition of linen, towels, and enamel bowls. I offered him supper. It was a poor affair, with nothing but a ham, a cheese and a dish of salt–pilchards to accompany the loaf, but he seemed grateful enough. To my amazement, when I offered to open a bottle of Muscadet, he announced that he had never tasted wine before.

'Well, what do you think of it?' I asked when I had watched him study and sniff the glass like a connoisseur, before tossing it off at a gulp. 'I'd hopes of it being more like rum,' was his diplomatic judgement, 'though I dare say you could serve it to the ladies in place of cider.' Still, he did not refuse my invitation to taste a second bottle, and took a third to bed with him, for fear that water might 'rot his stomach'!

I was alone when I woke on the morrow, for Provis had risen with the dawn and set off for more mattresses. The plan was for us to set up the church in the same way as the parlour, and for him to bring up the first of the patients in the afternoon. It was a strange morning, for I was alone with my excitement, but with nothing to do. The day was as still and sun-drenched as Friday, and for all that the Cornish turn their noses up at such weather – which they describe as 'dead' on account of there being no wind – I was delighted by it. After breakfast I stepped out onto the lawn, for the thought of my study could not be countenanced, and no sooner had I done so, than I decided to devote the morning to the bees. It was an incongruous thing to do in such circumstances, I grant you. And I felt uncommonly odd as I donned my veil and gloves, like a schoolboy who cuts his lessons and sneaks off to the back of the alehouse. However, my scientific curiosity soon got the better of me, for I was curious to see the extent of the summer's honey harvest, especially after the blight which did so much damage last year. You will remember that I had two hives constructed to my own design out upon the moor. They comprise of a central tower, for the queen and all her retinue, and two lateral annexes, which is where the bulk of the honey is deposited. The beauty of such a design is that the honey stores may be removed without overly disturbing the bees; one simply removes the annex, breaks it open and cuts out the comb, while the bulk of the hive remains intact. It was, I know, a good bit early to be gathering the honey, by at least a fortnight, but I was curious, and there were extenuating circumstances which drove me to it.

The yield was magnificent, with regard to both the quantity and the colour, which, if I am any judge, bodes exceedingly well. I had smoked off the bees and was just turning towards the kitchen to fetch the utensils necessary to scrape out the comb, when I became aware of a figure approaching the rectory from the lane. By a strange coincidence, it was that man Haddon, who of all the denizens of my parish, was the one man who shares any knowledge of apiculture. So I raised my arm in greeting, and bid him come over.

He agreed with my judgement of the honey, and was full of admiration for the chamber, deeming it 'ingenuous' – a rustic Malapropism which, I must confess, gave me cause to smile. 'And if you've a mind, twill be a relief to help'ee scrape it out,' he added, 'given as how working the bees be so soothin.' I agreed at once, and offered him the spare helmet. This he refused, saying that the bees didn't 'bate' him. Indeed they seemed not to, for although the bees were plentifully disturbed by our work, and crawled about his head and forearms, not one seemed to sting him.

Half an hour passed most amicably between us, and the comb was all but cut out, when Haddon indulged in that uncivil habit which I believe I have mentioned to you before: he cleared his lungs and spat upon the ground. Normally I would limit myself to letting my disapproval show upon my face, but in the present circumstances, I was horrified. Did he not know that the cholera could be transmitted exactly through such means? The old man scratched his head, taking the reproach thoughtfully.

'Tis a terrible plague, sir. I reckon those at Winnard's Mill have copped it.'

It was my turn to be taken aback. 'I beg your pardon?'

'Aye, sir. I were over that way this mornin, and twas deathly grim...'

'Good God, man, and we've been sitting here all this time discussing honey. Why didn't you tell me at once, you old ***' – and I confess, Isobel, I resorted to a term which my parishioners are unaccustomed to hear from my lips. I pressed him for more details, but the loon grew doubly incoherent. I left at once, commanding Haddon to order the hive as he saw fit. You may well imagine my thoughts as I rushed along the path, up over Polgarrick and down into the other valley: why it was but yesterday that I had left them healthy, quarantined, and taking every precaution against contact with the outside world. How could they possibly have become infected? And if they had done, to whom could they turn for help? Then when I remembered Dicky's request for sweets, and my own promise to return to them with news – which I had been too busy to fulfil – upon my word, I wept. I was at that stile where the path from Polgarrick meets the one by the stream, when the full force of my grief and anxiety overtook me. For a while I stood there trembling, my legs as weak as rotten stumps, and tears gushing from my eyes like a schoolgirl – Dicky's nicies! – I thought I could not go on. Yet go on I did. And that stretch of path by the weir, where it opens to the geese field, which has always struck me as the most picturesque pathway in the whole parish – why, it had become my Calvary.

Winnards's Mill did indeed present an aspect as grim and deathly as anything Haddon had hinted at. The goats were desperate with neglect. One had so tightly wound itself about the tree that I had to stop to untangle it, although you can imagine my impatience to reach the house. Then I thought to untie all three of them, and let them forage for food as best they could, for it was not likely that they would be tended by any human hand for a long while yet. The front door was half-open, and as I pushed my way in, I immediately sensed a chilliness in the interior which was due to more than the fire in the range having burnt itself out. Believe me, Isobel, the presence of death in a house is as palpable as the knowledge of night rain one has on waking. Yet even though I was prepared for it, the shock of what awaited me upstairs was formidable. The boy's hand was poking through the banisters. He lay sprawled on the boards, face down, at the top of the stairs. I stepped over him, and crept into the first of the bedchambers. Beth and the miller lay together across the bed, their contorted limbs more reminiscent of a pair of wrestlers than the peaceful couple we knew them for. Their blue lips and wide-agog eyes were sorry evidence of the violence of the cholera in its closing stages. I made the sign of the cross over them and went on to the end chamber. Jemma lay under a huddle of bed clothes. I was in the act of raising my right hand to mutter my inconsequential blessing over her too, when the bundle shivered. I confess I fled. It was only when I had seated myself at the kitchen table that my reason suggested that if the bed clothes had moved, it meant that Jemma was still alive. My first thought had been – well, I know not – I was atwang with fright, and heaven knows what superstitious gibberish was running through my mind. Nevertheless, before I could summon the courage to remount the stairs, I helped myself to a glass of the miller's brandy from the sideboard, then, seeing the bottle was almost empty, finished it off.

And so Jemma Lawson became the first patient of the fever hospital. When I did go back upstairs, I crouched by her bedside and made an examination of her. It is uncanny how quickly one gathers expertise in these matters when thrust through such an experience. Though I could not raise her to consciousness, and her face had the terrible colouring of the disease when a victim is within its grip, her eyes were still white and only a little bloodshot. This I knew to be a good sign. I uttered what words of comfort I could, though with little faith in her hearing me. I told her to lay still and that I would be back for her. I said a prayer for her recovery, although the words were ashes in my mouth. Then I said another for her soul, in case she died.

What was I to do? I could scarcely carry her to Lancaradoc a-piggy-back. I went outside and stood upon the footbridge, pondering my options carefully. I had to be home before long, as Provis was due to bring up the first of my patients before nightfall; yet there was nothing or nobody nearby to lend me any help. Porthcado lay too far off, and besides, those who were willing and able to lend succour had enough to do. I was just watching a pair of stippled trout circle round and round the pool below the bridge, when an idea struck me. Why not go to Parson Finch and ask him to help? If I cut up the side of the valley, through the woods behind the mill, Fretton should be less than half-an-hour away across the fields, and Finch must be persuaded to lend me one of his horses to get me home again. I'm no rider, Isobel, as you know, but necessity had given me the courage to do braver things in the last few days than sit astride a nag.

Finch met me with a blunderbuss. It had taken me longer than I had calculated to climb up the valley to Fretton, as the wooded hillside was steep and full of brambles, so that when I marched in at his drive and up to the door, I was as righteous to command Finch to do my bidding as any Old Testament prophet. I was sweating profusely. The bell pull evoked such a feeble little tinkle from within that I hesitated just long enough to wipe my brow before hammering on the front door. But here was a circumstance I had not envisaged: there was no answer. Where could the man have got to? It seemed absurd that my purpose in coming here – all my urgency to save Jemma's life – should be thwarted by such a capricious turn of events. Indeed, it was absurd, and I gave the bell pull a valedictory tug before skirting round the rose beds towards the stables.

Yet if it were my intention to turn horse–thief from the noblest of motives, the execution of such a purpose proved quite beyond me. Within the gloomy stalls I could make out three horses, and each seemed haughtier and more intimidating than its neighbours. I recoiled from the first when it made to bite my hand. The second pawed the straw with its hooves, and warned me with a toss of its head to keep my distance. And the third, why! it towered above the others: I felt I could no more have mounted it than scaled an Alpine peak. Next, though an array of equestrian paraphernalia was to be had in abundance, from a chamber just within the door, I had neither the knowledge nor the temerity to strap a saddle upon a horse's back, and as for the sundry leather straps and steel baubles that hung there – well, who was to show me how they were to be deployed as reins and harness, martingales, bit, stirrup and what have you?

It was clear that I needed assistance, and though I had no idea from which quarter it was to be had, I stumbled outside again. The light was so dazzling after the stables that I doubt if I would have even seen Finch if he hadn't hailed me. I looked up to discern him leaning out of an upstairs window, armed, moreover, with the belligerent apparatus I have alluded to. The gape of this antique weapon is an awesome sight, and as full of insolence as any lout you'll meet about the lanes. The shock of it was compounded by the sight of a nightcap on Finch's head, at an hour when all the world should be sitting down to lunch.

'Good God, man, have you succumbed to the fever?' The question was out despite me.

'Stand your ground!' And the order was accompanied by an ominous clunk from the contraption he was pointing at me.

'Are you ill, sir?'

'No. Nor do I intend to be. Which is why the only greeting you'll get from me is a pound of buckshot. And that was before I caught you snooping round my stables.'

'I can explain...'

'As can the Devil. Now, get off my lawn.' And he shook the weapon in his hands, to show he meant to use it.

It was at that moment that I noticed someone at a second window. A curious figure, and one I could not, on the instant, account for. Like Finch, he was a man well advanced in years, and so thin and frail that I was inclined to take this ethereal vision for a supernatural. He stood at the window immediately above Finch, and was dressed in a full-length cassock, the like of which I would love to introduce at Lancaradoc. And as soon as he saw that I had noticed him, he raised his finger to his lips, bidding me to conceal any knowledge of him.

I looked Finch squarely in the eyes. 'Now look here, I have need of a horse. It is a question of saving a life. You shall have it back tomorrow.'

'I shall count to five, Mudge, before you are a dead man.'

'I shall not contaminate your house, sir. You need have no fear on that score.'

'One!'

'God damn it man, have you no heart!'

'Two!'

'Put that infernal weapon down!'

'Three!'

I confess, I did not stay my ground or try to reason more.

I turned and fled towards the stable door. I had almost reached it, too, when the air was rent by a noise as loud as Doomsday. I threw myself in at the dark entrance, and remember marvelling at the discovery that the agony I felt on dying was nothing compared to the seering pain at my knees and elbows as I skidded across the stable floor.

An instant later, when I realised I was still very much in the world, I rolled over and looked out through the doorway. The mystery of my salvation was resolved at once: for now at the window where Finch had been there were two figures, tussling for possession of the gun – the vicar, in his white nightgown, and the ghost in the black cassock, who, it now occurred to me, must be the Father Benedict, the nun's confessor, whom I had heard them speak of. I dusted myself off and stepped forward into the yard. 'Gentlemen,' I yelled, but they were in no mood to hear me. Then my sight chanced upon a stone, and without thinking I picked it up and hurled it at the fighting clerics. It hit the window pane immediately above their heads. They were shocked by the shower of shattered glass. 'Gentlemen,' I called again, having clearly won their attention, 'will one of you please saddle me a horse!'

The three of us looked at each other, like three men who have simultaneously woken from a dream. I could clearly hear Finch and Father Benedict panting from their exertion. And as we woke to our surroundings we realised we were no longer alone, but at the centre of a large audience. The report from the gun had brought forth a scurry of nuns – they poured out of the door in the wall of Plumley's orchard like bees from a hive, and now ranged themselves around the yard, trying to make what sense they could of the drama that was unfolding. Finally, out through the orchard door stepped Mère Agathe, and all eyes turned upon her. She looked disdainfully first at me, then up at

123

the vicarage window, before demanding imperiously: 'May we 'ave an explanation of this preposterous noise?' And before she had an answer, she garbled away in French at Father Benedict, presumably asking the same question. From their expressions I believe my brothers in the cloth felt much as I did – like mere schoolboys suffering a rebuke for ragging in the yard.

The Frenchman began his answer on our behalf, hesitantly enough at first, but then with mounting excitement. My mastery of the French tongue, alas, was not up to such an animated speech, but from the way he indicated me, then Finch, with much gesturing of his hands, and an alarming coat hanger of a down–turned mouth, I could see he was making quite a tale of it, and that the villain of the piece was clearly Finch. There followed a swift interrogation from Mère Agathe, as a consequence of which the Frenchman left Finch at the window, to re–emerge, seconds later, brandishing a bottle of gin, as if in triumph. Finch hung his head ashamedly.

'So, you 'ave been drinking again?' said Mère Agathe with a scornful toss of her head. 'Père Mudge, I beg you to accept our apologies. Père Finch is a reformed man, but still he 'as 'is moments of crisis. Is that not so, Père Finch?' Finch replied with a sorry mumble, and looked most crestfallen. Then the abbess looked me up and down. 'Now, I understand he mistook you for an 'orsethief?'

'Perhaps not without reason, madam. I do have urgent need of a horse, although it was not my intention to steal one.'

'And why come all the way to Fretton to borrow a 'orse?'

I believe the explanation I gave was lucid enough. I spoke of Jemma at the mill, and the need to take her to Lancaradoc, which led to a description of the fever hospital.

'This is an excellent project. I hope you will allow us to offer our assistance.'

I accepted most willingly, my mind already turning to the chance of arranging food for my patients.

'Very well. Perhaps you would like to come to my study while Père Finch prepares your 'orse?'

When I returned half an hour later, I was in an altogether more optimistic frame of mind. Mère Agathe had offered to send two nuns to Lancaradoc daily to tend the wards; and as part of their duties they would cook a nutritious cauldron of broth. Furthermore the abbess would arrange for the provision of bread from her own ovens. Her offer was more than generous. By providing me with both nurses and food, she had resolved the most pressing problems surrounding the projected hospital at a single stroke. All I had to do was to keep out of my own kitchen for a few hours in the forenoon – a stipulation with which I could readily comply.

Moreover, to seal our agreement she sent for a bottle of the most excellent Burgundy wine and a small flat cheese, coated in what I took to be flour, although when I tasted it, it clearly was something else – I know not what – but with pears from her orchard and a loaf of white bread, she improvised a meal – although she partook of nothing but a sip of wine herself – which I was sorely in need of.

On returning to the vicarage stable yard, the repentant Finch proved himself a most punctilious ostler, testing and retesting the length of my stirrup when I was finally mounted and fussing over the reins; moreover he had insisted on saddling a second horse for me to lead, and took great pains to show me how best to secure Jemma's supine body for her safety and comfort.

And thus the foundations of my present life were laid. When I reached Lancaradoc I was to find myself already the director of a hopital, for Provis had brought the first five patients up in his wagon. Penworthy, who had accompanied him, burst out of the porch and demanded to know where the deuce I had been. But when he saw Jemma's form across the saddle he quickly regained his composure and apologised.

Shortly afterwards, Sam Shepherd arrived with another seven patients in his builder's cart, and Penworthy and I were kept busy transferring them to the parlour. In the lull that followed Penworthy suggested that we see what we could arrange in the way of nourishment, but the kitchen yielded such scant provisions that the two of us, untutored as we were, set to baking. If bread was what we were aiming at, we must have missed a crucial turning somewhere in the woods of culinary expertise, for what emerged from the oven were dusky lumps as hard as ship's biscuits. A little salt would have helped. I was doubly thankful that the nuns would be joining me on the morrow. 'Thank heavens that most our guests are too ill to eat,' I exclaimed to Penworthy on tasting our wares.

'Good grief man, what a callous remark!'

That he took it in this way caused my face to burn, for I could see that he was right, if somewhat humourless, and that my remark had lacked tact. We distributed our sorry supper among our guests, who did indeed eat little, but were grateful for our attention nonetheless.

* * *

It is just over a week since I broke off the above. I rose early on the morning after the events I have described to write this account for you through the night. If, indeed, I can be said to have risen at all, for I was in no mood for my bed that night, and having retired to my chamber I could not sleep, but dressed after an hour to tour the ward, carrying water where it was called for, then took up my pen.

The tale is confused, and over-agitated, but may stand. I

had scarcely finished my writing and was making another tour of the ward, when I heard the porch bell and went out to meet Soeur Madelaine and Soeur Ursula, at an hour when the sun was scarcely clear of the horizon: Mère Agathe had been as good as her word.

I will describe that first day in some detail, because those that followed – except for the changing faces of the nuns – have been its siblings.

The night before had ended busily: at sunset Provis returned with a third consignment of patients. Now that the rectory was filled to capacity, we decided that the sickest should lie in the parlour, where I could best observe them, whereas those who were beginning their recovery – and more in need of quarantine than care – should lay in the church. We were busy till eleven o'clock moving the patients round, but I have subsequently been grateful for the pains that we took on that first night.

However, I see that I have not written of my return to the mill, nor how I brought Jemma to the rectory, which is bound to interest you most in all this tale. And lest you read anxious of the outcome, I shall start by saying that Jemma is out of danger now, and was moved to the church on Wednesday morning.

I made my exit from Fretton Vicarage with as much aplomb as I could muster, careful not to dent what little reputation I may have with too obvious a display of my inability to sit a horse. It other words, though I was in a funk, I faked it! Yet it is a curious fact, that when a man is unable to perform a deed, either from fear, or incapacity – and my equestrian inadequacies are the result of both – he has only to act as though he can, and behold, he finds the strength to do the untenable. By this belief, actors would become the most valiant of men, able to assume the powers of kings and warlords and of all the antique heroes whom they ape, which proves, of course, that it is a folly, for who will not admit that those who practise the thespian trade are but vainglorious fops? – yet for me it seemed to work. I determined to ride out of Fretton with my head held high, and By God! I managed it. So perhaps it is no mistake to note that 'to act' is the first part of 'action', and that our noblest deeds are inspired by fictions.

But I digress. I merely wish to tell you that I managed the horse with more panache than I would have given myself credit for, although there were moments on the steep descent to Willard's Mill – when I no longer had an audience to play to – when I wished my feet were firm upon the ground.

I found Jemma just as I had left her. If there was any change it was that her coma now had more the appearance of a deep sleep, which is to say that she was breathing deeply and had a more peaceful countenance. I sat by her bed for nearly an hour to let her have the benefit of it. By five o'clock, however, I was mindful that I had other duties to attend to, and those most pressing, and that I would have to move her. I picked her up without difficulty, for all she is a big woman, and though she did not wake she put her arms about my neck, with all the instincts of a child. Once we were out through the mill door, I could bear her weight no longer, and allowed her body to slip down until her feet were on the ground. This caused an agitated reaction in her fevered mind, and she began to beat me with her fists. Her head lolled back, and she let out a stream of abuse and muddle-headed poppycock such as I have never heard from any woman before. Yet it was the disease, not Jemma, speaking, for she still did not wake. I was anxious lest I should not manage to lift her onto the horse in this state, but by leading her round the garden, with my arm about her shoulder, and whispering encouragement, I was able to calm her again. Then when I did pick her up and lay her across the saddle, she took to it as though it were a feather bed – either the motion of the ride, or the beast itself must have been responsible for inducing her to relapse into sleep, and though the going was slow, on the journey back up the hill to Lancaradoc she was as peaceful as Easter.

Mère Agathe has a policy of sending each of the nuns for two days, although she clearly sees Sister Ursula as the most reliable, as she has been here every day but one. Certainly Sister Ursula is composed, authoritative and a tireless worker. She comes from Bruges, from a family of financiers and bankers – and that she is used to commanding servants is evident from her firm handling of the wards, as well as her treatment of the other nuns. I do not wish to suggest that she is imperious, for she deals with everyone with great kindness, yet there is a steely purpose about this erect young woman which commands respect.

Yesterday and on Tuesday she was accompanied by Sister Brigette, who is as charming as a chaffinch. She is still in the first flush of girlish good humour, and scarce old enough to be wearing a habit. We have heard all about her three sisters, and her brother Artur who wants to be a soldier, her aunt Elène, who bakes so much better than her mother does, as well as sundry youths in the village of Briare, beside the Loire, where she comes from.

I still have my reservations about Sister Madelaine, who came with Sister Ursula on the first morning and again today. She seems to do her work begrudgingly. Twice when I have asked her to do something she has muttered a complaint in French: the first time I was unprepared for such insolence, but the second time, when I had asked her to check on Mrs Rowe, I would not let it go. 'Beg pardon?' I said, pretending her remark was addressed to me. 'Oh nothing,' was her reply, and she shrugged her shoulders. For all that, she is a handsome young woman.

On Thursday morning the sisters had a companion in tow: Judy Ruan, one of Farmer Ruan's girls – the second, I think. She was wanting to play Nurse Nightingale. Apparently she had risen at four to steal out of the house before anyone else was astir, and had then walked all the way to Fretton before she came here because she reckoned that if the sisters brought her to me I'd be less likely to turn her away. A cunning strategy, and it shows she's got her father's mind, though where she gets her heart from, isolated in such a family out on the stony uplands, the Lord alone knows! 'Parson,' she says straight out, 'I'm sixteen and not a girl no more. I know I can do the work, for I've nursed calves and lambs and even my sisters since I were a shrimpet. So you just show me where the sick'uns be to, and I'll bathe'un and feed'un. Besides, it'll give'un heart to see a local face alongside these Frenchies. I bain't afraid.'

But turn her away I had to, it was my plain duty. Yet not having the courage to tell her so bluntly, I sent her to one of the outhouses on the pretext that there was a cartload of chopped wood to sort, while I thought of a way to break the news tactfully.

Then an hour later, when I'd quite forgot her, Dennis Lobb's fly pulls into the yard: he was making show of his whip, and foul-mouthing as usual. He pulled up sharp against the porch, and jumped down so close to me that I was almost knocked to the ground. He'd heard that I'd opened a hospital and would I take his son in? I just gawped at him as he launched into a whole tirade of how this cholera was interfering with the harvest. According to Lobb, the entire epidemic was no more than a conspiracy the village had launched against him, to deprive him of his labourers. Even his lumox of a lad had been fooled into toppling off ladders and instead of directing the harvest by his father's side, was now lounging at home and needed nursing when there wasn't a pair of hands to spare.

What's more, Queenie Thorpe, who was tending him, was the best stook binder in the parish, and he could ill afford to waste her. Therefore, if I was adamant about making such a fuss over a touch of fever, then the least I could do would be to give his son a bed so that 'honest folk could get on and do an honest day's work'.

I was dumbfounded. I would have been hard put to answer whether it was the man's ignorance or his callousness which staggered me most. To see the epidemic as no more than an interference with the smooth running of his farm was one thing, but to consider sending his son into the infection wards all for the sake of relieving an extra pair of hands was abominable.

But before I could reply, Soeur Ursula, who had just then come out into the yard and must have heard the farmer's diatribe, gave a discreet cough to attract my attention. As no words followed I was momentarily at a loss to understand what she wanted of me. Then I realised the direction of her gaze, and that I was meant to follow it: she was staring at the outhouse where Judy Ruan was stacking logs.

I told Lobb exactly what was on my mind. I had never heard a more selfish request, and that the idea of sending William here was out and out wickedness. Did he not realise that half the village were in their coffins while he was only concerning himself with his harvest, and that to send his son here was as good as to consign him to their ranks?

A remark that was acknowledged with the merest grunt!

However, there was a solution at hand: what if I were to spare one of my nurses to tend William? I could see Lobb's eyes slither over Soeur Ursula's robes, and a look betwixt disdain and suspicion passed across his eyes. No, not one of the nuns, I said, but a local girl, and one whose qualities I could vouch for.

'Aye, well I'd have to feed her!'

'Yes Lobb, she would need that.' I was not prepared to give the bully an inch. He could take it or leave it. But that was the moment at which the farmer relented.

'It would save Will from having to be moved'. He shuffled from one foot to the other.

'If you want her, I'll ask her to walk up this afternoon.'

So off he rode, his fly raising a cloud of dust like one of the chariots of Egypt. All that remained now was to interview young Judy, and convince her that she would render better service not on the fever wards, but in her arch–rival's household. The task seemed such a daunting one that I conferred first with Soeur Ursula: we were in agreement that I should not mention our chief motive for our request – which was the girl's own safety – but she was as much as a loss about how to persuade her as I. What did impress me, though, was the nun's faith: if it was the right path, she assured me, then I had but to take the first step and let Heaven order the rest. It seemed an extraordinarily haphazard way to go about the Lord's business, and I was so intrigued by the logic of it, that I stumbled straight off into the woodshed, without a thought as to what I was going to say.

And would you believe that it worked? I got no farther than saying that I would like her to go over to Trebarton, where there was need of a nurse, and she accepted at once. There was no need of any justification at all to bolster my request. You see, Isobel, what I had failed to understand was that for all her show of pluck, the thought of the cholera terrified her, and my words must have sounded like a stay of execution to one who has already passed beneath the hangman's ladder. So Judy just thanked me and took out her handkerchief to blubber away as prettily as she could, and was all for setting straight off, except that I persuaded her that she ought to have lunch with us first.

We had another death in the night, bringing our losses to

nine. Old Jarvis. Sister Ursula told me she thought he had recovered consciousness when she was doing her rounds after supper, which gave me hope that he might mend, but it was not to be; I buried him first thing, not far from the lantern cross. He was seventy-three.

Later, an incident I would fain forget, but cannot, so I shall write it down. At lunchtime Sister Madelaine was helping me distribute our simple viands in the church: the usual bread, water, and a soup, today made of root vegetables such as swedes and parsnips. I was bending over Amanda Jarvis, near the font, when several people shrieked out, Jemma Lawson's voice being the loudest of them. I turned, and it took me a moment to discover the cause of all this commotion. A swallow had got in, and was flitting about between the columns, seeking the way out. Some of the women had mistook it for a bat, hence their hysteria. The poor creature was swooping and twisting and flying up at the windows, no doubt believing that the light there was indicative of an exit. Both for the bird's sake, and for my patients' peace of mind, I realised that it was imperative for me to take charge, for without help it would soon come to harm. The swallow is not a bird that will rest for an instant, and its constant motion increased the risk it ran of doing damage to itself, as well as the difficulty of our own task as its would–be rescuers. As I saw it, there were but two alternatives: either to trap the creature, and once caught, convey it from the building, or, by guile, to induce it to find its own way to freedom which, perforce, was through the porch door. Yet how were we to trap it? We had neither the nets nor long poles to serve us, and though such equipment could have been found in the rectory, there was no time to fetch it.

At once I saw how we must organise ourselves for the bird's salvation, and seeking a vantage point from which to give instructions, I hurried into the pulpit. I ordered all those who were able to, to move forward to the chancel, and the rest to lie quiet. There must have been a gaggle of a dozen or more who came forward, and I spread them out in a line that stretched from the vestry door to the wall of the south aisle, so that the whole church was covered. Next I instructed them to clap their hands, and process slowly forward down the body of the church. The bird was flitting around between the bell ropes, as far away from my chorus of 'beaters' as it could get. Every time the swallow turned towards us I gave the order to shout, and the sudden bellow of noise persuaded the swallow to turn back again. It was a strange sight, this whooping army advancing one pace at a time towards the bird, stepping over the bodies on the floor, and all for the sake of forcing it to freedom. I began to hope my plan would work, for I intended those in the nave to swing round and cut off the whole body of the church except for that space immediately before the porch door. Then, for a final offensive, I ordered the army to raise their hands and clap above their heads, hoping this would frighten the bird downwards and back out through the opening.

Yet this final manoeuvre was a mistake. Rather than forcing it towards the porch, the swallow flew straight at the human barrier that had been advancing to save it. It swerved upwards, and shot straight over their heads. From the pulpit I watched it cross the whole length of the church, as fleet as an arrow. It flew straight at the figure of the resurrected Christ in the great East window. And with a crack it hit the glass. Timidly, we gathered round it, where it lay on the slate floor behind the altar. It was clearly dead, for its neck was twisted at an impossible angle and a dab of blood dribbled from its beak. No one spoke. Then Soeure Ursula offered to take the tiny corpse away. But before she did, I blessed it, to console those who had tried to save it; for its death was felt as a most unlucky omen.

An unlucky omen of a more material sort – more of a proverbially bad penny, I suppose – is making her recovery on the ward. Do you remember Mrs Hawke, the old crone who so upset the Lawsons when you were here? Provis brought her over with two other casualties on Tuesday morning. Till now she has been too unwell to cause any mischief, but as she is eating again and beginning to harry the sisters with her ribaldry, it will soon be time to send her to the church, and I'm fearful of the reaction that the move will provoke.

*　　*　　*

Mudge to Isobel, July

Isobel dearest,

I am warmly recommended by Jemma to send you her greetings, and to assure you that she is well, and would be remembered to you. She came to me yesterday to announce that she has decided to sell the mill, for it is too much work for a woman to do on her own. Yet even more than the physical labour that the place requires, Winnard's Mill has become a burden to her spirits, haunted as it now is by her absent family. She came to me, she said, for advice, but her mind was already set on a sale: I can see that this is her wisest choice, although I am as afeared as she for what her future may hold. What she will do, alone in the world, and no longer in the first flowering of her youth, is a question that she can only answer on her knees, but I tried to assure her that she shall have an answer, and that I shall add my prayers to her own. Let us hope that the mill sells quickly and that it fetches the £430 pounds she anticipates from it.

But before all else, I feel that it is incumbent upon me to apologise for breaking off my account of the epidemic almost in mid–sentence. I was at my desk when Provis flew in, all of a lather, to announce that the Bideford packet had been sighted rounding The Pinnacles, and that Penworthy had ordered him to see what supplies I had need of at Lancaradoc. I knew he would also have to be entrusted with the account I had written for you if she were to leave, as her custom is, with the turn of the tide.

On Provis's suggestion we straightway left the house and rushed across the fields for a glimpse of her. But to see the packet pull into harbour again! As I squinted through his glass, I believe that I understood the emotion of a Crusoe who sights the sail that has come to rescue him – so like had been our predicament of solitude and terror over the past three weeks. It may have been a routine incident to have the packet call at Porthcado again, yet I cannot tell you how it gladdened our hearts. From that moment on, the parish began to reckon that we had come through the pestilence – it was as though the vessel heralded our deliverance. It is strange how such a supernatural thought can lodge itself in the mind, and even stranger that the same thought was admitted to by so many, as I was later to discover. With hindsight, it should have been evident that the epidemic was already receding: no-one had been admitted to the rectory's fever ward after Mrs Hawke; and Old Jarvis was the cholera's last victim. Daily, the atmosphere in the church was growing gayer, and the patients stronger. At the end, it was no longer the pestilence that was feared, but a lashing from the old crone's tongue!

On the Thursday morning – that is, at about noon of the day after the coming of the Bideford boat – Penworthy and Mère Agathe arrived together at Lancaradoc, that we might discuss the situation together, and we agreed that if there were no new cases in the meantime, and if those in quarantine in the church showed no symptoms of a relapse, then we should disband our hospital upon the Saturday. And thus it was done.

However, there was a terrible scene at the end. Hannah Hawke refused to go home. Already on the Friday night she was lamenting that she was being thrown out onto the streets.

'You've your cottage, be at peace woman, you should be thankful you're alive,' came the cries from the ward.

But no: Lancaradoc was nothing but a nest for vipers; she had been saved only that they might torture her with a slower death; she had been born among the most pitiless people on earth and no–one would spare an ounce of charity for an old widow.

This much I heard when I made my last round of the church at ten o'clock, and with such choice phrasing as I believe no other woman would be capable of. The fact was, Hannah Hawke had been enjoying herself: she had company, was comfortably provided for, and was loathe to return to the solitude of her slovenly cottage out along Fretton Lane. Later I heard that her complaints had carried on into the night, until the other patients grew tired of remonstrating with her.

Then, on Saturday morn, there was no sign of her. Initially it was thought that she had snuck off in the night. However, it later transpired that she had barricaded herself in. She must have stolen into the Pope's Chamber during the night and locked the door behind her – I'd little thought to remove the key, but then, who would have thought such a precaution necessary? We were running a hospital, not a prison.

As first light dawned through the church windows, splashing the grey walls within with dapples of colour, the ward woke in unaccustomed tranquillity. The knowledge that they were to go home rendered the day festive, not with outward show, but with a deep heartfelt happiness that was almost as tangible as the sunlight. Yet there was something else – a quietness that no–one could account for at first, for all it's being so evident: it was the absence of Hannah Hawke and her jeremiad. As soon as I stepped inside the church, which I did, as my recent custom has been, at a little before seven, I was told she had gone. Why should I, or anybody else, doubt the evidence of our eyes – or our ears? Mrs Hawke gone, her bedding gone, her sharp tongue gone.

We began to pack. Provis and Purvey were both bringing carts for nine o'clock: these to take a few frail patients and what scant possessions the rest could muster – for most of our charges were well enough to walk and were eager to stretch their limbs in the fresh air. I had agreed to accompany them to the outskirts of Porthcadoc, down through the woods as far as Long Meadow. Indeed, I was looking forward to leading them out of quarantine, much like Moses leading the lost tribe out of Egypt.

It was only when the carts were loaded, and most of us outside, lounging around the churchyard and awaiting our departure, that Sam Shepherd came across and said he'd heard a noise: he thought it came from the Pope's Chamber. Although I scarce gave his words credence, for that boy's not right in the head, I went back into the church with him; it did strike me as strange that the little door up above the rood screen was closed to, for it usually stood ajar. Shepherd was all for trying the latch, but I put a finger to my lips and approached the door as quietly as I could: I wanted to put my ear to the key hole and listen for noise within. And when I did so, it wasn't long before I heard a footstep.

I knocked. 'Who's in there?' There was no reply. I knocked again.

Shepherd, on the step behind me, must have guessed what had happened. 'It'll be that there Widder Hawke,' he said: 'this be her bid to stay put.'

'Mrs Hawke?' I tried her name tentatively at first, then again, louder. I must have called three or four times before we had a reply: 'I bain't goin' home.' Her voice was unmistakable.

I begged her to unlock the door, but it was no use. Then Provis came into the church – someone must have gone out and

138

explained the situation to him. He marched straight up the cramped little twist of stairs and thumped the door mighty hard. 'Now you come out drekkly, woman, or you'll be dragged out.'

'You shut yer gob, Provis. I'm not having you parting me from this gentleman.'

'Open the door, Hannah.'

'We'm proper snug here. Leave me be.' Then after a pause, she added: 'If I could bide here I'd be able to sweep through the church for you, Parson.'

'Mrs Hawke?' said I. 'Is there someone in there with you?'

No answer. Provis put a finger to his lips and beckoned me to back down from the door with him.

'Have you got a ladder?' he whispered, as soon as we were on the floor of the church.

'I'm afraid not – yes! There's the one in the bell–chamber, going up onto the roof.'

'Keep her talking, Parson. I's'll sneak round and shinny up through the window. Then we'll weavil her out, like a maggot from a lump o'cheese.'

I did as I was bidden. 'Now then, Mrs Hawke. Why don't you let me in and we can sit down and talk this out.'

All I got for an answer was a loud snort.

'Just a talk, I give you my word.' Silence. 'Surely you can trust me, Mrs Hawke?'

'Trust a priest? Why, I were married by one once. Tis one thing to have a man in yer skirts: tis quite another to have the parson say you've got to keep him there!'

'This is a public building, Hannah. Whoever heard of anyone living in a church?'

'I'd have some company.'

'Company, Mrs Hawke? When everyone's left you'll find this church a most lonely home, I can assure you.'

139

'I do coincide nicely with this 'ere gentleman, and his lady–love don't mind if I bide with the two of them.'

It suddenly dawned on me who these alusive companions were that she had been referring to: the portraits on the wall.

'If it's the pictures you like so well, Mrs Hawke, you can take them home with you.'

She tutted. 'Ain't got no nail.'

'I'm sure we can find you a nail.'

'Parson, you don't see how poor folk live: I ain't even got a wall straight enough to hang a picture on.' Pause. 'Now these walls be bootiful straight.'

We didn't get much beyond this when there was a sudden crash as the casement window was kicked in. Hawke screamed. Provis was in the room. The noise that followed was worse than a cock fight. Of course, Provis soon overwhelmed her – how could he not do? I heard the lock turn, and the door was yanked open. Provis had the old woman's arms pinioned behind her; she was bent double, and spitting with rage. 'I'll do you for this. There's plenty before you, Amos, who've learnt not to meddle with me. I'll see you dragged to hell.'

'Shut your beak, woman. I'm sure the parson doesn't want to hear your wicked tongue, specially not in his own church.'

And indeed I did not. Yet by the time I had walked down to Porthcado and back and stepped into the church– at about three in the afternoon, I found it so empty, and with only the lonely rectory awaiting me, that I could almost wish my flock of cholera victims back again, were it not that all of them – with the exception of Mrs Hawke – were so happy to have gone away from here, and would not give their sojourn in St Cadoc's church a single thought, except as a peril they were lucky to have survived.

How strange it was on the following morning to wake to an empty rectory. Nor, in the commotion of the day before had I thought to write a sermon. However, as I had had to forego the celebration of Communion for two Sundays running – replacing Lancaradoc's customary service with an extemporary prayer meeting – I saw no harm in leaving even today's homily to last minute inspiration. The return to customary routines has been like a convalescence, with each day bringing renewed use to inactive limbs. Sunday's service was an improvised affair with me stepping around the abandoned mattresses to reach the chancel, and, as I had expected, no–one for congregation. For my sermon I stuttered a few words of thanks and many words for the departed, until a thought came to mind of the congregation you had created for me for Sundays such as these. What a rush of blood to my face I felt when it occurred to me that those caricatures of Farmers Lobb and Ruan were stowed away in the bell tower, and had been but a few feet away from our convalescing guests. They were leaning up against the wall behind an unlocked door, and a glass door at that. I could hardly continue my sermon for shame at the thought of their discovery: I searched my mind for a memory of that door having been open, or of any word or gesture that might have betrayed that your paintings had been perused, and even though I could remember no such incident, my anxiety did not abate one jot.

I was in such a flummox when I came down from the pulpit that I confess I did not return to the chancel steps to begin the intercessions, but rushed straight to the bell tower. And wrenching open the door, I found myself facing a stretch of bare wall. I even ran my hand over the bricks to check that this was no illusion – the farmers had gone! How long they had been gone, and who may have took them – Isobel, I am sure you can imagine the conjectures that were racing through my head. I checked the

141

walls of the ringing chamber inch by inch, only to confirm what a cursory glance had already told me: they were not there. Then I dashed down to the vestry to fetch my keys and unlocked the door to the tower stairs. I climbed up to the bell chamber, but there was no sign of the farmers there either. I even took the ladder off the wall and pushed open the trap door onto the roof: nothing but slate and lichen.

Would you believe, Isobel, that I was in such turmoil over these missing figures that I searched the church from porch to altar, then went out and searched the churchyard too. It was all but two o'clock before I came back in again, exhausted, perplexed, and angry with myself that I had allowed this private mockery of my parishioners to escape abroad. Then, when I stood upon the chancel steps and turned back to face the empty church, I remembered that I had abandoned my celebration of communion in mid–service, and all for the sake of painted likenesses of one thin farmer and one fat one! And I began to laugh: I laughed until I was forced to my knees, and my cheeks were wet with tears.

As chance would have it, I was on my way to Porthcado on Monday, for my first foray down to the sea town for a fortnight, when I ran into Farmer George. I was coming off the path where it meets the lane at Block's Bridge. Lobb was astride a pony that was a couple of sizes too small for him, and wearing such a sunny disposition that I scarce knew what to make of him. I met his 'How be, Parson?' with a matching show of affability and asked after his sons.

'John's eye t'weren't nothing, just a scratch – and now he'm hale again, we'm sending him down Helston–way to learn commerce; my wife's cousin has a seed shop there, and John's always had a mind to go into commerce. As for young Will, he's been so well nursed I reckon he's beholden to Purvey for crackin' up his rib-cage.' So had Farmer Lobb been satisfied with the help I'd sent him? He replied to the effect that Judy Ruan was 'a proper tidy little baggage', then added something I didn't quite catch; however his jest was accompanied by such a lewd grimace that I thought it better not to seek further explanation.

*   *   *

Isobel to Mudge, August

Dearest Uncle,

How sad to hear of the terrible ordeal Porthcado has been afflicted with. I grieve especially for the awful fate which has befallen our friends at Winnard's Mill.

My only comfort is to know that you have survived the epidemic unscathed, and to read that you have been of such service to your parishioners in their hour of need.

If the news is of any consolation to you, I am delighted to announce that I was delivered of a baby girl, Emily Jane Wattling, on August 3rd: she came into the world weighing 3lbs and 4 ozs, and a healthier, quieter baby could not be wished for!

Percy joins me in sending you our warmest wishes,

Isobel.

1852

Dear Lucy,

This bleak winter provides a fitting end to such a year. The whole parish seems to be locked up by the snow as though it were a blanket of grief. In previous winters I have sometimes seen the uplands under the merest sprinkling of white, but I have never known anything like this: even the beaches are wrapped up beneath a white eiderdown to the water's edge, and the sea is such a broiling cauldron of angry grey cold that by comparison it is no mere fancy to envisage the snow as a blanket.

More treacherous than the snow, however, is the ice, especially on the steep streets of Porthcado. Jack Purvey, who surprised us all by recovering from the fever last summer, took a tumble on the glassy road before The Falcon, no doubt his sojourn there having done little to improve his balance, and broke the femur of one leg and the ankle of the other. There are those who say he will not get up again, but the old rogue has escaped his funeral blessing so often that I expect to see a score of villagers laid in the churchyard yet before Purvey is ready to make his way there.

No cart has been able to climb Harbour Hill for over a week now, and Miss Tingham's shop is out of eggs, not for any want of them about the farms, but because she is too timorous to risk her egg basket on the slope. One would have thought she was entrusted with the bank's ingots rather than a farthing's worth of eggs, but so small is the village economy that Miss Tingham's store of golden eggs might be accounted as Porthcado's equivalent of a vault of bullion in the coffers of the wider realm.

Yet the tribulations of a little adverse weather are nothing after what has befallen us: winter's difficulties do but toy with us, benignly perhaps, to distract our memories from the past. Moreover, this is a winter when men are so glad to be alive that they greet each other like beloved brothers safely returned from a hazardous journey. It is my belief that our celebration of the nativity has never been marked with such Christian good will as this year. And lest you suspect your brother of spinning such sentiments out of the air to adorn his Christmas sermon, there is a living proof of divine peace in our midst: Will Lobb and Judy Ruan are walking out together. Since she nursed him back to health they have become constant companions, and there is daily talk of their having been seen about the lanes. Nor is it the lascivious tavern talk which lovers are usually subjected to, for our parish is in wonderment at its village Juliet and her Romeo, and even more so on account of the seeming tolerance that this romance has met with in the houses of Montague and Capulet – by which I mean the farmsteads of Polgarrick and Trebarnon.

Moreover, I have my private reasons for rejoicing this winter: and though they concern matters of far more universal scope than the events of our small parish, they would not be readily understood here, so I must keep them to myself. Doctor McBride has written to me with an account of a discovery made recently by a certain Reverend Lorenzo Lorraine Langstroth of Philadelphia. It is of quite momentous significance, and is poised to transform the ancient craft of bee-keeping into the most modern of sciences. Langstroth has made the discovery that worker bees refuse to built across a gap if it is between five-sixteenths and three-eighths of an inch across. Why this should be is a mystery. If the gap is any smaller she will simply plug it with wax; if it is larger, the architect in her will design buttresses and supports to gird one section of comb to another. Yet for some mysterious reason, a gap of precisely the right dimensions, which is to say, about a quarter-of-an-inch wide, provides the bee with an insurmountable barrier.

The fact, you will say, is quaint. To the educated public it might prove curious. But can you imagine the implications of such beespace for the apiculturalist? We can now design hives which direct exactly how the bees will build their honeycombs. Consequently we can take as much honey as we like and need never disturb the Queen and her eggs. Langstroth's beespace has given us mastery of the perpetual hive. I have already drawn up a design for just such a hive, and have given George Honeycutt instructions to begin constructing it at once.

Who knows how long this letter will take to reach you in such a winter! Still the news is good, and good news, like good claret, can stand a little aging. My regards to Mr Kennington.

*   *   *

Mudge to Lucy, March

Lucy,

The enclosed handbill and reports from the papers will tell you much of recent events in the parish, and how Porthcado has again been plunged into a tempestuous flurry. What is left out is my continuing part in the story: for Provis has indeed gone into hiding and, as his friend, it behoves me to offer him what assistance I can.

Port of Porthcado

By Order of the Honourable Commissioners of Her Majesty's Customs.

On Saturday the 8th of March, inst, by Ten o'Clock in the Forenoon will be exposed to Public Sale at the Custom House in this Port, for Exportation to Foreign Parts, or Consumption aboard Vessels sailing for Foreign Parts, the undermentioned merchandise, viz.

BRANDY	.. .. ..	198 gallons
TOBACCO	.. .. ..	2,000 lbs
TEA	.. .. ..	420 lbs
SILK	.. .. ..	diverse articles

The above will be set up in several lots and sold to the highest Bidder, subject to the above–mentioned Conditions. Attendance will be given at the Custom House aforesaid, for viewing and sampling the same, Three Days before the Day of Sale.

*(from **The Western Daily Mercury**, March 4th)*

On the 23rd ult. the *Pydar Rose*, of Boscastle, through the vigilance of Capt. Clapp and the crew of the revenue cutter *Lurcher*, was seized off Cadoc's Zawn, and her Master, Wm Blunt, together with John Hodge, first mate, apprehended. The confiscated lugger appears to have been otherwise unmanned, and it is assumed that her crew were able to make their escape, for the ship's two galleys were gone, with the winching cables discovered to be still dangling from the stern. After a thorough search, there were found concealed in the bed–places and under the sails 84 bales containing 2,013 lbs of manufactured tobacco, 427 lbs of tea, a trunk containing sundry shawls and stockings of French silk, as well as 15 tubs of brandy. Moreover, the intrepid Capt. Clapp, suspecting that the brandy aboard represented only a fraction of the original cargo, has succeeded in retrieving a further 29 tubs from the sea bed through the employment of grapnels, or 'creepers', as they are locally known. The *Pydar Rose*, meanwhile, has been sailed into Porthcado harbour where she is presently moored and under armed guard, prior to being sawn in three in accordance with the due processes of Law. On 27th ult. Wm Blunt, and John Hodge, were brought before T. Eplett and F. Rosevear, Esqrs, County Magistrates at Bodmin. Capt. Clapp stated to the court that the duty on the goods amounted to £1,419.17sh. It appeared that she was last from Roscoff where the goods were taken on board. Both defendants pleaded guilty, and Blunt claimed, much to the consternation of the Court, that the two men had sailed her from France single–handed, and that whereas he knew the parties for whom the cargo was destined, and whose property it was, he would not divulge their names. The bench told him that there were circumstances of great aggravation in his case, he being master of the vessel; he was, therefore, committed to Bodmin Gaol for twelve calendar months, or until the sum of £150 be paid. Hodge was convicted to the same prison for four calendar months, but immediately expressed his willingness to serve his sentence with the Fleet.

*(from **The Western Daily Mercury**, March 11th 1852)*
A company of dragoons has been sent to Porthcado to quell the recent lawlessness there.

On the evening of 7th inst. rioting broke out in the Cornish sea town, during which the Custom House was plundered, and a substantial volume of confiscated merchandise was lost to the looters.

At around 9 o'clock in the evening, a large crowd from the town's several taverns began to congregate on the Platt, brandishing staves and agricultural implements, although some were armed with cutlasses and firearms. This rabble forced entrance into the aforementioned Custom House, where officials were forced to unlock the doors to the storerooms. Within minutes goods designated for auction, to a value estimated at £1,400, had been carried off. Thereafter, seemingly orchestrated by a small body of determined men, the mob proceded down Dolphin Street, to gather on the quayside. Initial attempts to board the *Pydar Rose* were repulsed thanks to the valience of Captain Clapp and the four men under his command. Thereafter one of the rioters feloniously fired several shots at the impounded vessel, grievously wounding Tidesman Neil Jarvis in the chest. News of this injury was enough to disperse the rioters, especially as Jarvis was a Porthcado man and two of his uncles were among the crowd. A Mrs Hawke, of Fretton, has come forward to report that the shots were fired by one Amos Provis, also of Porthcado, an accusation born out by Provis's subsequent flight into hiding.

On the following day a squadron of the Duke of Cornwall's Dragoons, under the command of Lieutenant Mason, was dispatched to Porthcado from Falmouth, both for the purposes of retrieving the purloined goods and to provide further protection for the *Pydar Rose* before she is broken up on Thursday next. Villagers who voluntarily surrender quantities of the looted goods to the Customs House are promised a free pardon.

* * *

Yes, Lucy, you will have guessed it: Provis is hidden away in the church. He came to me two days after the riot, on the morning that Neil Jarvis was reported to have died from his wounds. It was unnerving to conduct the funeral for the poor boy with Provis claiming the sanctuary of the Pope's Chamber, like a medieval fugitive. Nor am I running the risk you assume I am, for I assure you that since Jarvis was tucked away in the churchyard no one has come to Lancaradoc, and Provis would be safe enough in the kitchen, let alone ensconced in a secret hidey-hole in a corner of the church. Moreover, he is a cautious man, and most sensible of the risks he might expose his friends to: so much so, that he has refused several invitations to come even so far as the rectory – although I do believe he sometimes prowls around the churchyard at dead of night: this, partly for the good of his limbs, but also to permit himself a spot of touchpipes.

Moreover we have hit upon a scheme to deliver Provis from his present plight. Although we have no way of establishing his innocence, we can at least attempt to discredit the testimony against him. You will remember that the likeness between Provis and myself has been remarked upon: what, then, if we could arrange a meeting with his tormentor, which she will swear to before the court, then prove that it did not take place? Thereby the woman could be enticed into committing perjury. In essence our plan is simplicity itself: we send word to Mrs Hawke that Provis is willing to pay a substantial sum if she retracts her testimony against him, and Provis arranges to meet with her. She would surely boast of such a meeting in court, as it adds considerably to her scant allegations against him. Except that on the day that they supposedly meet, Provis is abroad, and we produce a dozen witnesses to show that the meeting with Hawke could not have taken place. How do we do this? Why, we but need to have Provis make one of his customary visits to Truro, while I go to talk with Mrs Hawke in his stead.

By way of preparation, I now have a three–day beard upon my chin, which itches damnably. Moreover, unlike Provis's black matt of whiskers, my own growth is as bright a red as the setting sun. I have sent to Miss Tingham to procure some dye.

* * *

Mudge to Lucy, April

150

Dearest Lucy,

While you have been with Isobel, I too was travelling, and all in the cause of saving Provis from his misfortunes. However, the story is much involved, and I must begin where I left off, with Provis in hiding.

Your picture of Salisbury moved me deeply, and I am pleased to hear that Isobel is so comfortable there. It seems but a while ago she was a babe with us in Frome, and but yesterday that she was sat opposite me here in the parlour chair. I have heard little from her of late, except for a rather terse letter in the autumn, congratulating me for having come through the horrors of last summer. No doubt the duties of motherhood, added to those of being a devoted wife, keep her concerns elsewhere. Indeed, your news spurs me to write to her, for there are events in the village which I know she will find of interest, and I'm working on a little gift from my pen which I hope to send her as a kickshaw.

The plan, as I wrote before, was that Provis should make a feint of buying his accuser off, while establishing an alibi elsewhere. Moreover, that I was to act as his counterfeit. Then, as soon as Mrs Hawke had been thus taken in, Provis was to hand himself over to the law, claiming that he had heard nothing of the accusations against him, as he had been seeking work and sleeping rough down Camborne way, and was now eager to clear his name. Moreover, it was imperative that we act quickly, for the sooner Provis constituted himself to the courts, the more plausible his tale would seem.

Yet act we could not. Something told us that our scheme was flawed, though talk it through as often as we did, we could not for the life of us – or, more truly, for the life of Provis – see where our error lay. On the grounds that my beard was never full enough, or that we did not know who would best act as our emissary to Mrs Hawke, we always found an excuse to procrastinate for a few more days. This went on till Provis had been in hiding a full month; finally the Sunday came when, strengthened by the morning's service, as well as a fine pheasant and a plate of parsnips, I visited his chamber determined to persuade him to action. Besides, we had to arrange our meeting for a Friday, to coincide with Truro market, so unless we began our negotiations early in the week, another fortnight was like to slip by.

I had scarce got Provis to consent, than I was out with my hat and stick and off up the valley to talk to Haddon – for that old rustic was Provis's final choice of go–between with Mrs Hawke. And indeed the simpleton showed such an immediate understanding of our intentions and such readiness to do what we asked of him, that I traipsed home convinced that Provis had better sense in his choice of go–between than I had given him credit for.

Yet that same evening, Lucy, I cannot tell you what an agony of silence we passed in the Pope's Chamber! The fat was truly in the fire, and in spite of all our preparations our doubts still stained the atmosphere like the stench of rancid bacon. Provis paced up and down, up and down, in a fug of tobacco smoke I hadn't had the heart to deny him that night. 'It won't do, Parson. She's goin te see'ee.' And as soon as his words were out, we were both convinced of the truth of them. So what could we do? 'There's but one road out. I must see'er meself. You'll have to go down to Truro, and play me there.'

The idea was preposterous. To pass myself off as a Cornish labourer for half an hour before an audience of one – and a purblind old crone at that – was one thing, but to sustain the act before a public of hundreds for an entire day was quite another. It couldn't be done. On that I was adamant.

'Listen, Parson, you only have to sit snug in the Market Arms for an hour with my coat about ee and a mug of ale afore ee, and we'll find a dozen men ready to swear that they saw what they expected to see: Amos Provis come to Truro all reg'lar–like. You'm won't even have to speak to anyone. Purvey will take you down on his cart, and if you'm ply him with a drop o' Cousin Jack and if I tell him – proper friendly–like – what he can expect if he gabs, he'll keep his trap shut.'

It was no good my protesting. Provis was more adamant than I. And if I hadn't much hope of carrying off the impersonation he was urging on me, I was yet as convinced as he that Hannah Hawke would tumble to our deception at once should I be the one to meet her in his stead. Perhaps I was as influenced by her reputation as the rest of Porthcado – I don't know. I only know that from fear of the old witch I let Provis talk me into this new scheme, mad as it was, and that I agreed to set out with Purvey at daybreak on Thursday morn.

When the day arrived, I was up an hour before dawn. I made coffee – a luxury I had been sent by Mère Agate – and took a cup over to Provis in the church. He, thank heaven, was in a most sanguine and sturdy frame of mind, and quite light–hearted about the morrow's interview with Mrs Hawke. He even advised me wisely with regard to Purvey, suggesting that as well as offering him a guinea for the fare, I should show him the brandy I proposed to give him, but promise that he should have it on our return: there was too much risk that a man like Purvey might take a tipple while I was with him, and that he would consequently lose whatever discretion and native wit the man possessed. Provis then handed me a bundle of his clothes. From habit I took them to the vestry to put them on; it was a strange, but fitting, sensation to go there to pull on his breeches and smock over my underclothes, in a ritual that was reminiscent of

153

my robing on a Sunday. Provis came in and pronounced his satisfaction with me. And indeed, at first glance, my beard, which I had dyed the evening before, looked almost as black and fierce as his own.

Then before I left him, I asked him if he would kneel with me on the chancel step and join me in a prayer for our venture. He assented with a nod and we knelt down as like as twin brothers. To my surprise, when I had finished, Provis added a most heart–felt extemporary prayer of his own, most full of compassion for Tidesman Jarvis, but also commending me to the Almighty in terms of such gratitude and affection that I had a job to hide my tears from him.

I returned to my parlour and waited. Purvey tapped at the window at precisely half–past–six, as we had arranged. I showed him the brandy and offered to cook us both some bacon. Purvey was all for trying the brandy with his breakfast, but I insisted it would have to wait. When we sat down to eat, Purvey's eyes were scuttling all over the kitchen. Clearly he found it difficult to swallow his bacon without a glass of liquor at his elbow: I offered him tea and he shuddered. Before I knew it, my offer of breakfast had turned into a challenge of wills: Purvey wanted a drink and I was denying it to him. Of course the antagonism which I had unwittingly set up was absurd, so I went to fetch the bottle of Madeira from the parlour sideboard; and though it was but a quarter full, it was enough to appease him.

We stepped outside a little after seven. It was a cold morn, with a fret that seemed undecided as to whether to lift or turn to drizzle. By the time we had climbed Fretton hill, the sky was beginning to lighten and the mist showed signs of lifting. By 9 o'clock we reached the Bodmin road and stopped at an inn for refreshment – in my case, a glass of milk: for Purvey, a mug of ale – and hay for the donkeys. Thereafter there was even a little warmth in the air.

Purvey was a changed man once he was up on his cart. He's usually such a mischievous ferret of a man, yet perched up on the cart, behind his donkeys, he was almost serene. He even indulged in a little tuneless whistling, especially on the downhill slopes. It was I who was not happy: I was balanced precariously among the sacks and packing cases, and with more than mere discomfort to depress my spirits. Perhaps I should have ventured some conversation by way of distraction but I could not bring myself to do so: my thoughts were wound about the task I was embarking on; also, I was ignorant of how much Provis had told the carter and was shy of talk with such a sensitive mission in the air. Besides, I did not know what to say to a man like Purvey.

We put up for the night at Tresillian, at a modest inn which backs onto the creek. This village lies some five miles out of Truro, where it seemed we were far enough away to run no risk of being recognised, and could relax before the day ahead. The landlady served us a most succulent chicken each, and thereafter I retired to our room, whereas Purvey stayed down in the taproom, to wake me by his clumsy entrance in the small hours.

And thence to Truro! Oh Lucy, I am ashamed to tell you how deplorably I conducted myself there.

We rode in at a little after nine in the morning, and, both because it was my purpose to be seen, and because Purvey insisted it would allay my nervousness, we called in at an ale-house in the High Street. Next, to another opposite St Mary's. And two more before we reached the Market Arms at noon. What possessed me to think that I could match Purvey glass for glass I do not know – but it was my undoing. By the time we had reached our lunchtime rendez-vous, where it will be remembered I was to provide a mummer's likeness of Provis, sitting quietly at his customary table, I was so fuddle–headed I believed I could play the man in all his swagger. So I slapped backs, offered a drink to any man who would call me Amos, and lit up the clay I found in his shirt pocket. I even joined in – nay, instigated – a chorus of snatch–songs.

Whether I was taken for Provis, I know not. Indeed, I was past caring. That rascal Purvey, fool that he is, seemed delighted with my performance, and did all that he could to encourage me in my debauchery. It was late in the afternoon when we staggered outside, and he led me to the cart. The market had closed, most of the stalls had been dismantled, and ours was one of the last carts to leave the square.

Then – oh horror! – the worst scene of all. I had just climbed atop the cart, and now assailed by the gusts of a wet wind, my muddle–headed euphoria was having to contend with the alarms of a nauseous stomach, when I saw two clerics turn the corner at the bottom of Lemon Street. And woe for me that I still had enough of my senses about me to recognise them. For one was my good friend Dean Dangerfield and the other was that Welsh martinet, Doctor Rees.

Lord knows what nonsense was churning through my head as the cart trundled down the cobbled street towards them. I only know that I sighted a small turnip in a corner of the wagon, and that this seemed to my preposterously drunken senses to have been sent as a piece of God-given ammunition. Then, just before we drew level, the two men stopped, and – for which I should be thankful – the good Dean took himself into a shop – I believe it was a printer's shop. But at least he was not to witness what followed. Poor Rees was left on the curb, immobile, casually surveying the square, and no more than ten feet away. I yelled at him in the broadest Cornish accent I could muster: 'Here, Taffy, this be a gift from the Children of Brychan'. And I hurled the turnip at him with all my force. I was aiming at his nose: it struck him on the shoulder. To see him standing there, so outraged, so perplexed, brought my euphoria to a climax: our eyes were locked onto one-another's, and for an instant I experienced the sweetest sense of hubris in revenge for all the humiliation and frustration which that pedantic Welshman had heaped upon me. But only for the briefest moment: for in the next I was engulfed by wave upon wave of nausea. Doctor Rees was still staring after me when I leaned over the back of the cart and was formidably sick.

It is one of nature's consolations not only to be blessed with unconsciousness in times of gross physical strain, but also that in our minds certain painful events should become obscured from memory. For the next two days my thoughts were spared the ability to revisit my ignominious behaviour: it was as though every time I tried to think of my conduct in Truro, when, instead of acting to save that good man Provis, my drunken pantomime was exposing him to mortal danger, or when, in particular, I was tempted to dwell on that brief but violent encounter with Doctor Rees, there was an angel standing guard over my recollections, whose job it was to drop a decorous drape over the events of that shameful day.

And if I am trying to describe the torments of the mind at such a moment, it is not because my body was free from tribulation, but because my physical plight was self–induced, temporary, and in the nature of a just punishment. Of the rest of that day I can remember little, but on the morrow how the flesh suffered! – my head and stomach most sorely.

In the late afternoon, on leaving Truro, Purvey rode as far as Probus, a dozen miles off. There, we put up at an inn of exceptional comfort, or so I'm told: my only memory of it is of a cold bed and a white enamel bucket. Purvey woke me early but I would not rise. He left me while he had his breakfast and hitched up the cart, and when he returned at half–past eight he had to wake me again. He had news: one of the donkeys was lame and would need re–shoeing. Purvey left to find a blacksmith and I slept again. Nor did I wake till well past the hour for lunch, and though part of me toyed with the calamity that would befall should we fail to make Lancaradoc that night – for I should be missed from church in the morning, and I was puzzled by Purvey's long absence – yet another side of me was content that I had been given this chance to rest.

I rang for hot water and bathed. I still had a change of fresh linen, which at such times is as good a tonic as anything a doctor can prescribe. Yet once I had donned my underclothes I had to pull on Provis's smock and breeches and these garments tortured me with self–reproach. My toilet done, I could neither bring myself to read nor pray, but sat at the window as glum as a pollack. Purvey came in at four, the smell of liquor on his breath, then went out again a few minutes later. Evidently he had found the blacksmith congenial company. I had not the heart to chide him, nor, indeed, could I have brought myself to do anything so hypocritical. I assumed that we would stay in Probus for a second night, given the hour, and was resigned to it. To my surprise, when Purvey returned some ten minutes later, he announced that we were ready to leave.

Needless to say, we didn't make Lancaradoc that night. We put up in Lanivet, a village on the highroad, a few miles west of Bodmin. I woke on Sunday morning in a most sorry frame of mind: my absence from church was sure to compound the harm I had already done Provis, and I could not hope to escape a congregation either, for last Sunday the farmers came, and during the week Mrs Lorneville had taken up her summer residence; I have never known her to miss her Sabbath observances.

The rascally carter seemed quite unperturbed. He took to whistling cheerfully the nearer we approached home. I could not find it in my heart to blame him: the failure of our mission was entirely my own. It was, besides, a most radiant morning, full of sun and scudding cloud and the promise of spring. Consequently we made light work of the four-hour drive and came upon familiar landscapes sooner than I had expected. Of a sudden we could see Fretton before us and, having climbed the hill, had our first glimpse of the sea. Purvey was all for stopping in the Fretton Arms for sustenance, but I insisted we carry on. Porthcado lay tantalisingly close, just beyond the Pinnacles, and I could see the fold in the valley that hid Lancaradoc. Even if I had little to look forward to, I was eager to be home.

I intended to make a full confession at once. I would say to Provis: 'I am sorry, my friend, I have acted ignominiously. Through my own foolishness and irresponsibility I have let you down. I have failed to establish the alibi you need and my only advice is for you to flee these parts while there is still time to save yourself.' It would be a painful disclosure, yet once the words were out, like a rankling tooth, some comfort would ensue: for me, at least, the worst would be over.

So eager was I to meet Provis that I slipped down from the cart as soon as we reached the rectory gates, paid Purvey his guinea in fare, and bid him a perfunctory farewell. I let myself in, deposited my bundle of clothes on the kitchen table, and without even bothering to change out of Provis's attire, rushed out again across the lawn, and clambered the wall into the top corner of the churchyard.

'Afternoon to ye, Parson'. So unexpected were the words, spoken in that deserted place, seemingly by the soft spring air, that I blanched: they seemed to have come from an antique slate–

topped tombstone beside the yew tree. And my evident perplexity caused that ghostly voice to laugh – a laugh which I recognised at once as Provis's. In that very instant he sat up, his head appearing above the tomb; he had a clay in his mouth, and a quite inappropriately benevolent grin upon his face. He must have been taking advantage of the tree's shade for an afternoon nap, and I saw at once that he had been lounging on the grass dressed in my best Sunday cassock, which irritated me unreasonably.

'Good grief man, this is no time for such tomfoolery!'

'I never meant to fright'ee.'

'Aye, well it's the sight of myself in my own graveyard. Sprawled out like that...'

'I do the parson rather well. Leastways, I did this morning, so there's no need to fret.'

'I'm sorry you were put to that. Nothing in Truro occurred quite as we expected...'

'Twas no trouble, now. Only had that Lorneville woman to church, and I can scan my way through a prayer book as well as the next man.'

I could imagine it! How that great lummoxing labourer must have burred and stumbled his way through the psalms. Yet it was nothing now, as I meant to explain.

'Beside, she seemed quite happy with me judgin' from our little pallyvoo in the porch afterward.'

I was about to ask him what he meant. Except that at that precise instant the peacocks began to shriek: clearly there was someone on the rectory lawn.

'Quick, man, hide yourself!'

'No, sir, tis you that has to hide. Get down 'ere.' And as he spoke, I felt one hand upon my collar, and the other in the small of my back, pushing me roughly down behind the tombstone.

He was right, of course. How stupid of me! – for all the world to see, he was attired as the parson, and I was still Provis. I breathed in the scent of earth and grass and tried to calm myself.

'You can stand up, Parson. Tis only Purvey.'

He was crossing the lawn. We watched him descend the steps into the lane. When he reached the lynch gate he put his hand to his mouth and hollered: ''Ere Parson, what about that Cousin Jack?'

As if we hadn't more important things on our mind! Yet knowing the individual as I do, I could see that we wouldn't be rid of Purvey till he had warmed his belly with a few glasses of cognac, or at least could see his way clear to doing so. I waved back at him, and indicated that he should go back to the house. I would join him forthwith.

'Don't you worry about him, Parson. He may be adle-headed but in a pinch he can be trusted.'

'I'm quite sure.' The look on my face, however, belied the confidence of my words: nor was my expression lost on Provis.

'He hasn't blathered, has 'ee?'

I shook my head. 'It's not Purvey. It's myself: I'm not sure I played you so convincingly in Truro'

'Someone tumbled to it, you mean?'

'Not exactly. But I rather overdid it in the Market Arms...'

'After this morning, I daresay that Lorneville woman won't take Parson Mudge for no saint, neither. Best get rid of Purvey.' He nodded towards the rectory.

We shook hands, and I left him. How downcast I felt as I plodded back up towards the house: how full of self–reproach. Not only had I put the man in mortal danger, but I hadn't even found the courage to make a clean breast of it. I resolved to be rid of the carter as quick as I could, then to finish my duty.

'You'll sample it with me, won't you Parson?' commanded Purvey, when I brought out his gallon tub from the pantry. On any other occasion I would have refused, but under the current circumstances I had neither the wit nor the fortitude to supply a ready excuse. As we sat down at the kitchen table, however, I made it quite clear that I was busy and would only take the one glass.

Nor did I finish that; we were disturbed by the doorbell.

'Tis that Mrs Lorneville,' hissed Purvey, sidling across to the window and peering out.

'What on earth can she want? Still, I'd better let her in. Thank you, Purvey.'

'In that attire?'

He was right. 'You let her in then. Tell her you're the new gardener – tell her anything.' And I dashed up the stairs to get changed.

When I returned, a minute later, I was horrified to find Mrs Lorneville, in her best tea gown, sat at the kitchen table with the carter, a glass of Purvey's Cousin Jack before her. 'My dear lady!'

By way of reply, she gave me such a sweet smile of tolerant understanding that I could see that my apologies were less necessary than I had assumed.

'Good afternoon Parson, I trust I do not disturb you.'

Purvey tossed off his glass and scraped back his chair. 'I'd best be on my way.' And picking up his cap, he tucked the brandy barrel beneath his arm, and walked out through the door as determined as a mill mule, without giving us a backwards glance.

What Vanessa Lorneville had come for was tea, and though I was hardly in the mood for it, I clearly had no option but to offer her a cup. Moreover, although the lady is usually so bright and civil, I found her in a most trying frame of mind. She looked quite vexed when I suggested she move into the parlour while I put the kettle on, and when I brought the tea through, she just sat and stared at me, without a word of what the locals call 'mouth-speech'.

'I hope your journey down was not too tiring.'

'Yes.' She was winding and unwinding a green silk handkerchief about her fingers. I was searching for something to say to allay her distress, when she suddenly reached out and grabbed my arm, just above the wrist. 'How can you stand to live alone like this!'

I confess to being somewhat taken aback. Such concern for my domestic arrangements, and expressed so ardently! 'I do know how to look after myself,' I explained, gesturing at the tea-tray between us. 'Besides, I have a girl from the village. She comes three days a week.'

The answer seemed to do nothing to reassure Mrs Lorneville. She sank back in her chair and glowered at me.

It was, I can assure you, a most taxing hour. I had Provis on my mind. My lady visitor would not go, and yet she seemed to have lost the ability to converse. I was beginning to dread that she was expecting me to walk her home. But she did eventually rise, and I showed her to the door. Her leave-taking was as queer as the rest of her visit: I was enfolded in an embrace of startling intensity, and she whispered something in my ear: I believe what I heard was 'Richard!'

Whatever her predicament was, I had little time for it. As soon as she reached the gate, I dashed through the house and out through the back door.

I believe I was already filled with a presentiment that something was amiss. Do you know that sensation one has on entering a house where one is expecting to find someone at home, and yet it is empty? That is exactly what I felt as I turned the iron ring that lifts the heavy latch of the south door. I knew at once that Provis had gone. At first I was reluctant to accept it. I went to the Pope's Chamber, but even as I climbed the stairs I could see that the door had been left wide open and there was no one within. Not finding him in the church, I thought he might still be about the churchyard, even though the sun had gone an hour ago. However, I had hardly got outside again when it occurred to me that, pen-shy though he was, a man like Provis would not go without me leaving a note, so I retraced my steps, and went back up to the chamber with a candle. Sure enough, tucked into the frame of one of the paintings was a sheet of paper; and so evident was the whiteness of it against the dark background of the cavalier's mistress that had I not been so perturbed previously I should have seen it even in the gloaming. I took it down and turned it over, for all that I had already read the large scrawl of its message. 'Put to Bodmin. Amos'.

At least there was humour in it, I suppose: if someone is 'put' to Bodmin, then they are in the asylum for the county's lunatics; those in the gaol are said to have been 'took' to Bodmin. No doubt Provis had wished to reassure me that he had gone to meet his fate with a light heart. Poor wretch! With this note still in my hand I stumbled down the steps and sank into the front pew. I had but one thought: this piece of paper was as good as a death warrant. Oh why had I not told him what had passed in Truro? Not for lack of courage, surely, because I had meant to tell him. I had simply bungled.

How long I sat in that cold pew, I cannot tell you, Lucy. It seemed like a night's vigil, but I was probably not there above an hour. Do you think I prayed for my friend? I tried. Yet I could not lift my thoughts to the Almighty, for they were stuck in the mire of my own incompetence. After worrying uselessly for Provis on my knees, my only consolation came with the impulse to unburden myself by setting everything down in this letter. Perhaps that impulse was itself the answer to my prayer. So eventually I rose and let myself out with a leaden heart. My five-week guest had gone; the church felt as empty as an eggshell.

*   *   *

Mudge to Lucy, June

Dear Lucy,

You are right. It is the older generation's duty to maintain family contacts, and although I have felt Isobel to be little interested in us since little Emily was born, I must confess that I too have been a laggardly correspondent. Perhaps the pace of events here will excuse that.

My chief news is of Provis, and of the Bodmin trial that has just concluded. When I think back now to the first days in the court room, it is hard to credit how it has turned out. From the first, it seemed that the machinery of law had already decided on his guilt and that its chief purpose was to make an example of him. On the opening morning Provis was forced to walk the mile from the gaol to the court house on Mount Folly in chains, a custom usually reserved for the most depraved of murderers. All of Bodmin was out on the street to watch him. And even if the crowds were not necessarily hostile to a smuggler, they were still a Bodmin crowd, which is to say they were not a Porthcado crowd, and so had little reason to show him sympathy. A month in that dreadful place had reduced him terribly. He could scarcely stutter out a confirmation of his name before the court.

I had engaged a local advocate to conduct the defence, a Mr Judd, a solid man, but lacklustre. When Judge Epplet began to harangue the court with apoplectic zeal, it was immediately apparent that Judd meant to defer to him, and would limit himself to citing from his dusty law books: there were times, by damn! when I would have liked to take a stick to him, the way

Purvey goads his donkey.

First Captain Clapp was called upon to give his account of the assault on the *Rose*, which he did most fairly, and was ready to admit, upon cross–examination, that he had no idea of who had fired the shot that did for young Jarvis, nor did he believe that anyone on deck could have distinguished individual faces from among the crowd. Two of Clapp's men were called, then several of the officers from the Custom's House. The best part of three days were devoted to the testimony of the excisemen, establishing the facts of the riot, but without a shred of evidence to point to Provis as having taken part in any particularly violent fashion. None of the witnesses were even able to identify him as one of the rioters, although Provis freely admitted that he had been both among the crowds that entered the custom house, and later on, with those upon the quay.

Then on the Thursday morning, Rosevear, the prosecutor, called Hannah Hawke to the bar. I must say, she spoke out to the court as though born to it, putting aside that terrible fury she is capable of, and presenting herself as a very model of sweet reason and cooperation.

'Mrs Hawke, tell the court where you were standing, and how far you were from the defendant when you say he fired the flintlock.'

'I can tell'ee zackly wur we waz to. I waz up against the bollard where they tie *The Queen o' May* and hanging onto a post there lest I end up in the sea. There waz a great shove aback o'me, and I was right on the water's edge. Him there,' – she pointed at Provis – 'wur right beside me. No more 'un the width o' my kitchen away from wur I wer stood.'

'Now Mrs Hawke, you will appreciate that there are few here who have the privilege of knowing your kitchen. In terms of this courtroom, can you explain to us, as near as you can, the distance there was between yourself and the defendant?'

'From here to the edge o' that thur table. About half the distance there be between us now.' And so saying she looked Provis straight in the eye. I saw that look: it was one of cold triumph. Seeing Hannah Hawke like that, in her hat and fawn-coloured gown, her great turkey jowls powdered, trying to pass herself off as a harmless widow, whose only motivation was concern for the Jarvises – why, Lucy, I hated her for it. If I had had the power to damn her to hell, in that moment I would have done so.

Judd began his cross examination: 'Tell me, Mrs Hawke, in that substantial crowd, were there no others standing between yourself and Mr Provis?'

'O'course they wer. We were packed tighter'n salt pilchards. But I believe I got a plain look of 'em: he had to stand forward to fire his shot.'

'If his actions were witnessed by so many, is it not strange that there are not more witnesses ready to support your testimony?'

'Not when they all do come from Porthcado, Yer 'Onour. Besides, Amos Provis has always been well liked in the town.'

In short, the case against Provis lay on Hawke's testimony alone, and against the claims that at night, and in such a crowd, the old woman might have been mistaken, she held her ground, but without insistence – a tactic which more than any other lent her accusations a veneer of plausibility. Knowing what was to come, everything about widow Hawke's performance struck me as so much play acting; I alone, apart from Provis, knew what she and Rosevear had in store for the court, and once it was claimed that he had tried to buy her off, the events on the quayside would scarcely count. Yet the rest of that first week played itself out with the cross examination of a score of

Porthcado men who had been alongside the *Pydar Rose* on the night of the riot. None of them felt they could give any indication of who might have fired the fateful shot, so that when the court was adjourned on Friday afternoon, Judge Eplett was in a most irritable mood, and there was hardly a man in the courthouse who felt there was enough evidence against Provis to press for a conviction.

I passed a fearful weekend. On the Saturday morning Judd and I sought permission from the prison governor to meet with Provis, but it was refused. Nonetheless, Provis was able to send letters out: a note of gracious thanks to Judd, albeit coarsely worded, and to myself a private letter in which he wrote that he had every faith in the strength of our rebuttal against the accusations that Hannah Hawke was about to make. Imagine my consternation when I read it: I alone knew that this defence would be a farce; the very men on whom Provis relied to provide his alibi were sure to condemn him, for they would speak of the buffooning clown who had aped him, and even granted their charitable disposition towards him, some suspicion that Provis's trip to Truro had not been quite as regular as we were claiming was bound to out.

Twice I was tempted to go to Judd and make a clean breast of it. We had just parted after reading Provis's letters together in the Mason's Arms. I had an hour to wait before the chaise was leaving for Porthcado. I even had my bag with me, so I had no need to return to my lodgings. After walking up and down the High Street, I came back to Mount Folly, which is the town's main square. There, hard by the courthouse, was the door to Judd's chambers. From the clock, I could see that I still had ample time to air my worries. I resolved to see him at once and crossed the square. But at the last something stayed my hand from ringing the bell. It was my confusion, most like. I had not thought the thing through: what, after all, would be gained by making a confession to Judd at this stage? Perhaps he could find a solution, and to do that he would need to be forewarned. But once he knew that our defence was based on deliberate trickery, what then? Even if he was still prepared to argue for us, might not his performance lack conviction? The only conviction I could count on was poor Provis's. I tell you, Lucy, the turmoil in which my thoughts were embroiled knew no end.

Nor did the night I spent back in Lancaradoc help me. I arrived at a cold house, to find that the maid had forgotten to buy in the provisions I'd asked for. I was exhausted by the journey, and slept fitfully. Mrs Lorneville was all my congregation on Sunday, and though she is devout at her prayers, and as attentive of her priest as any clergyman could wish for, I preached a sorry sermon, for I was all too eager to be alone with my thoughts. After a cold lunch I hurried out to be on the highway in time to meet the Bodmin coach. The break had resolved nothing: I returned to Bodmin feeling as confused and inadequate as when I had left it.

I had not been back in my room above a quarter of an hour before my feet were eager to carry me out again. Moreover, despite all the remonstrance's that I had made with myself, I found myself walking out of town and up the hill towards Judd's house in Grenville Road. Thank heavens the maid who answered the door announced that her master was not at home! I was saved by providence from an interview which I was not prepared for, and which I knew in my heart was folly.

Would you believe that all my anxiety had been in vain? And that my own part in providing Provis with an alibi slid by undetected? The second week of the trial went much as Provis and Judd had predicted it would – and ended in disaster.

At ten o'clock on Monday morning, after Epplet had

strutted in, to be welcomed by the court with much bowing and scraping, Rosevear rose to his feet, and with a modesty that was commendable, announced that he had further evidence of Provis's guilt to lay before the court. Epplet met his request to call Mrs Hawke back to the witness box with a curt nod.

'Mrs Hawke, if I were to say to you that, as an elderly woman, whose eyes are not what they used to be, at night, and in such a crowd, your ocular testimony is not alone sufficient to identify Amos Provis as Jarvis's murderer, how would you respond?'

'That twas'ee what did it, sir.'

'The court is hardly convinced. After all, we have seen that no one has been found to confirm your evidence.'

'But there's more.'

'Meaning?'

For answer, Mrs Hawke slipped off her gloves and undid the top three buttons of her gown. The eyes of the court room were all upon her. She extracted a cotton purse that hung about her neck, and tipped a handful of money into her hand. Looking straight at Provis she arranged ten piles of sovereigns, each six coins high, along the wooden rail of the witness stand. It was a consummate piece of play-acting. Then she glanced coyly towards the judge's bench: 'He tried to buy me off, Yer 'Onour.'

In the momentary silence which ensued, Epplet could be heard to grunt with satisfaction, before a tide of astonished whispers began to ripple through the court.

In response to Rosevear's questioning, Hawke narrated the circumstances in which she had the money from Provis. And of course she told the tale convincingly, because, for once, she was telling the truth. What is more, she had the money – as it happened, my money – to lend her words credibility.

When she had finished Rosevear nodded to the judge

then sat down, giving his coat–tails a satisfied flourish.

Epplet turned menacingly towards the accused. 'Have you anything to say for yourself?' Judd rose to his feet, signalling to Provis to keep silent. Provis lifted his right hand, in a gesture that was at once both a rebuttal to the lawyer but which also suggested a solemn swearing: 'She says it was a Friday I was supposed to have paid her off? The Friday after Easter?'

'T'was an' all!' Hannah Hawke shrieked across the courtroom.

'Then I can prove she'm lying – that day I was in Truro, Your Worship.'

At that point, Judd's excitement knew no bounds. He scurried first to Provis and, grabbing him by the sleeve, forced him to his seat. Epplet had to resort to his gavel to quieten the court. When Judd had finished the conference with his client, he rushed across to the bench to talk to Epplet. The court was in uproar. There were several minutes of this pandemonium, with Judd scuttling back and forth, and Epplet summoning first one lawyer then the other, before Epplet took up his gavel again, and it was clear that he was about to make an announcement. Although his message was for the benefit of the whole court, he addressed himself to Rosevear, who at that moment was conferring with Mrs Hawke: 'The counsel for the defence informs me that they wish to establish that Mr Provis was abroad on business on the day when this alleged colloquy took place. To do so they need time to round up their witnesses. The court is therefore in recess until Wednesday.'

'We need more than that, Your Honour. At least a week.'

'Very well, you are granted an extension – but only until Thursday, Mr Judd.'

When the court reconvened on Thursday morning we only managed to produce two witnesses from the Market Arms:

the landlord's daughter and one Roger Japes, a trinket-seller, who I remembered for his loud but tuneless singing. The landlord's daughter recounted how she had served Provis his lunch well enough – and so she should, for I had eaten heartily, and the stew of tripe had been uncommonly good; but under cross examination Rosevear confused her so much with dates that even she could not swear to it's having been on a Friday that she had served him. Japes was an entirely different kettle of fish. As a stallholder, Japes had the advantage of only coming to town for market, which should have established the date beyond doubt, yet there was something so seamy about the man, and he was so ready to ingratiate himself with all parties, that even Judd had a job to make him sound convincing, and Rosevear had him looking like the lowest form of gutter–snipe.

By the afternoon we were also able to produce one Bill Bruford, an honest but slow–witted labourer, and two more of Provis's drinking cronies were present on the Friday. To my surprise, none of them showed the least doubt as to Provis's identity, despite my debauched impersonation of him. Rosevear, however, was so adept at confusing them over dates, as well as our witnesses being such an ill–mannered gaggle of simpletons, that once my own fears were put to rest, even I was wincing for the ingenuousness and crudity of their replies.

Epplet, alas, had far less patience than I. On the Friday afternoon he announced that he had listened quite long enough to the dubious testimonies of such riff-raff, and that if Provis had found sixty sovereigns to buy off Mrs Hawke, he had no doubt that such people could be bought for far less. Unless there were any further developments he intended to conclude the case on Monday. And with a bang of his gavel we were dismissed.

I walked out into Mount Folly Square stunned by the injustice of it. Provis was to be hanged for little more than

Epplet's prejudice against the lower orders. I walked down the short hill towards St Petroc's. Rooks were cawing in the elms beyond. Looking up I read the church clock: twenty to four. There was just time to return to my lodgings and catch the chaise at four. It was a base thought at such a time: my duty was clearly to visit Provis in his cell and give him what comfort I could. But I could not do it, Lucy. I took the chaise.

The sun had set by the time I reached Lancaradoc. I let myself in and lit a fire. For supper there was bread and brisket: I opened a bottle of claret for consolation. However, it was a sober evening, for all that I drank the bottle off. It was much like a wake, for Provis was as good as dead. Yet in some strange way the day had brought not only Provis's condemnation, but my acquital: at least if he was to go to the gallows it would not be through my own bungling, but because he had had the misfortune to cross the paths of such as Hawke and Epplet. That Provis was innocent of Jarvis's death I had no doubt. Yet Mrs Hawke had seen her chance to do for him, and Provis's attempts to save himself had come to nought. Although the instruments that had cut him down were all too human, his end was as impersonal as the cholera. I went to bed reflecting on the indifferent stars that had allowed such a random destiny.

The same mood of cowed acceptance clung to me throughout the following day. I believed that Provis was beyond all help. I only wished to put him from my mind, although of course I could not. What could I do but busy myself, tending that tiny plot of trivial concerns that was my life? After breakfast I went out to the hives. I have rather neglected the bees of late. By lunchtime I had gone through the hives against the churchyard wall, checking for queen cells and healthy brood. Then I inspected those on the moor, two of which have swarmed recently, and discovered that one was inexplicably empty. By mid-afternoon, whether from the morning's exertion, or the accumulated anxiety of a week in Bodmin, I was exhausted, and slept nearly three hours. Then, if I tell you that in the evening I failed to write out my sermon, you will realise how far the events in Bodmin have upset my customary routines.

And would you believe that when I woke on Sunday morning, everything had changed. Rees! Why had I not thought of him before? He had seen Provis in Truro that Friday, and surely Epplet would accept the testimony of such a man! I bounded out of bed and rushed to my study to write him a letter. The thought of Rees must have been slipped into my dream by an angel. You do believe in angels, don't you, Lucy? And what if he was no longer in Truro? What if he had returned to Pembrokeshire in the intervening weeks? Such matters were not in my hands. But as much as I could do, I would. And who should take the letter? Not Purvey. I could not trust him to make the necessary haste, and needed someone who could lend his own persuasion to that of the letter. Besides, what if Rees had seen Purvey and were to have remembered him? While I was getting dressed, the solution came to me: I would ask William Lobb to go. He was a fine upstanding lad, and could ride one of his father's horses.

I sealed the letter and put on my coat. Then I took it off again. What if the Lobbs were on the way to church? They had been coming irregularly over the last few weeks: it would be just my luck to miss them because I was heading over the fields towards Trebarton just as they were riding to Lancaradoc by the lane.

So at half-past nine I went down to the church and loitered about the porch. Ten minutes later I heard the lych-gate open. On peeping out, imagine my disappointment when I saw that it was but Mrs Lorneville. Indeed, I snuck round behind the porch so that she could come into church without meeting me. Her presence there was, I must confess, little more than an irritant, for it distracted my mind with thoughts of the sermon I had not written, and the prayers I had no intention of conducting. My only wish was to talk to William Lobb, and to hear him say that he would ride to Truro for me, and at once!

By ten-past-ten it was clear that I should have no other congregation than the respectable Mrs Lorneville – least of all the Lobbs. So I was all for setting off to Trebarton immediately, seeing as I had already lost the best part of an hour since finishing the letter, but an instinct of vestigial politeness made me turn back towards my church to tell the good woman within that there would be no Communion that morning.

'Mrs Lorneville, I must apologise: I have kept you waiting, and I am bound to disappoint you still further.' This was how I began when I reached her at the front of the nave. I was somewhat unnerved, because she had not been devoutly on her knees when I stepped into the church, as I had expected, but sitting languorously with her feet dangling upon the pew, as though it were a chaise longue, and had been facing the south door so as to better scrutinise my entrance.

She put her hand upon the sleeve of my cassock: 'Believe me, Rector, you shall never be a disappointment to me.' The familiarity of her remark took me aback.

'What I mean, Mrs Lorneville, is that there shall be no service this morning.'

She blushed. 'Very well, Richard. What would you have us do?'

'Do, madam? Why go home of course. I have important matters to attend to: matters – and I make no exaggeration – of life and death.'

Far from ending our conversation there, for I thought I

had made myself clear – and to my utter amazement – Mrs Lorneville encircled my waist with her arm and pulled me towards her. There was nothing I could do to prevent her from burying her face against my stomach, in what seemed a most intimate and compromising posture.

'Mrs Lorneville!' But my protests were in vain. The poor woman was sobbing – I was going to say 'inconsolably', but subsequently discovered that a few gentle caresses on my part went some way towards consoling her.

Eventually I untangled her arms and insisted that I had to leave: 'Mrs Lorneville, please – whatever it is that distresses you, we shall soon find time to discuss it. Only now I have an appointment which I must keep. Believe me, something of such overriding importance that I must abandon both the duties of my calling, and your good self.' And thus saying I backed towards the porch.

At the kitchen door of Trebarton Farm, Mrs Lobb explained that her husband and son were at work in Sidman's Copse. This stretch of woodland lies in a sheltered side–valley adjacent to Lancaradoc, and provides an ideal site for the raising of pheasants. However, as it is half a mile inland from the rectory, reaching them would involve me in the frustration of retracing my steps. I set off at once, despairing that it would take me the best part of half-an-hour to get there, and that this circumstance would delay William's departure by at least another hour.

I found them repairing a gate. The farmer gave his son a broad wink at my approach: 'Here, Will – the parson has come to tell'ee that old man Ruan won't let his daughter marry a Lobb after all. Still, it'll save me having to sit down to dinner with him, so what's bad news for thee, be good for me.'

'Nothing of the kind, William. But I have urgent need of you. It's about poor Provis.'

The two men lay down their hammers and gave me their attention. Farmer Lobb was full of concern and questions, but his son, with all the self-containment of youth, listened in silence to what I had to ask of him. I charged William not just to seek out Rees if he were still be found in Truro and to give him my letter, but also to remonstrate with the Welsh cleric and convince him that he alone had the power to save an innocent man's life. Moreover, as I was returning to Bodmin that night, William would have to come and find me there, by lunchtime tomorrow at the latest, as it would take me all my influence to delay Epplet from passing sentence before then. Indeed, secretly, I doubted if even this were possible, but I had to try – there was no alternative.

'Of course he'll ride to Truro for you, Parson,' the farmer replied on his son's behalf when I had finished. 'Won't you, Will?'

'Yes, Father.' Yet even as he said it, I could see that there was something vexing William. He packed up his tool bag and we took our leave of the farmer. We walked up through the wood in silence. So steep was it that I had to go sideways, sometimes clinging onto the trees for support. The strange thing about a North Cornish wood is that the trees are entirely stunted and misshapen by the winds, and their boughs so bearded with grey and yellow lichens, that they are scarce recognisable as relatives of their English cousins: Sidman's Copse consists mostly of oaks, but it was only this physical contact with the trees that brought me to recognise them as such.

I was short of breath when we reached the top. William slipped dexterously over the fence into the field, and waited for me to clamber over it, which in a cassock is no mean feat. As I looked up I caught him giving me a look of such despairing resentment that I decided to have it out with him at once. 'Something's up boy. What is it about this undertaking that you

177

find so irksome?'

William gave a guilty smile and denied that there was any problem. 'Nothing, sir. Especially if Mr Provis's fate depends on it. My misgiving is a puny and selfish thing – only I've arranged to walk out with Miss Ruan this afternoon, and now I see that I shall have to disappoint her.'

Well if that was all it was, then perhaps I could go in his stead, to explain his absence and walk her home. Where was their tryst to be? Two o'clock at Bartlett's Cave, and should I go young William would be most grateful. And with that settled, we parted, for Lancaradoc lay straight ahead across the fields, whereas the boy's way was to follow the hedge round towards Trebarton.

I scarce had time for an improvised luncheon at noon before it was time to set off to meet William's girl. Luckily there was a plate of stewed leeks in the pantry, which, together with a small loaf, some cheese and a mug of ale, would provide sustenance enough to see me through the afternoon. Bartlett's Cave is out at Cadoc's Zawn, and although the shortest path from here is the one through Polgarrick, I decided to follow the valley down into Porthcado first, then follow the cliff path round the Pinnacles. That would allow me to drop in at the Falcon and satisfy the sea-town's appetite for the news from Bodmin. Yet my report of the week's events, and Landlord Barret's crestfallen reception of it, was a glum affair, and I continued my walk in a sombre mood, and little confident that by sending William to Truro I could redeem poor Provis.

At the eastern end of Cadoc's Zawn a finger of rock juts out into the sea, beyond which is a patch of sand and a great sea-cave. At full tide this side of the beach is quite cut off – indeed, one can see from the cliff that the cave is filled with the churning waves – but at low tide, and on summer afternoons such as this, Bartlett's Cave, as this corner of the zawn is known, is a favourite meeting place for romantic assignations. As I clambered over the rocks I could see Judy Ruan sitting on a rock at the mouth of the cave. She was wearing a red dress, her straw bonnet upon her knee. I hailed her and waved my arms. I could tell from the way she rose that I had alarmed her, for I expect that I was the last person she expected to see coming over the rocks towards her. A priest has a reputation as sorry as any crow's as a bringer of news, and whatever fears the sight of me provoked, I felt I ought to dispel them at once. That will no doubt explain why I rushed so recklessly over the stones, and slipped on a patch of emerald seaweed. The consequences could not have been more unfortunate – with my footing lost, I slithered into a puddle of seawater, and bruised my posterior most fearsomely. Moreover, if Judy had been flustered by my appearance, she was now quite alarmed by my antics. With the help of her hand, however, I was soon on my feet again, and limping a little sorely across the sand.

It was the work of a moment to explain my arrival in lieu of her fiancé, and to allay her fears. Miss Ruan took the news most graciously, for she is sweet–natured girl. Standing there at the sea's edge, it occurred to me that Will Lob is going to find himself with an exemplary wife. I offered to see her home. She took my arm, and we began to pick our way most carefully back over the rocks.

We had no sooner reached the crest of this natural barrier when we became aware of a figure coming towards us on the footpath, at the base of the cliff. It was a female figure in a striped pink dress; she was carrying a folded parasol of the same material, and was waving it over our head, clearly intent on catching our attention.

'Why, I do believe it be Mrs Lorneville,' exclaimed Judy, whose eyesight is so much younger than mine.

I had scarcely been able to ascertain this for myself than

Mrs Lorneville was on the sand before us, and from her red face and contorted mouth, it was abundantly clear that something was amiss.

I had no idea that I might be responsible for her rage until I felt her parasol about my ears. Luckily, my reactions were quick enough for me to ward off the worst of the blows with my arms, but together with the injuries from my fall, this last week the bruises to my elbows have caused me considerable discomfort.

'How dare you! You philandering, deceitful hypocrite. So this is your overriding importance, is it? Your matter of life and death? How dare you make love to me, then rush off to this insolent chit of a thing.' Then she turned towards Judy and lunged out at her with her parasol. 'Hussy!'

I grabbed her wrist, snatched the offending weapon from her, and snapped it in two over my knee. 'Mrs Lorneville! Now that's enough!' I fair bellowed at her, which had the effect of damping her rage. Indeed, her face crumpled, she extracted a lace handkerchief, and began to snivel. 'Now, please, would you explain what on earth you mean by this?'

Alas, my reasonable words only aggravated the situation, for she struck out at me with her fists, then, once I had secured these with my own hands, she had at my shins with her feet. I have never been subjected to such inexplicable wrath by a member of the gentler sex.

This second attack exhausted itself in a frenzy of tears. I noticed that Judy Ruan, with exquisite tact, and perhaps an instinct for self-preservation, had removed herself out of hearing range, and was now walking at the water's edge under the furthermost cliff. So in a gentler voice, I repeated my request to Mrs Lorneville that she explain herself to me.

'I shall not be toyed with!' Mrs Lorneville drew herself up

with considerable dignity. 'It is enough that our relationship must flourish in the shade, away from the glare of convention. After all, I am a widow, and you are my priest. Any attachment that there is between is bound to provoke tittle–tattle, and possibly criticism. So a modicum of discretion, even reticence, on your part was something I was prepared for. I was even foolish enough to imagine that it did you credit. But that you should try to deny everything is beyond my understanding.' And here she looked towards the shore line, in the direction of Miss Ruan. 'Clearly, however, you have more experience in making love to your female parishoners than I surmised.'

'Did you follow me here?' As soon as I had blurted it out, I realised my indiscretion, for Mrs Lorneville would only take such a question as proof of her preposterous accusations. Yet in that instant, a sudden conviction that I had indeed been followed along the cliff path out from Porthcado – for this alone would explain Mrs Lorneville's appearance in such a wilderness – had seized my mind, and I could not prevent myself from giving utterance to it.

For answer I was met with a steely glare. Then Mrs Lorneville held out her hand. For an moment I thought that she meant for me to take it, in a gesture of peace – then I realised that she only wanted the wreck of her parasol, which was still dangling from my hand. As I handed it over, it was evident that Mrs Lorneville had more to say. 'Not only are you a disgrace to your calling, but I believe that you are quite the most insolent, cowardly man I have ever had the misfortune to meet. Good day to you.' And with these words buzzing about my ears, she turned upon her heel, and marched off across the sand.

As you may imagine, sister, our walk back to Polgarrick was not the most cheerful. Neither of us could bring ourselves to speak. I saw Judy Ruan to her door, and bid her farewell as civilly as I could, although I believe I was quite red–faced with the embarrassment of what we had been subjected to. And thence I traipsed home to the rectory, not for the life of me able to understand the attack that had been made against me, yet feeling unaccountably ashamed of myself nonetheless.

It was fortunate that I had the Bodmin coach to catch at half-past-four. Preparations for the journey at least necessitated a flurry of activity and prevented me from dwelling on the afternoon's absurd encounter with the widow of Guildford: I found the whole incomprehensible affair humiliating and unnerving. Moreover, there was to be plenty of time for brooding once I was ensconced within the tottering coach, in that suffocating cell of cracked leather and horse blanket. My only travelling companion was a man with green teeth and a brandy flask. From his suit I took him to be some sort of sales tout. Once I'd declined his offer of a drink, I huddled into my cloak and stared out of the window – the last thing I desired was to get into conversation with such a man, which was what had been implied by his offer of the flask. And everywhere I looked, at the dark outlines of hills and in the contorted branches of the trees, I could feel that woman's foolish anger and failed to account for it.

To all intents and purposes, it must have looked as though I were asleep. Yet I was not. My thoughts were flinging themselves, again and again, against this enigma. And like the smallest fissure in a rock, still seemingly intact after it has withstood the countless onslaught of the puny waves, the tiniest crevice of understanding began to open up within me. Somehow Provis was at the bottom of this. It was nothing more than a suspicion at first, but with the coming of night, and the monotonous rocking of the coach, my suspicion began to take the shape of a tiny crystal in a core of dull stone. Why, Provis must have taking advantage of the poor woman while I was away in Truro, and there on his behalf! What liberties had he taken in my guise – what schemes of seduction? Yet this was mad: I could not credit that he might have drawn close enough to touch her, for surely the deception of our identities would have been unmasked. We were not that alike! Yet it must have been Provis who had made love to Mrs Lorneville in my absence – what else could explain my now finding myself so compromised with that grotesque lady? Why, Provis was a caitiff: nothing but a degenerate ingrate! I had acted as his friend, risking everything to protect him, and this is how he had repaid me. Well may he go hang! And what was I to do about it? I could hardly ask him to explain his conduct, not on the eve of his sentencing. Besides, even if I were able to gain admittance to him at such an hour, I could hardly interrogate him with regard to the Lorneville woman at such a juncture.

By the time I reached Bodmin, I was more exhausted than agitated. I took my bag round to my lodgings, to find, much as I had expected, that there was no news from Will. Indeed, given the distance to Truro, I hardly expected to hear from him before the morrow, and if he had managed to push his horse as far as Truro and back in a single day, it would only be to bring the news that Rees had returned to Wales. If he were successful, and had managed to persuade the Welshman to come to Bodmin, then they would perforce arrive on Monday. I wrote a note to Judd, asking to meet him in the coffee house at eight the next morning, and gave it to the landlady's boy to deliver. Then I went out to find what consolation I could in a fine dinner at The Royal Hotel. No doubt Pontius Pilot ate as heartily on the night he decided to wash his hands of Our Lord. I was past caring. I even slept well: more soundly than for weeks.

It was twenty-to-nine when Judd showed up the next morning. The coffee room was crowded – I had not thought that there would be such a throng so early on a Monday. He shook his head after I had explained my hopes of producing Rees. 'I can't see that Epplet will hear another witness. It would be most irregular at this stage. Besides, it's clear his mind is made up.'

'We can at least ask.'

Judd sucked in his cheeks, pondering a thousand legal nicities of which I was unaware.

'Damn it man, it's the only chance we have.'

'You fail to understand that it is not in our interests to disaccomodate Judge Epplet in this way. The machinery of the law is a delicate affair, Mudge. I have to work with His Honour in a plethora of cases. Nothing is to be gained by antagonising him unnecessarily.'

'Unnecessarily? You call the saving of an innocent man from the gallows unnecessary?'

'Provis has already been found guilty.'

'Mr Judd, I am paying you your fees, am I not?'

'Yes, indeed. You are paying me for my professional advice, which I have given you, whether it is what you wish to hear or otherwise.'

'Fiddlesticks!' I flung down twenty florins before him. 'Just take these and ask.'

The clatter of silver on the table caused quite a stir in that crowded room, and brought our argument to public attention. In the ensuing silence Judd picked up the coins one by one and placed them in his coat pocket. I watched the corner of his mouth twitch. He rose and nodded, with all the formality and sanctimoniousness of an undertaker. 'I believe you are wasting your money,' he sneered. 'However, if those are your instructions, I have no alternative but to comply.'

I took a turn about the square before the assizes were due to begin. Judd's opposition had been the last straw. I could scarcely bring myself to go within: I only wished to stand out beneath the grey skies and scuttling clouds. Yet in I must, for half of Bodmin had packed into the courthouse before me, and the last act was about to start. Provis was already in the dock, sunken into the stool that had been provided for him, and apparently oblivious of his surroundings. He cut such a haggard and deflated figure that despite myself my stomach lurched in pity for him. I spotted Hannah Hawke among the spectators at the back of the court: she was sporting a new hat, obscenely elegant for such an old hag, and absurdly decorated with a sprig of buddleia. The court rose. Epplet came in, looking a veritable ogre of irritability. He was bleary–eyed and jaundiced. As Judd approached the bench I feared that the lawyer had been right, and that I had allowed my enthusiasm to get the better of sound judgement.

I watched them whispering together. Judge Epplet glanced at me a couple of times in the course of their colloquy. Then I saw his hand emerge from the sleeve of his toga and a wagging finger gestured at me to join them. As I crossed the courtroom floor, Provis looked up for the first time that morning. I forced myself to give him a weak smile. Epplet's features looked even more intemperate at close quarters, and his breath was fetid with drink. 'Mr Judd tells me that you wish to produce another witness to testify that the accused was seen in Truro. Is he a gentleman?'

'He's a clergyman, Your Honour.'

'That is hardly an answer to my question. However, the court will hear him. Can you produce him tomorrow morning?'

I can hardly tell you the emotions that were coursing through my veins at that moment: renewed hope, the sting of Epplet's deliberate insult, a thrill of victory, and the need to risk all on a lie. Words failed me. I merely stuttered a nod – if a nod can be stuttered – and heard Epplet dismiss the court until nine o'clock the next morning.

I caught up with Judd on the courthouse steps. He muttered something about the adjournment being most irregular, and Provis having the Devil's own luck. 'I tell you, Mudge, if Epplet hadn't been so indisposed this morning, he'd have donned his black stoll by now and Provis would be listening to the music for his gallows dance. It's ironic – but if your smuggler friend gets his reprieve, it'll be because Epplet over-indulged his fondness for a glass of Cousin Jack last night.'

I needed to get away. You may imagine what a quandary I was in at that moment, how at the mercy of news from Truro, how dependent on patience, which is a virtue I have never possessed in any great quantity. I was longing for woods, and thought to walk besides the brook that leads from the town down to the River Camel. My footsteps took me below the very walls of the gaol, which towers up over the stream like a hideous castle. My hour's walk brought me no respite.

As it turned out, this hour of self–inflicted misery was quite needless. Will Lobb was waiting for me in my lodgings, and, so said my landlady, had arrived early, some ten minutes after I had left the house that morning. Although he was alone, his whole aspect bespoke the success of his mission. He must have been asleep in my arm chair before I came in, but woke effortlessly and rose to greet me with a firm handshake and a relaxed smile.

'He'll be here tonight. He only asks that you find him a comfortable bed.'

'God be praised! How did he receive my letter?'

'With a great deal of indignation, Parson. Then he looked up from it and said of course he remembered the incident, for he had been both insulted and abused by the man.'

'Was he reluctant to come?'

'Only a bit vexed. He did say, though, that the law could hang all such villains as far as he was concerned, but it was his duty to come and take a look at the rogue, and tell the court if it was the same as had accosted him. He wouldn't have any man's death on his conscience.'

'And you are sure he'll be here tonight? It's vital that he is in court tomorrow morning.'

'He was already making arrangements for the journey before I left.'

'Come, Will. I'll secure a room for him at The Royal, then treat you to as fine a lunch as Bodmin can offer. You must be hungry.'

And, indeed, though the fare had clearly been prepared for diners who predated us, the food was plentiful, and we washed it down with three bottles of a very fine Bordeaux wine and several tumblers of brandy. Will, though not used to drinking, was clearly enjoying himself, and took up my offer of the bed afterwards, where he slept for two hours before mounting his now rested horse to head for the coast.

I didn't see Rees until we met in court. I was round at The Royal Hotel to be sure, several times: as soon as Will had ridden off, and again before supper, then at nine, immediately afterwards. On this last trip I was informed that the gentleman I was waiting for had indeed arrived, but had taken to his room after issuing a volley of instructions, among which was that he was on no account to be disturbed. I had to content myself with the news that at least he had made it to Bodmin, and would be in court the next day. Moreover, I ran into Captain Clapp in the bar, and was invited to join his friends in a game of backgammon: and though I finished the evening slightly out of pocket, I could scarce have had greater fortune, for the excitement of the game quite took my mind off the trial.

The next morning, I had my first sight of Rees in the street, while I was on my way to the coffee house: the same slight, erect figure, the same intense, unmistakable gait as I remember. I have always thought him such a handsome man, although his dark hair has grown noticeably thinner. He did not see me, however, and I withdrew into a doorway, covetous of the little time I had to myself. Perhaps this was cowardly of me, or at the very least, ungrateful. Yet I have never been at my most sociable while still bereft of a breakfast, and besides, though Rees was necessary to Provis's defence, I had little stomach for the company of either of them. When we did meet, in the foyer of the courtroom, Rees failed to shake my hand and his bearing was marked with the disdain which had formerly rendered him such a tedious houseguest. Our paths crossed but for a second, yet I cannot say that his manners unsettled me. I was simply grateful that he had come. What's more, his aloof dignity stood him in good stead with the court, and even Epplet was inclined to treat him with respect.

Judd did a sterling job in establishing Rees's story. How that he had been assaulted, and insulted, by the man in the dock, in Truro, while standing outside a bookseller's on Lemon Quay. And that Rees had no recollection of ever having seen this man before, although his assailant clearly knew him. Moreover, the nature of the insults clearly recognised Rees as a Welshman: Rees thought that this may have been explicable on account of his visit to Porthcado three years ago. Rees was invited to imagine a motive for Provis's behaviour, but thought that his drunken state was itself sufficient explanation. And thank you, your honour, the counsel for the defence has no more questions.

Rosevear began his cross–examination. As before, he hoped to snare our witness by confusing him over dates, but the tactic which had proved so effective with the denizens of the

Market Arms was no match for an Oxford–educated clergyman. 'And can you be sure of the exact date on which this man accosted you?' asked Judd, after Rees had identified Provis.

'Why, certainly. It was on the day in question.'

'A Friday?'

'I believe I may be trusted to know the days of the week.'

At this point Epplet interrupted, leaning forward to bellow across the courtroom: 'Mr Rees, there may be no doubt in your own mind on this point, but as there is considerable doubt in the mind of the court as to the whereabouts of the defendant on Friday 17th April, any evidence to support your assertion would be highly pertinent.'

'Very well.' Rees pulled up a leather holdall from under his feet and began to undo its straps. He pulled out three books and held them up for all to see. 'These are 'The Kingdom of Christ' by F.D Maurice, a volume of Robertson's Sermons, and Praed's 'The Red Fisherman', for a total of two pounds, thirteen shillings and a penny. These are the very books which Dean Dangerfield was purchasing while I was standing before the bookseller's, to be accosted by this drunken ruffian.' Rees opened the largest of the volumes and took out a folded sheet of paper. 'And this is a receipt of sale from Smithgay's Printing and Fine Manuscripts for the same sum, dated April 17th.' The paper was taken to Epplet for his perusal. The magistrate then called Judd and Rosevear to the bench and showed the document to them. After a whispered debate with the two lawyers he addressed the witness box. 'Thank you, Mr Rees. This would appear to be conclusive. The court is now adjourned. I shall make my pronouncement at two o'clock.'

There was a cheer from the gallery. Poor Provis did not appear to comprehend that with these words his freedom was all but guaranteed. Judd went up to wring Rees by the hand: he was grinning from ear to ear. I too rushed to thank Rees, and was surprised to discover that the Welsh scholar's handshake exhibited no more enthusiasm for the triumphant emotions that he was the cause of than would a dead mackerel.

When we reassembled, although Epplet kept us waiting till nearly three o'clock while he dined, the proceedings lasted no more than a minute. Epplet's verdict was that there was insufficient evidence against Provis. Moreover – and here Epplet's perspicacity surprised me, as it did many – the only testimony against him came from 'a woman who was a byword for spitefulness and vindictiveness': and Hannah Hawke was fined sixty sovereigns for perjury. It could not have been a more fitting sentence. And yet, watching her face broil with anger and humiliation, I decided there and then that as soon as I returned to Lancaradoc I would visit Widow Hawke in her hovel, and offer her this very sum – again! It would become blood–money else, and there would be no end to her schemes and wickedness.

And so, Lucy, the trial was at an end, and against all my expectations, Provis had been acquitted. We returned together by coach later the same afternoon, but Provis was such a husk of his former self that I have not had the heart to think ill of him. He may have taken advantage of the Lorneville woman, and played light with my reputation in order to do so. I scarcely cared. What I do know is that since his return he has gone to ground: I had not seen him till yesterday, and am happy to report that he was much closer to his former self. However, he cannot have gone far off in the last fortnight, for he has been behind the rumours that have begun to circulate about Portscado: how I succoured him, and saved him from the gallows; how, when all hope of a reprieve had vanished, I had ridden to Truro and miraculously persuaded a lord of the church to intervene on his behalf. Why, had I done half the things I am credited with, I still would not deserve half

190

the praise, and yet my reputation in the village has never stood so high. Even the attendance at St Cadoc's has improved, and on Sunday last I had one short of thirty communicants.

If you have followed my tale this far, Lucy, you will understand why, despite the happy outcome, my own role in this affair has left me feeling little better than a charlatan.

There is one further incident which I have still to tell you. I retired to The Royal with Doctor Rees after the trial: with Judd, too – so it was therefore a rather formal hour the three of us spent together. And although Rees did ask me at one point if I had kept up my scholarly interests, too much stood between us for my reply to be anything other than evasive. We went outside when it was time for me to catch my coach. Provis was already waiting for me in the square, where we had our appointment. When Rees saw us together I thought I saw him start. He shook hands with each of us, first Provis, then myself. When we were settled in the coach he put his head in at the window and stared hard at us both. 'So, Mudge, you still espouse the Children of Brychan?' These were his parting words. I still do not know what he meant by them; only that Rees had evidently reached his own conclusions concerning the trial and the favour I had asked him to perform.

*   *   *

Dear Isobel,

Forgive me on intruding on a young mother's seclusion, but yesterday I visited Hannah Hawke, which I must tell you of, for I have gleaned surprising information thereby. Furthermore, I hope to solicit news of your life in Salisbury, and to hear in your own words how little Emily is fairing, if she is proving a healthy babe, and whether she has her mother's looks?

Hannah Hawke's cottage, on a lane out of Fretton, turns

out not at all to be the hovel I had imagined, though very cramped: it lies in a valley bottom, by a stream, and is set back a little from the road, standing in a copse of raggedy elms. I knocked at the door, out of sorts, for it had been a long traipse on a damp afternoon, and I was encumbered by the portrait I had brought her.

I thought at first that Mrs Hawke was not at home, it took her so long before she came to unbolt the door. Nor was her reception of me exactly friendly.

'Well if it ain't Amos Provis's little pet. Come to gloat, have'ee? Come to see an old widda reduced to destitution?'

'Not exactly. I want to talk. To try to make amends.'

'He sent you, did 'ee?'

'I've come on my own account – Provis doesn't even know I'm here. Besides, I've brought some gifts for you.'

'There's a surprise. Didn't think you would piss, Parson, without you seeking 'is permission first – if you will excuse me for putting it so vulgar.' The sneer that accompanied her apology left me in no doubt that I was being mocked.

Anyway she bid me come in. There was but the one room downstairs, and I doubt there was space for more than one above. The wall to the right of the door was filled by an ancient range. I had to duck between festoons of linen – sheets and undergarments, from what I could make out – that hung down from the rafters. The cottage was like an effete chandler's shop, or the laundry of a bawdy house, with so many sheets hanging down that her kitchen resembled the deck of a full-rigged ship set to sail.

'Now you're here, you'd better have some nettle tay.' That, I realised, along with the laundry, was what gave the room such a distinct aroma, and one which was not altogether unpleasant. I nodded, wishing perhaps for a more familiar beverage, but when I drank it I found it not unpalatable.

'So, gifts you say?'

I took out a pound jar of honey and placed it on the table.

'Ugh, can't abide the stuff!' And the face she pulled would have confirmed her dislike even more than did her words.

'Aye, Mrs Hawke, but this is something I know you will like.' And I slid the portrait towards her across the slate flags.

She put her hand on top of the wrapped rectangular parcel and surveyed it for a moment, somewhat distrustfully. Then she lent over and with her other hand ripped off the paper in a single savage gesture.

'Oh, ee is handsome!' She picked the picture up and dawdled it on her knees. Then she propped it on the table and smiled at me. I was able to count her teeth: precisely three – two below and one above; two on the right and one on the left. She gazed back at the portrait before giving me a wink. I must say that to see such amorousness in old Turkey Jowls quite put me off my nettle tea, which I found a taxing enough beverage to begin with.

'Ee's the kind that be the undoing of us poor maids. Well, thank God I be past all that! Why is it, Parson, that they do blight our lives, and can maim a young maid more quicker than you can snap off a twig of apple blossom, yet still we hanker for 'un?'

'Ah the intrigues of romance, Mrs Hawke. Who can say what part they play in God's plan for the world!'

I judged that the moment had come, given the gentler disposition that the Laughing Cavalier had bestowed on her, to broach the real object of my visit. 'There is something else I wish to give you, Mrs Hawke. Though I wouldn't wish to be misunderstood: it isn't my intention to offend you.'

She watched me over the rim of her cup, her eyes as cold and sharp as the creature she was named for. I extracted the purse I had prepared from my coat pocket, and beneath that chilly gaze laid out the sixty gold coins it contained along the edge of the table.

'What be thee intending to buy?'

'Nothing, I assure you.'

The old woman tipped her chair back till it leant against the wall. 'Now you listen, Parson. I can guess what you are up to, if, as you do say, twas your own idea to sweeten me up, and not that sly bugger Provis. So you just put those glittery sovereigns back in your pocket and take'un along home. I won't be bought.'

'Really Mrs Hawke, I'm not trying to buy anything.'

'No? Not even a fair end to that bugger trial? Or your own peace of mind?'

I considered her accusation most carefully – wondering whether it perhaps contained an element of truth – before making a reply. 'I suppose I did hope to put an end to whatever animosity you may still feel towards Mr Provis. Perhaps because I feel a certain amount of responsibility for what has happened. After all, he was acting under my authority the day he manhandled you out of church.'

Turkey Jowls cackled. 'Why you're a fool, Parson, if you think our quarrel do only stem from that.'

'Why, I was not aware that there were other motives for...'

'Strikes I that you bain't aware o'much, Parson. What's more I think you'll find that that's the considerable opinion hereabouts.' She delivered this judgement with such a malicious smirk that I took the one course of action that I felt was open to me: I scooped up the money I had brought her and returned it to the purse.

'I believe you are a sad and malicious old woman, Mrs Hawke, and it is that which is the considered opinion hereabouts.

And if you refuse to accept a hand that is offered you in friendship then I am much saddened. Not for myself, you understand, but because I doubt that you will be offered many more such chances.'

'You'd better leave, Parson, before words are spoken which you bain't going to like to hear.' The voice was scarcely audible, and I thought I detected that sinister note of a threat for which she was renowned. And yet, as I rose to leave, she held out her hand to me. I took it: it was a cold and papery talon.

As I was ducking through the lines of white drapery, trying to avoid entangling my head in pillow cases and starched corsets and I–know–not–what, I became aware of the front door opening and another figure entering the cottage. I only glimpsed a pair of brown shoes and the hem of a brown serge skirt at first. The visitor, like myself, was ducking between the sheets and crossing the room; it was impossible, in the narrow confines of Mrs Hawke's kitchen, that I should not collide with the stranger in the middle. So I stretched out and pushed aside the washing line in front of me with my hand, thinking to avert such an accident. And who do you think I should see standing before me in that forest of lingerie? Mrs T! Enveiled as she was in sheets, why, I almost mistook her apparition for a ghost. Not that my appearance had a similar effect on her, for she took my presence most coolly. She bid me a good afternoon and indicated that I take hold of the corner of the sheet that was pegged up by my right ear, to help her fold it.

I was too dumbfounded to speak. We moved down the lines in this way, silently unpegging and folding the voluminous quantities of washing, which Mrs T then piled into a basket on a chair by the kitchen range.

'I believe you know my cousin,' said Hannah Hawke as the last white nightdress came down from the line. She was still sitting at the deal table.

'Your cousin? I was not aware...'

Mrs Hawke chuckled. 'Tis as I said, Parson. You don't know the smell o' your own fart.'

And before I could think what to reply, before this last insult had even sunken in, I heard the latch of the cottage door click to. I turned round. The basket of laundry had gone, and so too had my former housekeeper.

'What's the matter? You do look as if you've seen a ghost.'

'Mrs T – I'd no idea she had come back.'

'Back, Parson? Where do you reckon she's been to – the jungles o' Peru? She's been up to Fretton since she left you. Says Parson Finch has more use for a housekeeper than ever you did – if you follow my meaning.'

'So all those sheets – they're from the convent?'

'That's right. We take in washing for the nuns. Brings us some pin money.'

'And Mr Tredennick? Is he with her?'

'Ah, now you're asking! You'd all of you like to know where the 'pothecary's to, but we'm who wish 'im well, and might have an inklin, we bain't prepared to tell. Vanished into thin air, he be, and that's the safest place for'un.'

Too bemused by this disclosure to know what reply to make of it, I turned towards the door. As I reached my hand towards the latch, Mrs Hawke spoke again.

'Now, think on, Parson, you'd better not blab a word about Mrs Tredennick down Porthcado way, for 'tis more than her life be worth.'

'I can assure you, I have no wish to meddle in her affairs. Though she may have left as she did, Mrs T served me as an excellent housekeeper. Impeccable. I shall not forget that.'

'Aye, well, there's something else you shouldn't forget,

196

Parson. My cousin has suffered somewhat dreadful at the hands of certain friends of yours, and I don't intend to stand by and see her suffer no more. And if you want my advice, you'll steer well clear of Amos Provis – that man's blighted more lives hereabouts than last year's dose o'the cholic.'

'Really, Mrs Hawke, you carry your animosity against Mr Provis too far...'

'I have my reasons. You may think I'm a daft old varmint for acting like I done – but I were only trying to protect my own. That man's a murderer and a cheat.'

'Mrs Hawke, let me speak very plainly: whoever shot young Jarvis it was not Amos Provis. You have already tried to have him convicted for a crime he had no hand in –'

'Tisn't Jarvis I'm talking of. 'Tis Plumley.'

'Sir Henry? Good grief, woman, the man hanged himself!'

'Oh, did he? That's where Provis had you all. Plumley were a nasty, lonely old bugger, and if he went an strung isself up, that's just the end you'd all have wanted for 'im. But I know it were Provis, which is why I blamed him for Jarvis, see.'

At that point I found myself slumping down again at the deal table. I must have left the doorway and walked back across the room, though I have no recollection of doing so. Even if her new accusation was nonsense, yet another example of the old woman's obsessions, I was intrigued: for she was finally admitting that she had accused Provis on a trumped up charge, and I wanted to hear where her crazed logic would lead.

'Mrs Hawke, why on earth would Amos Provis have wanted to murder Sir Plumley?'

'For sellin' out the *Rose*!'

'The *Pydar Rose*?'

'How else d'you think the excise got at her? Besides,

197

Plumley needed the money to pay off his debts.'

For an instant I was prepared to entertain the idea – but only for an instant. 'Really, Mrs Hawke, very fanciful! But there isn't a shred of evidence…'

'Course there ain't. It's Tredennick who had the evidence – that's why he scarpered. Provis were going to kill 'im an'all.'

My incredulity must have shown on my face, for Mrs Hawke reached out and pinned my hand to the table with her talon. 'Now look 'ere, Parson, why do you think my cousin and her husband left Porthcado in such a tither? Because they were scared of the plague? Surely you knew Tredennick better than that? He were a good man, Parson, who knew his duty, and certainly no coward.'

I grunted. I wanted to say something about 'by their actions you shall know them', but before I could recall the phrase, Mrs Hawke went on.

'Tredennick found something, see. Oh rather he were given somat. Twere a note from one of the fishermen. That's what scared im. Twas old Cridden before the plague took 'im, God rest is soul. Now it just happened that Tredennick came straight out to speak to his wife, who was here at the time.'

'You mean – you were present?'

'I was n' all.'

'Well, go on. What did it say – this note?'

Turkey Jowls paused. I could see she was flustered. At first I thought she was reluctant to trust me, but when she did go on, I realised that her hesitation had another cause.

'T'was in Latin.'

'Which surely Tredennick would have translated for you?'

'Well that's it. He couldn't get the sense of it. It was something like 'I've lost everything and will give you the Rose' –

and when the apothecary showed it to us I could make out the word Rose plain enough.'

'Mrs Hawke, you cannot expect me to believe this garbled story, surely? That he found a note, the meaning of which, on your own admittance, wasn't even clear...'

'It were clear plain enough afterwards, Parson. When he showed it to they nuns he learnt what it said alright, and it were enough to convince him to flee to the ends of the earth.'

'The nuns?'

'Aye, if I remember right you're to thank for that. Hadn't you been over yourself to ask for some help with your Latin, Parson? Leastways, Mrs T said as much.'

'What did it say?'

'Darned if I know! If I knew that, you can be bloody sure I'd have had Provis strung up by now. Whatever it was, though, it scared the 'pothecary right out of his wits. He made off for the furthest corner of empire – told his wife to keep her head low and bide while he sent for her, and that's what she's been doing.'

'Then surely Mrs T would ...'

'Knows nothing, Parson. Tredennick thought the less she knew the safest she'd be, and he were right. So we've been puzzling our heads along with the rest of Porthcado, but it's plainer than the ziggy-zaggy down an adder's back that someone must have turned over the *Rose*, and Tredennick swore that note were written in Plumley's hand all right.'

And there you have it, Isobel. You can imagine how churned up my thoughts were afterwards; I hardly noticed that my feet were tramping the lanes on the way back to Lancaradoc. Mrs Hawke will not renounce her resentments, but seems to have bound her grudges against Provis in ever–thickening coils of intrigue!

Provis, incidentally, appears to have recovered much of

his former vigour of late, and I have heard talk at the Falcon that he is behind a plan to buy a Normandy gig. Let us hope that Porthcado may regain some of the trade that was lost after the *Pydar Rose* was seized.

I have other news of those who were once – and, as I have every reason to believe, still are – dear to you. You may be as shocked as I was to read this: Veen came out to the rectory on Thursday afternoon to tell me that he has resigned as captain of the seine fleet and that he, along with the twins, who are all that he now has for family, propose to try their lot in the Antipodes. Moreover, Jemma Lawson has sold the mill and has decided to travel with them. Down west, an army of Cornish lads have already left the farms and the mines, and with our own fisherman now following them, and even men of such standing as Veen, one wonders if the flight is to become universal. Soon there'll be no Cornishmen left. Yet fear as I do for our community, the letters that have reached Porthcado from those who have survived the voyage are encouraging. Only last week Miss Tingham showed me a letter from her niece who was able to find work in a millener's within a week of her arrival in Adelaide, and – what impressed me more – recounts how she has been able to have dentures made, specifically for herself, and for only three shillings.

If Jemma and the good Mr Veen have a chance to prosper in this new land, who am I to begrudge them for deserting us? So I put a brave front to my regrets and asked Veen, for it is not common knowledge, whether he knew that the city of Sydney is named for one of our Cornish saints? Veen confessed he had heard no such thing, so thinking that the story might bring him a little comfort in the new life he is embarking on, I narrated the following tale:

Lost dogs

St Sithney is reputed to have been a right curmudgeonly character, for all his devotion. They tell a story that one day, while he was at his prayers, neck–deep in a moorland stream, in winter, the Good Lord was so impressed by his rectitude that he sent an angel to Sithney, to ask if he would consider becoming the patron saint of girls – for there were few even among the saints who could be trusted with such a task.

'Young maidens?' said Sithney, 'More trouble than they're worth! They don't need a saint – t'would save time commending them drekkly to Old Nick hisself.' And off flew the angel with ruffled feathers.

So the Almighty ruminated on St Sithney for a while, troubled that for all his piety a good saint should have such a stony heart, and then called for his angel again. This time, when the angel appeared on the banks of the river, Sithney threw a rock at it, believing that it was his right not to be disturbed while at his devotions. 'Sithney,' said the angel, 'I have been sent from the Lord with another proposition. How would you like to be the patron saint of dogs?'

'Dogs?' Sithney scratched his head for a moment, then his face lit up with glee. 'Aye, dogs'll do nicely.'

So it is that in Cornwall a lost dog is looked for by first dropping a ha'penny down Sithney's well, and I dare say the Australians chose him knowingly as the patron of their metropolis, for they say that their country is no place for the gentler sex.

* * *

On consideration, I may not have been so wise to repeat this legend to Veen, for he asked me what I knew of the customs of the Antipodeans with regard to women. Nothing, said I; and it is true, for I was merely repeating a piece of idle hearsay. But

201

seeing how Veen is travelling in the company of three ladies, for whom he takes responsibility, I was alarmed that my tale had given him cause for anxiety: all I had in mind was to proffer a little entertainment along with a touch of erudition.

And indeed, we are sorely in need of a modicum of light-heartedness these days, after the troubles which have afflicted Porthcado of late. Yet for all our tribulations, there is news of a happier kind: Polgarrick and Trebarton are to be tied by matrimony. Will Lobb has been courting Judy Ruan since the autumn and a week since their fathers trooped into the parlour to ask me to read the banns. You should have seen them, Isobel! Those mortal enemies, both cap-in-hand, winking and nudging one another like unruly schoolboys. Well, Sirs, this calls for a celebration, says I, and insist on our sharing a bottle of sherry. Yet with much shuffling of feet – for neither would be outdone by accepting a seat before the other – they refuse. Come, gentlemen, this is no time for teetotalism, and if you have taken the pledge, which I hadn't heard of you, then foreswear it, at least this once, for my sake. But it emerges that that is not the problem, either. Eventually it is Ruan who spits it out: 'By your leave, Parson, we've already thought on it, and we reckon if we've got to celebrate we'd better see it done proper.' And taking my perplexity for a yes, Lobb slips out to the yard and comes back with a gallon of brandy, three loaves, a cheese and enough cold mutton to feed the harvest lunch. It was four in the morning before I found my bed, and there was such evidence of our debauchery the next day that I am glad I no longer have a housekeeper to account to. Where the farmers slept I do not know, for I am sure that their cart was still outside when I crept down to the kitchen for water sometime in the morning, but gone by the time I had slept off my indisposition.

The which is all my news. If you have the time, Isobel,

drop me a line and tell me of the little girl. I am eager to hear how she sleeps, what she eats, whether she keeps it down, and when she starts to teethe – I shall absorb all such nursery news with the attentiveness of a fond uncle.

And finally, I have thought to send you another of my stories. This one has been long in the making but I am rather proud of it. However, the portrait of piety which emerges has been sketched from an original angle, so that I know not who else I might show it to beside yourself.

St Selevan's supper

When a poor-little-rich-girl marries a handsome hulk of a man, she should not be surprised if he occasionally comes home in the small hours red-eyed, foul-tempered and unrepentant. What Olwenna, the squint-eyed daughter of King Tewdrig, could not understand, is why when Bernan returned to her bed in such a condition, he should invariably stink of fish.

They had been married a year before by St Selevan, and as they stood together before the altar, neither of them could believe their luck: Olwenna, because she had such a broad-chested, black–bearded husband, and Bernan because he need never put out to sea again, but could lounge around all day on badger skins in a snug hut, and call for Olwenna's servant girls to refill his mead cup – something they were far from reluctant to do.

In the winter Olwenna gave birth to a son, and when the weather improved Bernan would strap him to his back and take him down the valley to the cove where his mother and five brothers lived in a rickety shelter at the base of a dismal cliff. For a while, Bernan was perfectly content with the prince's welcome he received in his own home, and to have a chortling child to dangle on his mother's knee, and he didn't mind that his wife was ugly to the point of deformity, and squint-eyed to boot, for by her he had gained great advancement in the world.

But then the boy died, and was buried by St Selevan beneath a rosemary bush on the banks of the Fowey river.

Olwenna was inconsolable; not just for the loss of her son, who – so Selevan assured her – had only strayed as far as heaven, but because she had lost her husband too; and he, she was sure, was straying as far as other women's beds.

But that still did not explain the overpowering stench of fish.

Olwenna resolved to take her worries to confession – after all, Selevan was renowned for his skill as a fisherman. Although he never set foot in a boat, he spent long hours out at Lamegoat Head with a willow rod, and a lamp by night, pulling fish from the sea as deftly as a child picks berries at Alban Elued. The incredulous believed that those he caught he preached homilies to, before throwing them back into the sea; the cynical pointed to the saint's round belly, and commented on how tasty fresh mackerel was between the teeth. Yet Selevan knew what all fishermen know: the contentment that comes from silent waiting by deep waters, which is akin to the contentment of prayer.

What advice could he give her? He had his suspicions of what Bernan was up to, but they were not of a kind to share with a young woman of noble birth, especially one who was still in mourning for the death of her only child. So he sent her home and told her to leave matters with him.

This was in the month of the hunter's moon, at Samhain – a moon so bright that anyone looking out towards Lamegoat Point could see that Selevan's tallow lamp illuminated an expanse of flat and empty rocks. But there were none to look: at that hour the young and lusty were busy with their wicked business, while the feeble good were indoors, intent upon their comforts.

A casual glance noted the yellow lamp across the bay, and assumed that the good saint was beside it. But Selevan spent the nights of the hunter's moon under a tarpaulin in the fishhouses, crouching down between the pilchard barrels, waiting for Bernan.

On the twelfth night, Selevan's vigil was rewarded. Bernan came into the fishhouses with Prua, who was fifteen and tipsy; the prettiest girl between Rame Head and Dodman. And if Selevan kept his eyes open to watch the abomination which Bernan forced her to, then he did it to strengthen his prayers for the fish, for whom the saint had an especial sympathy.

And if afterwards, as Selevan followed the cliff–top path out to Lamegoat, under a moon that lit the way more clearly than the sun on many a winter afternoon, and he was lost in thought, it needn't be imagined that he judged Bernan and Prua too harshly after what he had seen: for Bernan's perversion was the result of his grief, and as for Prua – like any young maid, she was curious to see what madness her charms could provoke a man to. Besides, like many of the saints, Selevan was disposed to look upon the peccadilloes of the flesh with leniency, and as he collected up his lamp and tackle he was serene enough.

Which he wouldn't have been had he known that he wasn't the only witness to Bernan's despoiling Prua among the piles of fish that night.

And that Olwenna was besides herself with fury.

For a week she shunned her husband's caresses. If he walked into the room, she walked out of it. She served him at meal times, but sat across in silence at the table while he ate, stony–faced. Then one morning Bernan woke to find her smiling down at him, with a tray of honey–sweetened milk and saffron cakes. Her mood had passed like the thunder clouds above Carn Brea. Inexplicably, and for the next week, Olwenna became as

205

pliant, and as doting, as in the days of their courtship. Better –
for she had learnt how to touch him to bring him to pleasure, and
now she never troubled him for kisses. She brought him
sweetmeats she had made in the kitchen, and saw that his mead
cup was never empty. And if he kept away from her all
afternoon, she forgave him and met him with a smile on his
return.

So on the night she suggested a walk in the moonlight
after dinner, Bernan was ready to indulge her. She wanted to
walk to the sea, she said, so they did. She wanted to sit on the
rocks again, holding hands. Bernan even managed a few sweet
nothings in her ear. It was a warm night. They walked out along
the jetty to where the fishing boats jostled like sleeping sea-birds.
To his surprise, Bernan realised that he didn't even resent his
wife for insisting that they walk arm–in–arm like this in public.
Then they walked back again, until they stood in the shadow of
the fishhouses.

Olwenna lifted the latch and led him in. At first they
stood side by side in the darkness, holding hands, but as their
eyes became accustomed to their surroundings, Olwenna found
that the interior was lit by a glow of moonlight that filtered
through the row of fist-sized holes, at waist height, that served to
air the building, and that in the middle of the floor the day's
catch – where it waited to be sorted, and salted, or soaked in
brine – gleamed like silver treasure.

She reached up and put her hands around Bernan's neck.
The smell of fish was overpowering. As his tongue found hers,
she thought of their squirming bodies, the slap of a bass's tail, the
knobbliness of sea–urchins beneath her back, of crabs still
scheming beneath that half–dead mass, and broke away from
him.

'Not here,' she whispered.

'Yes, here,' he hissed back. His hands were already at the fastenings of her dress.

And when she stood naked before him, Bernan put his hands around her hips, lifted her up, and flung her, like a recalcitrant dog-fish, onto the top of the pile.

As Bernan threw his weight across her, Olwenna writhed and squirmed to be free of him, but the more she struggled, the deeper she slithered in among the fish. Resistance was useless. She lay still and took a long, slow breath, forcing her mind to think of forests and sunlight, and anything that was far away – and as she did so, in that minute act of relaxation, oh wonder of wonders!, a miracle occurred. For suddenly the repulsive bed of fish beneath her felt as cool and as soft as the silkiest sheets, and as she breathed in, she inhaled the perfume of the sea. She was in the great ocean, her body as lithe as a dolphin, and Bernan's body was above her, touching her at every point; it had the warmth and strength of the sun, engendering life in the watery depths. Olwenna started to laugh. The fish tickled. She was dancing in silver. As Bernan's cavorting above her shuddered to a halt, she opened her eyes. She was smiling. Then, a new wave of delight broke over her, stronger by far than any merely physical pleasure he had given her: for as she looked up at her husband, she saw the grimace of horror that was stamped across his face.

On the pillow of fish next to her own, was Prua's severed head.

Its eyes had been gouged out of their sockets by lobster claws, and an elver was feeding on the tongue. As Bernan's love-making had forced his wife deeper and deeper into their slippery bed, it had brought them closer and closer to this little surprise his wife had prepared for him.

Selevan knew nothing of Olwenna's matrimonial reversals. Only that in the spring she was waiting for motherhood again, and every Sunday left his church as happy as a chorister, with her morose but handsome husband trotting devotedly along behind her.

It was a balmy afternoon in June when Olwenna and Bernan, parents once more, were coming to tea with the silver-haired hermit, to discuss the arrangements for their daughter's christening, and Selevan was out at Lamegoat Point, hoping to catch something he could offer them for supper.

The sea was a motionless cobalt mass. There were no waves, and only small patches of the surface rippled occasionally with the passing of a stray breeze. At ten minute intervals the enormity of the water would shudder, like the sighing of a leviathan, then sink into inertia once again. Selevan sighed too, for he knew that fish never bite on a day like this. He held the rod limply in his hand. His eyes were entranced by the distant horizon.

With a sudden wrench, his rod bent double, almost leaping out of his lazy hand. He felt his catch lunge towards the sea bed, and jumped up, yanking the willow-pole heavenwards. He ran along his ledge of rock to take up the slack. For minutes the fight hung in the balance, then, slowly at first, he felt the line jerk with less conviction. A minute more and the battle was won.

On his hook was not one, but two, sea bream. He marvelled at the improbability of it: how could two fish have swallowed his hook at the same time? But there it was, piercing both brittle little jaws. Two fish flapped upon the rock, and both looked up at him with their imploring eyes. Perhaps it was a sign; anyway, he would have a fit supper to offer his guests.

When the fish were set before them, Olwenna felt her stomach flip over, and Bernan's flesh went as cold as cod meat. They both blanched; they pushed their plates away, and excused themselves, for they could not eat them.

'You must, my children, for they were sent especially for you,' insisted Selevan, and he told them the miraculous story of how both fish had been caught on the one hook.

Husband and wife listened in silence. Their newborn daughter slept at Olwenna's side. This was their punishment. At Selevan's table, bathed by the setting summer sun, Olwenna knew that her husband's weakness would bring him to confession. She stretched out and took a handful of the hermit's oatcakes and crammed them into her mouth. She picked up her knife and fork and forced herself to eat the fish. Bernan felt his wife's eyes upon him, compelling him to do the same.

And Selevan watched, perplexed, as they ate, blank–eyed, then collapsed beneath his table, gagging and retching and gasping for air. They writhed and squirmed in agony, their insides pierced by fish-bones, their gullets stoppered with oatmeal. Theirs was a horrible death and Selevan looked on, unable to help.

Which is why, to this day along the south coast of Cornwall, chad, or young sea bream, are known as 'chuck–cheeld' (or choke–child) – although the only child present, St Adwen, slept peacefully through that short summer night, and in the morning she was taken into Selevan's household as his adopted daughter. And she too is remembered in Cornish prayers.

* * *

Mudge to Lucy, August

Dear Lucy,

Has Isobel told you that she proposes to visit? I received a letter from her yesterday and she is to arrive in three weeks time. What has decided her to come in this precipitous fashion I cannot fathom, although I am delighted at the news. But here I am with no housekeeper, and after spending most of the summer in

Bodmin the rectory's become a sloven's den.

And yet she comes at a most propitious time in the affairs of the village, her affection for which can hardly have diminished over the last three years. Moreover, she will be here in time to meet Jemma before she sails; Porthcado, still intoxicated with the news of Provis's release, is enjoying a truly festive season, and extra help for the house can always be hired from the village.

And Lucy, please, if you write to her before she leaves Salisbury, I beg you, do not disclose what I now tell you: I want it to be a surprise! Jemma is to be married. Veen has offered her his hand and they are to be joined in matrimony prior to leaving for the Australias. Is it not fortuitous that Isobel will be able to attend her friend's wedding? Moreover it is to be an event the like of which Lancaradoc church has not witnessed in a hundred years – a double wedding! For Mr Veen has asked me if he may take his bride at the same ceremony in which Will Lobb marries Judy Ruan: all parties have given their consent, and the parish is determined to make of this event a public celebration.

*　*　*

Isobel to Percy, September

Dear Percy,

No sooner had I placed foot on firm soil on Thursday last, at an hour before noon, than I was met by such a stench of pilchards, that had my already queasy stomach had its way, I would have returned immediately to my berth upon the packet. Indeed, on my remarking upon it, Uncle said that when the wind blows up the valley from the sea, the stink from the fish houses has been known to stop the church clock, though I am sure he spoke in jest, for he also remarked that the odour is by now so very familiar to him that he has ceased to notice it.

He is not as debilitated as his account of the epidemic, or those scandalous stories, have lead us to believe. Grey about the temples, yes, older and more tired, but such is only to be expected given his situation, and the horrors he has lived through. Let us say that his eccentricities are more deeply engrained than ever, but talk no more of derangement. For the most part his conversation is conventional enough, with perhaps just that hint of garrulousness and impropriety which afflicts the lonely, so that, on occasion, he still launches into tiresome discourses upon those subjects which so obsess him.

What gives me greatest hope for his sanity, however, is the reception he receives from the villagers: whenever we go down into Porthcado together, he is met with greetings by all and sundry, and seems the very shepherd of his flock, which is quite the reverse of the cold treatment I remember him receiving when I was last here.

If I may speak to you frankly, there is something which gives me cause for concern, and it lies in his excessive use of laudanum. He has the trembling fingers, and the redness about the eyes, that are sympomatic of immoderate usage. Perhaps herein lies the explanation of his muddle-headedness. That, and the grief to which he has been subjected, might explain his extraordinary claims concerning the Lawson boy, who was carried off by the recent epidemic. It is true that I was on the closest terms with the family at Winnard's Mill during my stay here, and could not but have been caught up in the excitement over the birth of their firstborn. Yet Uncle's assertions concerning his godson's parentage, had they been made by anyone less inclined to eccentricity, would surely be considered offensive - nay, slanderous!

Percy, please abide by my judgement in this: we must humour Uncle - to take the matter further would only overburden a weakened mind, and cause distress to the child's grief-stricken relatives.

Uncle has made me promise to bide with him a full fortnight, but I shall sail on the 26th, and cut my stay in Frome to a minimum.

Well, Percy, never was wife a better advertisement for her husband's business! To judge from the stares which my salmon-pink travelling dress evoked, there is a fortune to be made here in the west. Why, but send them last year's fashions and you would win the custom of Cornish matrons, and of their goosy daughters, as readily as the Hottentot is won over by a handful of beads!

A bientot,

Your devoted wife

*   *   *

Mudge to Lucy, September

My dear sister,

Isobel is asleep in her old bedchamber. Yet she is not the old Isobel: she is not as free in her conversation as she once was, and in our evenings together I have grown quite shy of her.

I do not wish to sound querulous. She has grown most stately, this beautiful daughter of yours, but now she is so grave and matronly. I am not even sure that the reasons for her coldness lie in me, for I have seen her walk about the town greeting former acquaintances with a similar aloofness – even Jemma, who was almost a sister to her.

Yet I shall never forget my first sight of her last Wednesday. She made such a picture on the foredeck of the Bideford packet, standing as erect and as opulent as one of those Romish statues that are paraded upon boats in Mediterranean sea towns, like a veritable Lady of Salvation in her pink gown and fluttering curls. Those townsfolk who were on the quayside were gawping at her, remembering her no doubt from her previous visit, and impressed by the transformations wrought by a few short summers. I had to have words with Sam Shepherd and tell him to mend his manners, for his attention bordered on the insolent. Isobel was pale and tired, but a night's rest soon restored her.

I wonder if her reserve is not due to her grief over the boy, for although she has not said a word about him, I have frequently seen her slipping down to the churchyard when she assumed that I was engaged, and that she was unobserved. I pointed out his headstone on the afternoon she arrived, but she paused at it no longer than before the grave of the Lawsons, or of others she had known, who are buried nearby.

Shortly we are to have an entertainment here at the rectory, as a prelude to the forthcoming wedding. It is likely to be an unbuttoned, licentious affair, after the customs of these parts, and I am concerned that Isobel will disapprove of our antics.

*   *   *

Mudge to Lucy, September

Lucy, dearest,

Lest you are alarmed by my last letter, I have thought to write to you again to assure you that Isobel is well, and that perhaps the portrait I painted of her reflected more my own feelings than your daughter's actual condition. She has certainly been looking happier these last few days, and joined in our pre-nuptial dinner with a gaiety I would not have anticipated.

However, I cannot pretend that our evening was a genteel affair. Provis and Mr Honeycutt have a reputation as two of the town's most implacable drinking men, and the farmers were out to celebrate their new-found alliance with as much relish as they previously brought to their enmity. Young William, too, shows himself to be very much his father's son once he has taken a drink, and entertained us from a trove of salubrious stories which a colour sergeant would have been proud of. Even Mr Veen, who is generally much restrained on account of his Methody sympathies, became surprisingly boisterous, and led the company through some lewd songs when we reached the pudding. But then, not only has he got his bride and a new life to celebrate, but I gather that Provis has handed him a staggering amount of money to obtain a controlling interest in the seine fleet. Given the paucity of the pilchard shoal in recent years, I can only surmise that Provis has catches other than fish in mind for the Porthcado boats, which may be straying closer to the French coast in future than they are used to. Indeed, the prospect that Porthcado may soon be flourishing again was much in the air, and added considerably to the evening's rowdiness. So much so that by the time the plates were cleared our guests were all calling for brandy, and I had to tell them that I had none. However, I did have wines answering every description, and in copious quantities.

'What, no brandy, Rector? Fetch me a ladder and I'll soon rector-fy that,' piped up Mr Honeycutt with a wink, and most pleased at his own joke.

So I rose, and we all traipsed down to the church to admire the ladder where it hung in the ringing chamber, Isobel included. Mr Honeycutt took it down off its nail and led us back to the rectory and round to one the kitchen windows, where he set it against the side of the house. Meanwhile Mr Provis went down the drive to his cart to return with a length of rope and an evil–looking grappelling hook. Then, with Ruan holding the ladder firm, Honeycutt shimmied up and before I knew it, he was sitting astride the roof, and removing the conical pot from the top of one of the chimneys. The rest of us were all standing around my vegetable plot to watch, and though I resisted the urge to reprimand him, I thought that Mr Lobb, as a farmer, should have had more sense than to trample the carrots the way he did. There was a steady rain falling and it was a cold night. It was then that I realised that this particular chimney was not above any of the rectory fires – neither the parlour, nor the study, nor any of the bedrooms – but that it was aligned with that curious hollow shaft that had so intrigued me about the house when I first arrived here. And I had no sooner made this discovery than Mr Honeycutt began to haul upon the rope and my companions burst into applause as a small firkin emerged, attached to his grappelling hook. Provis rushed up the ladder and Mr Honeycutt rolled the barrel down the roof to him. Then Honeycutt dangled his line down the chimney again, and in a much shorter time on this attempt, hoiked out a second barrel.

The brandy was uncommonly good. When we were on our second glass, and the fire was blazing fiercely to counter the effects of the drizzle, I remarked on what a curious feature of the house this vertical shaft was, and how when I had first arrived, Mrs T had explained to me the strange custom hereabouts of constructing spirit chimneys.

'Spirit chimney? Why, a liquor 'ole is what we do call it, in good plain Cornish,' retorted Honeycutt. And though the remark was the cause of much mirth, it set me wondering whether Mrs T's explanation was to be taken at face value. Perhaps, after all, it was merely a disused chimney which more recent generations had adapted to serve another purpose.

And having thought on Mrs T, I mentioned that I had met with her recently, and that she was living up at Fretton – a piece of news which excited the company, and especially Provis. Afterwards, Isobel berated me most severely for betraying a confidence, and although I admit that the disclosure may have been a little tactless, I cannot see that any harm can come of it.

But this wedding is going to be a fine affair! The sea-town has decided to make a celebration to match any of the pomp put on for a royal occasion: indeed, more so, because it is something of our very own we are celebrating. There will be dancing on the Platt and a show of fireworks from the end of the jetty. Harbour Hill is already festooned with bunting, and Mr Barret is rumoured to be at work on brewing a hogshead of wedding ale of formidable potency.

Last night, having just added the finishing touches to my sermon for the great day, I took a turn about the lawn. It was that hour when the sun has gone down but when, with the western ocean stretching endlessly before us, there is enough light in the summer sky for it be coloured with the last of the day for at least an hour longer. I watched the heavens change colour constantly, first from yellow to ochre, then taking on strange taints of green and muddy red, before descending into indigo and black night – and I observed to myself that it was much like watching the healing of a bruise, but in reverse.

And do you know, sister, I experienced such an hour of beatitude, mingled with a sense of quiet triumph, that I felt I have no right to expect such happiness this side of paradise – or perhaps, outside the closing pages of a triple–decker novel! For am I not to preside over such a wedding as one finds in the old romances? And have I not finally achieved the goal that has eluded me through all these years, and become at last the father of my flock?

So please, Lucy, take up the copy of the sermon which I am sending you, and as you read it, join myself and my parishoners in our most solemn, most triumphant, nuptial celebrations.

* * *

The sermon preached by the Revd. Richard Lancelot Mudge at the double wedding of William Lobb to Judith Ruan and of Matthew Veen to Jemmima Lawson at St Cadoc's church, Lancaradoc, on

216

September 20th 1852.

Dearly beloved brethren, I take my text today from our Old Testament reading, in the fourteenth chapter of the Book of Judges: 'Out of the eater came forth meat, and out of strength came forth sweetness.'

I am sure that you will all remember the incident, when Samson returns to the carcass of the lion that he has killed, and finds that a swarm of bees have made their hive in the lion's ribcage. But perhaps you are less familiar with the narrative in which this incident occurs.

Let me remind you of it. For that too is the story of a wedding, and of an opportunity for an ancient enmity to be healed. It is also the story of a riddle, of treachery, of an oppressed people, and of love and death.

Samson, much to his parents' alarm, falls in love with the girl from the town of Timnath, a daughter of the despised Philistines – it is as though a good Cornish lad were to travel beyond the Tamar, to Plymouth perhaps, and announce on his return that he wishes to marry a girl from abroad. 'Why,' says Samson's father, 'Are there not plenty of nice Jewish girls for you to marry? Must you choose a girl from a house that oppresses us?'

Samson's birth, you will remember, had been heralded by an angel, who had promised great things of him, and commanded that he should be brought up under the strict precepts of the Nazarites, and had prophesied that one day Samson would deliver Israel out of the hands of the Philistines. How could all this be, if Samson were to marry a daughter of Timnath?

Still, their fondness as parents got the better of them, and his mother and father agreed to accompany Samson to Timnath, and open negotiations for the marriage to the girl their son had fallen in love with. It was while they were there that Samson was

217

out walking and came up against a young lion in the vineyard, and slaughtered it with his bare hands. Later, and with the marriage settlement successfully concluded, he walks that way again, and comes across the bees that have made their hive in the lion's carcass.

Imagine him: a country boy, a fine strong lad, as our Will here, in the full flush of his love for a shapely young maid whom he is soon to marry. No wonder he is so full of himself at the marriage feast. He takes a glass too many; and then he falls to boasting. 'Which one of you knows the answer to this?' he says, for there are thirty Philistine lads at the table, all of them friends of the bride or her family. And to spice things up a bit, he suggests a bet: a new suit and a set of sheets for each of them if they should guess, or the same from each of them to him, should they fail. They take the wager up. But then he poses them a question that is worthy of the Exeter Book of Riddles: 'Out of the eater came forth meat, and out of strength came forth sweetness – now, what's that supposed to mean?' Well, it has them flummoxed! They've a week to find the answer, and they haven't got a clue! So what do you think they do? They go sneaking up to Samson's bride and persuade her to wheedle the answer out of him. Which she agrees to, for she's a foolish cheeld: she ballyrags him for a week till he tells her. And when they give him his answer, saying it's bees of course, which happen to have made their hive in the carcass of a lion, Samson's dander gets sent right up: 'If ye had not ploughed with my heifer, ye had not found out my riddle', he says – calling his bride a proper baggage, in other words. Then he lays out and slays the lot of them.

And it's only when these thirty lads are laid out on their funeral slabs, that Samson reveals the real meaning of the riddle: the fine raiment he was to give them are their best suits, which they've been dressed up for burial in, and the new sheets are nothing other than their shrouds.

Of course, we wouldn't wish any such outcome to today's wedding, although we too are expecting as fine a feast as any in Timnath, as well – I dare say – as a bit of ribbing. So where's the moral? What has Samson's story got to tell us, here in St Cadoc's church, today?

Many things, I would suggest. But I would like to start with bees. For bees have a riddle of their own, and one the answer to which has only now become known.

Paradise itself is pictured as the land of milk and honey. John the Baptist lived off locusts and wild honey in the Sinai desert in preparation for his ministry. As we gather here this morning to join these good people in holy matrimony, I would like you all to reflect that the institution of marriage is entered into for the purposes of constructing the human hive, that is to say the family, and that the joys of matrimony are the sweet honey which the Lord has provided to console us on our journey through life's wilderness.

In my few words to you today I wish to elaborate on the honey–bee and its activities as a metaphor for marriage, and to draw out certain insights and conclusions much as sweet honey is extracted from the hive.

Forgive me, however, if I now enter on what may appear to be a digression. It concerns a man who only last year, in the American state of Philadelphia, made a momentous discovery – a man who I am privileged to say follows the same calling as myself. That man is the Reverend Lorenzo Lorraine Langstroth; and his discovery has to do with the way in which bees construct their hives.

Now, we know that as long as Man has left a record of his doings, he has not only valued honey but has tried to ensure a ready supply of it close at hand. From prehistoric Africa to

Mexico to ancient China, there is evidence of mankind constructing hives for bees to live in; the clay hives of Mesopotamia date back at least five thousand years. Man built the hive; he then went out into the forests in search of a colony of bees; he brought the wild bees back with him to house in this new home – enslaving them if you like, but under the mildest and most benevolent of tyrannies – and when the hive dripped full with honey, he would rend it asunder for this sweetest of plunder! Such a partnership between Man and Bee has continued unchanged since time immemorial. Improvements have been made – modifications to the design of hives, to suit different climates or changing conditions – yet the relationship between Man and Bee remained essentially static, in a fixed and time-honoured practice.

There is nothing very remarkable in that, is what most of you are no doubt thinking! Bee-keeping is such a well-established, immutable practice that it hardly warrants our consideration.

Yet the Reverend Lorenzo Lorraine Langstroth's work heralds an entirely new covenant between Man and Bee!

For Langstroth has discovered that there is a gap across which bees cannot build. Think of it – these wonderful architects of their own homes, who can construct their hives in the tops of trees, or below the ground, and even in the ribcage of a lion – are at a loss when they are confronted with a space that is approximately a quarter of an inch wide. The precise measurements of this gap – or 'beespace' as Langstroth calls it – are fixed at a lower limit of three-eighths and an upper limit of five-sixteenths of an inch. And although she is a consummate constructor, the honeybee is totally unable to bridge a gap of such dimensions. Why this should be is a mystery. Yet its implications are profound. For the first time we can now design a hive as a series of drawers. If the distance between them is of the requisite width, each drawer can then be extracted and the honeycomb removed without disturbing the bees, let alone destroying them. In a sense, what Langstroth offers is eternal life to the hive!

I put it to you that the discovery of beespace stands in our own day as did the fact of the resurrection for Our Lord's disciples; it is the model for a new covenant. It teaches us to accept those mysteries across which we cannot build. For despite all the progress of Learning and of Science, we still have no answers concerning final matters. And neither I as your priest, nor the church I represent, can explain away the bewilderment that is rightly felt in the face of life's perplexities and suffering. We cannot justify the ways of God to Man. We can only repeat the old stories, whether those of the scriptures, or of the church's holy men – yes, even the doings of the saints who once walked here in Cornwall – in the hope that mankind may not be daunted by those questions to which there are no answers.

The Revd Langstroth offers us a new covenant between Man and Bee. He has shown us is that we can harness the power of mystery for a greater good, regardless of whether we can penetrate that mystery. The mystery of the resurrection shows us that we will eventually triumph over the powers of death. And on this wedding today, are we not now gathering sweetness from the very carcass of the epidemic which ravaged our parish last year? 'Out of the eater came forth meat!'

The love of Judy and Will, born as it was in the midst of our recent calamities, proves that there is remedy even for the antique enmities that have marked our community. Jemma, here, and Matt Veen, have come to the marriage table after losing so many of their loved ones to the cholera; they, like so many thousands of our Cornish brethren, are about to leave these shores to begin a new life in a distant land. For where today will you find a Cornish family which is undivided, which has not sent a son or a daughter to the dominions? Indeed, it would appear that the Cornish themselves are vanishing from this land, like the saints and the piskies before them.

And are not the seas, the mighty oceans, which separate us from Australia, from Canada and from South Africa – are not these oceans yet another instance of beespace?

We are the bees who work to garner up the Lord's honey. The mysteries of Love and Death are like the upper and lower limits of Divine Beespace: they are the barriers which we cannot cross. We may imagine the Kingdom of God as a hive ordered by the Almighty Beekeeper himself. And we must trust that the mysteries that we cannot see beyond, but which we are asked to accept, are ordered for a holy purpose, and for our own greatest good. I.T.N.O.T.F., A.O.T.S., A.O.T.H.G., Amen.

* * *

Isobel to Percy, September

Forgive me, Percy, if a confused account of this day is all I can offer, but I have been so shocked and unsettled by these vulgar Cornish folk that my only desire is to leave Lancaradoc and obtain the security of my own home as quickly as possible.

How can I explain what has happened? It has been all so ridiculous and at the same time rather frightening. Uncle has disappeared. He drank more than he should have at the wedding breakfast and has gone off somewhere to sleep it off. I am alone in the rectory, and my one thought now, in this draughty, uncomfortable house, is of the Bideford packet. But alas, she isn't due to put in at Porthcado until next Friday.

This morning's nuptial celebration was a calamity. As soon as we left the rectory and were coming down the lawn, it was clear that something was amiss; we were aware of voices that were clearly not the contented murmur of wedding guests. As I was mounting the stile into the lane, Uncle went on ahead as far as the lych-gate. He returned, mopping his brow with an old and yellowing lace kerchief, looking most anxious.

'Who is it? What has happened uncle?'

'Take no notice. We must brave them out.' He took me by the elbow and led me into the churchyard. We were not halfway along the path when I began to distinguish not the faces of the gaggle of protesters who were standing before the church porch, but what they were carrying. Why, they bore aloft the very caricatures of the farmers whose children were about to be married, which I had fashioned and painted when I was last here! Thinking to salve Uncle's nervousness I bent down to pluck a few stalks of wild garlic from the hedge bottom, and having thus caused him to stop, while still out of earshot and well away from the church, said, 'They certainly mean to enjoy themselves. I suppose this must be another of your quaint local customs.'

'Quaint? They are here to do mischief, Isobel.'

I smiled as sweetly as I could, putting my hand on the crook of Uncle's arm, and led him onwards. As we came towards the church, I could make out that there were four of them, three women and an old man, and to my surprise, I saw that it was my friend Mrs Tredennick who was holding one of the placards, although she would not meet my eye. I was even more dumbfounded to see Mrs Lorneville with her, and in one of her finest hats! The other placard was held by a woman whom I did not recognise. She glared at us fiercely, and was of such ugliness that she could have withered rosebuds quicker than frost. Much to my relief, as we drew level, they hung their heads in sullen silence and allowed us to push past them, although I believe that the man spat upon the ground as we did so. At such close proximity it became clear, from their bloodshot eyes and the foul fug of their breath, even out in the open air, that a night's heavy drinking united them, and was no doubt a large part of the explanation for their incivility.

Within, it was comforting to find that the wedding guests were arraigned much as they should have been. Mrs Ruan had outdone herself with the flowers, especially with two wonderful sprays of magnolia on either side of the altar. The bridegrooms were standing on the chancel steps, but most casually, conversing with their families and friends. Our entrance caused quite a scurrying into pews, and this informality being so much the rule with the Cornish, neither they nor I myself felt the oddness of a priest conducting his processional with a lady on his arm – and one, if I may be allowed to boast, who was quite the match in elegance for either of the brides! Uncle stopped half way down the aisle to see me to my pew, yet I was still close enough to him to hear what he whispered to Mr Lobb – something to the effect that he thought it would be prudent if Mr Lobb slipped to the porch once the brides had entered to bolt the door.

No doubt the ceremony would have been delectable had we not been intimidated by the rabble outside. A double wedding is such a touching affair! Normally at a marriage ceremony one's eyes are all on the bride and groom, so that it becomes a personal celebration between the two people who are to be married, and that the clergy, like the guests, are there merely to witness their happiness. Yet to have first Jemma, then the Ruan girl, parade down the aisle and take their places next to their respective husbands – why, Percy, there was poetry in it! It was as though we were being reminded that this was one of the great gates that all humanity is called to walk through. I was put in mind of my own wedding: and began to think about how many doors are closed by marriage, how many old and childish dreams have to be put away – and yet it does lead to a new life, and one, invariably, that is quite different from anything we might have

224

imagined.

These were my musings as the ceremony began. Would that they could have continued in a similar vein! But then began that extraordinary series of events that has left me stranded here, and Uncle who knows where.

Uncle had just mounted the steps to the pulpit when a great shout was heard from without. And the horror of what they were shouting! For although the clamour was at first indistinct, it soon became apparent that their insults were couched in the most foul language.

Uncle, who had just begun with the reading of his sermon, faltered. 'Get on with it, man!' urged Dennis Lobb. And when this encouraged Uncle to go on with his sermon, the farmer shouted out again, but in a louder voice than before: 'Get on with the blasted wedding – never mind your randicle!'

So Uncle left off his preaching almost as soon as he had begun it, and stumbled down from the pulpit. By this time there was a continuous hammering at the door. The locked door would have been enough to keep the protesters out, I am sure of it, but they were now making so much noise that the exchange of marriage vows was quite drowned out by it. And no sooner had Uncle pronounced both couples man and wife – to a mere spattering of applause, for his congregation was anxious, and scarce able to follow the ceremony because of the commotion outside – than he stepped forward and beckoned several members of the church to join him. They stood in huddled consultation, but what was said was soon whispered round the pews; I heard it from Eliza Purvey, who was sitting on my left. Uncle had decided to invite the protesters into the church to hear their grievances. Nor was I reassured by the uneasy smile that Uncle gave me as he and Farmer Lobb passed by on their way to the porch, for Uncle looked quite at a loss at how to deal with this rude intrusion into his little church.

When Mr Lobb slid the bolt and pulled the porch door open, the hollering ceased immediately. No doubt the old biddies were taken unawares. After a muttered exchanged Uncle led the way back towards the chancel, followed by the protesters, with Dennis Lobb bringing up the rear.

When he reached the chancel step, Uncle asked the Lobbs and the Ruans to move from the front pews and bade the intruders sit down. When they had done so, he addressed them sternly: 'You have seen fit to ruin these poor people's wedding day. Now what is it that you want?' However, given that he had every cause to rebuke these rabble-rousers, and even to send for a magistrate, his invitation could scarcely have been more conciliatory.

It was not an easy interview. First the old man leapt up, flapping his fist at Jemma. As he began to shout I recognised him: it was that strange little man who helps Uncle with the bees. 'The blessed church should be drownin' witches, not marryin'um. She's the one that brought the plague upon us – we know all about that there giddy-'oss from foreign parts. Mrs Tredennick here have seen it all. Though he weren't no more than a babe, he picked that hossy up and brought it into our homes the way that flighty gyppo queen in olden times did carry a viper to her bossom. That's how the cholera was snuck into Porthcado. Besides, who was the first patient in Mudge's hospital?' – he jabbed his finger at Jemma – 'and bain't she the boy's own aunt? No wonder she were the first to fall sick – she were living under the same slates as the 'fectious lad! And now Parson's blessin'er up for marriage n' sendin'er off to Demon's Land '

As I was beginning to piece his fantastical beliefs together they all began to shout out at once, so that their tirade became as confused as the noise they had been making without. It seemed that because the Lawsons had suffered so dreadfully from the epidemic, and Jemma had been the first patient here in Uncle's hospital, she was now being accused of deliberately introducing it. But as their jabbering diminished, one voice could be heard loud above the rest – it was that of the old hag: 'You'm through with Lancaradoc, Parson. We'll torch this bastard church, then see what the Excise make of the skellingtons they find in the crypt.'

How Uncle would have responded to these new accusations I do not know, for just then the beekeeper leapt from his pew and lunged at Judy Ruan, who, of all the wedding party, happened to be standing closest to the protesters. She let out a scream that was loud enough to rattle the glass. And though her attacker was soon thrust back into his seat, he had been able to grab the sleeve of Judy's dress and rip it, so that it hung half off from where it was torn at the shoulder. Uncle's voice boomed out in anger: 'Ye Gods and little fishes! May I ask you people to remember where you are?' He stepped forward and put an arm around the younger bride.

However, even this protective gesture was too much for Mrs Lorneville. She stepped past Farmer Lobb and stood in the centre of the aisle. 'Now you listen here, Mudge. I, for one, will not stand by and listen to you protecting these thieves and miscreants. Why, I have never known such brazen impudence in a parson – taking advantage of a widow's loneliness to importune her with the most unseemly advances, while living openly with a girl from the village, and now I hear that you are in league with these ruffians to succour their illicit trade with France. Oh you may presume upon your legends of West Barbary to justify and disguise your lechery, but let me remind you that this is the nineteenth century, Mr Mudge. Even in Lancaradoc it is the nineteenth century! And if you fail to recognise what that means, then I am sure your bishop will explain it to you. For believe me, I fully intend to write to him and describe what reprehensible behaviour you have been indulging in, and just what a libertine he has allowed to represent the established church in this parish.'

Uncle merely gawped at her in astonishment. I do not know what reply he would have made if Provis hadn't taken Mrs Lorneville by the elbow, and whispered something in her ear – something which caused the grand dame from Godalming to blush to the roots of her hair.

It was at that moment that Mrs Tredennick leapt up like an avenging demon and shouted something at Uncle, which, though incomprehensible to his congregation, had the most devastating effect on our Rector. I thought he was going to collapse. I could see his knees buckle beneath him. He turned to me, his own flesh and blood, in the expectation, perhaps, that I could say something to sustain him at this moment of crisis, and though I stretched out my hand towards him, I could find no words to comfort him. We stared at one another for a second, and then he turned. Stunned into silence now, we watched him shamble down the aisle, head bowed, then duck out through the open door. When he had gone, the congregation turned towards me; no doubt they expected me to follow Uncle outside – for was I not, after all, his own flesh and blood?. Yet I could not. I sank to my knees and wept.

Percy, we must be brave. I have much to tell you that cannot be put in a letter. Some of what I have to say you have long suspected – that I know. But my faults are more grievous than anything you can have guessed at. If I write this now, it is so that I shall not be able to draw back from telling you everything when we meet.

It was Jemma who led me out of that place. She sat me up upon the wagon, between herself and her husband, and put her

228

arm around me. And though I could not bring myself to speak as we drove out to Trebarton, I was conscious that I had never received a greater kindness.

Uncle came in with the last of the guests. He must have walked from Lancaradoc. Fresh air and reflection seemed to have restored his spirits, for he was in a sanguine, even jovial mood. However he was drinking heavily. Moreover, when we mounted the carts to accompany the Veens to the sea-town I called out to invite him to sit with me. And hear me though he must have, he turned and clambered up behind Purvey, the carter, who had a flagon of brandy to share. I felt my cheeks redden, and dared not trust my voice to offer the small coin of conversation to my neighbours, for I had received a deliberate snub.

It was only when we drove into the yard at Polgarrick, having bid the Veens farewell, that his absence was noted. And despite the several jests that Barret's wedding brew had done for him, and that he must be sleeping off its effects somewhere, I fear that the real reasons for his leaving us are more sinister. What he will say tomorrow I know not; however, he will be sober, and his interview with me is likely to be far from pleasant. He has just cause.

*   *   *

*(from **The Western Daily Mercury**, September 28th)*
Magistrates who convened at the Falcon Inn, in Porthcado, on Thursday 25th inst., have been unable to confirm Reverend Mudge's demise or to ascertain the exact nature of his departure from the parish. The Revd Richard Lancelot Mudge, Rector of Lancaradoc, disappeared, and is presumed to have drowned, after putting to sea in a barrel from Porthcado harbour last Saturday, an hour before sunset.

The Reverend Mudge conducted a double marriage service on the morning of the incident, in circumstances which were themselves unusual, as a party of protesters disrupted the ceremony, so that the wedding had to be hurriedly and indecorously concluded.

The Rector was last reported in the party accompanying one of the wedding couples, Mr and Mrs Veen, to the harbour, where the newlyweds boarded a lugger taking them to Plymouth on the first stage of their voyage to Australia. Amid the boisterousness of the Veens' farewell, no one witnessed Mudge's disappearance. It seems that although his sudden departure from the party was commented on by several of the remaining revellers, no clear picture began to emerge of what had happened until seven in the evening, when a barrel was sighted off Crad Head, a quarter of a mile beyond the harbour wall. The alarm was raised by Samuel Shepherd of Dolphin Street, but as most of the villagers had by this time set off to Polgarrick Farm to continue the nuptial festivities there, vital time was lost before a rescue party could be organised. According to Mr Shepherd's account, two large white birds were perched on the lip of the barrel, obscuring a clear view of the rector himself; his fantastical description of the scene – for Mr Shepherd insisted on describing these birds as 'white phoenixes, half swan and half albatross' – the fact that he had clearly been celebrating, together with his reputation for soft–headedness, were all motives which further delayed the rescue operation.

The Reverend Richard Lancelot Mudge was last sighted off the Pinnacles shortly after sunset. And whereas several vessels put out at first light on Sunday morning, all efforts to recuperate either the priest, or his corpse, or the barrel, have proved to no avail. Excise officers along the coast have been alerted to the case, and as well as exercising their vigilance in the discovery of the clergyman's remains, are being urged to report the sighting of an empty barrel, or of any timbers constituting the wreckage thereof.

The motives for the rector's ill-fated voyage are far from clear. Little credit can be given to the several rumours abroad which purport to explain the tragedy. Some would connect the incident with the protests which took place at the marriage service earlier on the same day. Is it possible that the Reverend Mudge was forced to embark on his sea journey by the protesters? However, no witnesses have come forward to substantiate the theory that Mudge was forced into the barrel, or that he undertook the voyage against his will. Several of the wedding guests have remarked that Mudge seemed deeply agitated by a remark made by Cheryl Tredennick, his former housekeeper, so much so that on hearing it he left the church in a clearly disturbed state of mind. However, as no one appears to have heard the remark clearly, or to have grasped its intent, and as Mrs Tredennick herself refuses to discuss the matter, its relevance to the Rector's disappearance must remain a matter of speculation.

Another explanation for the clergyman's dramatic disappearance centres on the suggestion that the Revd Mudge wished to emulate the Celtic saints, of whom he was a notable scholar. As legends of these fanatical hermits include many episodes of their undertaking sea–voyages employing such unlikely craft as millstones, altars, roodscreens and dolphins, it is not beyond the bounds of possibility that the Rector of Lancaradoc thought fit to experiment with a similarly improbable vessel.

A third current of opinion holds that Mudge set out to sea after over-zealously lending his support to the wedding celebrations. And although the suggestion of an advanced state of inebriation reflects poorly on the clergyman's character, it would at least seem to provide the most rational explanation for last

231

week's tragedy in Porthcado.

The magistrates are to meet again next Friday, when it is thought that they will proclaim a verdict of death by misadventure. However, under such circumstances, the law stipulates that the presumed death cannot be registered with the courts for a year and a day following the date of the clergyman's disappearance.

*　*　*

Isobel to Revd. Penworthy, October

Dear Reverend Penworthy,

I owe you not only my heartfelt thanks, but also, I believe, an explanation; nay, several explanations.

You could scarcely have arrived at a more crucial moment, and if I greeted your appearance at the convent with tears of gratitude, and an almost hysterical account of the predicament you saved me from, yet even from the safe distance of Wiltshire, and with a fortnight to reflect calmly on the events of that afternoon, I am forced to reach the same conclusion: I believe that I was in grave danger in Fretton Hall – of exactly what I could not say, but it was all the more sinister for that – and it was only by your fortuitous arrival that I was able to make my escape.

As you may have gathered from my jabberings, I had gone to the Fretton nuns to ask for help with a translation, as I know my uncle had once done before me. The document in question was but a slip of paper, with a mere four words written upon in, and though I have enough Latin to pick out the gist of what was written, I could not comprehend its meaning, nor why such a short message should have been of such import that it had to be hid, or that one man had fled the country, in fear of his life, after it had passed through his hands. I only knew, or thought I knew, that it concerned those sinister nocturnal dealings for

232

which the county of Cornwall is famed, by which so many there are fed, and through which colossal fortunes can be made, albeit snatched from the shadows of the hangman's tree. In short, I believed that the document that had come into my possession was in the nature a smugglers' pact.

Why, though, the nuns should have reacted to this note the way they did, that is something I still cannot understand. But first I should explain how I came to have this coded message.

Yet I cannot – for that story depends upon another. For a week now I have been agonising over this: should I bury what I know in the silence of my heart, or should I relate my experiences, in the hope that others will be able to make more sense of them than I have done? For you see, Mr Penworthy, I believe I know why my uncle put out to sea.

Do you remember Mrs T's shriek at the wedding – the words with which she taunted him? They were incomprehensible to most who heard them, but not to me, and nor, when the penny dropped, to my uncle: 'There's many a spring flower who'll open her petals right up for a hoary sun, Parson. Aye, even for old Bellows' Breath.'

Behind that ugly and incomprehensible phrase there lies a tale – and it is my tale. If I tell it to you now, I hope that you will accept it in the spirit of a confession, both because it explains why my uncle chose to leave us as he did, and because I hope to rid my conscience of an unbearable weight of guilt.

I do not know, Mr Penworthy, how far you are acquainted with my story. That I first came to Lancaradoc to have a child, and that this was the same child brought up by the Lawsons, this much, no doubt, is common knowledge, and has been part of the parish's beer-house tittle-tattle for the past three years. More fool me, then, for thinking I could return and play the lady.

233

What is not known, is the identity of the father of that child. For I had told no one. Nor that the child was conceived from such spite and shame and vanity, the result of such an act of monstrous selfishness on my part, that I denied his existence even to myself, and knowledge of the facts of his conception to all the world. How, then, Mrs Tredennick came by my secret, and should blurt it out in public, I knew not.

You see, the child's father was my mother's husband, Arthur Kennington. That is the secret that Mrs Tredennick's words conveyed to my uncle. On the instant, I failed to understand them, but their import was clear enough – is it any wonder that learning this should have unhinged him? I had no idea, however, that this information would cause him to act the way he did. Afterwards, at the wedding breakfast, he shunned me: he was distressed, I could see that, and he took a great deal to drink. To tell you the truth, I was frightened, but my fear was for what he might say to me, not for any thought that he might be planning to harm himself. When he disappeared, I assumed he was sleeping it off somewhere. I fully expected I would have to face him in the morning.

That night I wrote to my husband. Events had forced me to do what it has long been in my heart to accomplish. I intended to make my husband a full confession, and wrote in such a way that – or so I thought – I would be committed to telling him the whole, sordid story.

How odd it is that two people can live side by side with the chill of a monstrous shadow between them, and yet carry on their lives as though nothing had changed! Yet so it is. I hinted to my husband that I had grim news to tell him, yet he has not the courage to ask me what it is, and I am too much of a coward to go through with telling him.

However, to return to events at Lancaradoc: on the

morning after the wedding, I walked down the valley to the sea town to post my letter at Miss Tingham's shop. And that is when I heard about my uncle. I saw a group of fishermen talking together on The Platt – and from the looks they gave me, I realised that something was amiss. So I asked them. I did not know who they were. I walked up, and said, 'Excuse me, but has something happened?' 'Aye,' said one, 'We fear your uncle be lost at sea.' Then the whole story came out. I said nothing. I went to Miss Tingham and posted my letter. After that I walked as far as Crad Head to clear my thoughts. That's when I made up my mind to speak to Mrs T.

I knew from uncle that she has been working for Parson Finch in the capacity of housekeeper. So I resolved to go out to Fretton and ask at the vicarage if he knew where I could find her. As it happened, she opened the door to me.

I could tell from the expression on her face that she too was ready to make a confession. I mean, her look was a mixture of fear, regret, and something akin to relief. 'You'm better come through', was all she said, and she led me to a little sitting room off the kitchen. It was a sort of converted larder.

When we sat down, in that cramped room, our knees almost touching, she took one of my gloved hands in both of hers: 'I'm sorry, dearie. I never knowed it would come to this.' I started to cry. It was the first time I had cried since I came to Lancaradoc, and once I began I gave myself up to such a fit of sobbing the like of which I have never experienced before. Believe me, Mr Penworthy, I am not usually given to such displays of emotion. Mrs Tredennick took me in her arms. When she had calmed me, we began to talk.

'I'm not proud of what I did, child. I were puddled, see. Proper puddled. Then, Cousin Hannah had been working on me all night – she can work up a lather better'n saddle soap. Of course, I was angry – proper angry. If I hadn't been she wouldn't have had nothin' to work on, would 'er? I were so irate with yourm uncle. What right had he to go blurtin' out to Provis that I be abroad, and where I be to? Smug old busket! So I guess it just ripped through me, like 'twer some great malodorous wind o' somat. Instinctive like.

'Listen, dearie, he weren't a bad man. Just foolish. And so wrapped up in his own little world that he weren't aware of what were going on round about 'im. Then when that great clod Provis got 'is mitts upon him, the parson's meddlin were like to cause pandemonium.'

I blew my nose. 'Was it? I know you have your own reasons for shunning Provis, but he is hardly Bluebeard...'

Mrs T flashed me such a look that I abandoned my attempts to mollify her. 'Bain't he? There's blood on that man's hands, dearie. Why do you think my husband fled and I be lying low?'

'Mrs Tredennick, do you really share your cousin's conviction that Provis is a murderer? A rogue, he may be...'

'And worse, believe you me!'

'... but this story of his murdering Plumley is utter nonsense.'

'Who told you that?' Mrs T glared at me – suddenly we were back in the church on the morning before: the woman, sober though she may now be, spat the words out with the same indignant hatred. 'Lord, so he did do some blabberin' – God rest his soul!'

'I'm sorry. He used to write to me. He was a very lonely man, Mrs Tredennick – he told me everything in his letters.'

'Everything? Don't 'spect he knew much, all alone in that old house. He certainly didn't hear much from me.'

'As I understand it, Uncle thought your husband left

236

because of the epidemic. However, he was persuaded by Mrs Hawke that Tredennick fled the parish for quite different reasons. Some story about finding a note, and how this concerned Sir Harry?'

'Aye, that were the long and short of it.'

'And what happened to the note?' Mrs T just shrugged her shoulders, as though she neither knew nor cared. I tried another tack: 'Do you believe that Provis murdered Sir Henry?'

Mrs T let out a long sigh. 'I tell you, I know nothing. What cousin Hannah knows is what she wants to know. She's always been that way.'

'Didn't your husband tell you anything? Perhaps a few words for you in private before he left?'

'All he said was, the less I knew, the safer I'd be.'

'And where is your husband now? Is he well?'

'Don't you worry, dearie. He's alright. That's one story that'll come right soon enough.'

So you see, Mr Penworthy, it was a very inconclusive interview. Mrs Tredennick was clearly keeping something back. I understood that she was frightened, but also that she neither knew, nor cared, for the intrigues of the village, except in that they had touched her husband and taken him from her. As for her part in causing my uncle's accident, she was guilty in much the same way, and to much the same extent, as myself: our behaviour had led him to act as he did, yet neither of us could have predicted, nor ever wanted, any such outcome. Not for the first time, I found myself sharing a curious fellowship with Mrs Tredennick. We are sisters in shame.

There was, however, one other question which I felt I had to ask before my interview was over. It was the question that had been on my mind all along. How did she know? About Dicky's father, that is. I asked her.

'Well for one thing, you'm as good as told me yourself. Leastways, you told me it wasn't Captain Edward, and if it weren't your true love, it had to be someone else. Then when Kennington came, and I saw that man holding the baby, as frightened as a rabbit given a baby ferret to look after, well that's when the penny dropped, like. I said something to him once, too, about a family resemblance, and I could see from his face – for it turned the colour o' scalded tripe – that I'd found yourm little secret alright…'

So there I had it: a lucky guess. Shortly after, I rose to go. We embraced at the door. 'Mrs Tredennick, if there is anything I can do for you – anything – you will let me know, won't you?'

'Don't you worry about me, dear. He'll turn up yet, you'll see.' At first I thought she meant her husband, but then I realised she was referring to Uncle.

'I do hope so, Mrs T. Goodbye.'

My hand was on the gate when she called out: 'Isobel, there was one little thing my husband did say afore he left: 'If anything happens to me, you remember this, the secret lies with the Pope'.'

'Meaning?'

'Drat if I know – 'spose that whatever this is all about, those French maids over the road, they'll know the answer.'

It was strange, but as I walked the three miles back towards Lancaradoc, between the high stone hedges topped with briars, where gateways and turnings offer occasional glimpses towards the Atlantic, whose wildness had swallowed up my uncle, it was those elusive words of the apothecary, rather than my uncle's plight, or my interview with Mrs T, that haunted me. The secret lies with the Pope?

I cannot say when the conundrum resolved itself, that strange eureka moment when one suddenly sees a familiar

238

problem in a new light, for I turned those words over and over in my head until they had become as familiar as a loose tooth, but I think it was while I was making the fire, which refused to take – for I found the rectory doubly cold, the sun having already set when I reached it – when a new understanding struck me. The Pope's Chamber! Perhaps Mr Tredennick had meant the Pope's Chamber. And late as it was, I lit a lantern and went out to the church.

However, once inside, my enthusiasm left me. The little candle I was holding threw long and tremulous shadows, and served only to emphasise the quantity of darkness beneath the cold church vault. I forced myself up the narrow twisted stair that led to the hidden room, but having glanced around its walls, I realised that my search would have to wait till morning. Besides, what was it I was expecting to find there? Deciding that I was on a fool's errand, agitated by solitude and frayed nerves, I went back to the rectory, and took what comfort I could from the spluttering fire.

Then, as is so often the case, the morning brought fresh hope. I was still laying curled beneath the sheets, when I remembered the work that Tredennick had done on the floorboards. It occurred to me that if were to have hidden anything in that room, he would have hidden it there. Surely that's why the Tredennicks had insisted on coming to the rectory before they fled the parish! I leapt out of bed, pulled on a dressing robe, pushed my bare feet into a pair of shoes and rushed out to the church, still in my nightgown. Moreover, I had the presence of mind to arm myself with a hammer from the kitchen – one of those clawed hammers – and once I was in the Pope's Chamber, it was the work of seconds to turn back the rug and pull up one of the white, unvarnished boards from the new section of the floor. I put my hand in and groped around: sure enough, there was a tea caddy, with, as I suspected, the note inside.

Perdendo vobis Rosam do. I now know the words by heart, for I must have repeated them to myself a thousand times. Though I may not have understood them, they made mention of the Rose – that much was clear enough.

Yet to have this slip of paper in my hand brought me no nearer to understanding its significance.

So you see, Mr Penworthy, it was not just inadequate Latin which took me to Fretton Hall, but a lingering suspicion that Mrs Tredennick may have been right: whatever the mystery surrounding the note, perhaps the nuns, after all, were party to it. And by confronting them with the note, I hoped to learn whatever secret they kept, if indeed, they knew anything at all, which I doubted.

I was shown straight into Mère Agathe's private apartment. I was given tea. The abbess could not have shown more sympathy: would I like to stay as their guest until the time for my return to Wiltshire? Had I enough money for the voyage home? Could she send two of her nuns to look after the rectory until my uncle was found, as surely he must be? This diminutive lady, with her melodious French accent and dark blue eyes was so charming that my one thought as I listened to her was a wish to sketch her! I almost asked her, then and there, if she would like to sit for her portrait, but had the good sense to realise how whimsical and inappropriate such a desire would sound at such a time.

Throughout this interview, however, my thoughts were on the note. How was I to bring the subject up? Faced with so much solicitude on the abbess's part, it seemed almost callous of me to announce that I needed her help with a translation. However, while I was turning this problem over, Mère Agathe offered me the very opening I needed. 'But tell me, my child, given that we can be of no practical 'elp to you at such a distressing time, surely there must be some reason for your walking all the way to Fretton to see us?'

'Well, actually, Ma'am, there is...' I did not know how best to address a French abbess, and the 'Ma'am' came to me more or less instinctively. 'I understand that my uncle, the rector, asked you to help him with the translation of a commercial document.' Mère Agathe raised an eyebrow, clearly puzzled by the turn the conversation was taking, but I was determined to push on. 'I understand that one of your sisters wrote a letter for him in Italian.'

'Ma oui, Soeur Madeleine. But you do not wish to tell me that there has arrived a reply?'

Not wishing to commit myself to uttering any falsehood, I simply said that I would like to talk to the sister, if that were at all possible.

'Certainly. Come with me, and I shall have her sent for toute suite.'

The abbess led me downstairs, and showed me into the dining room, which is the room you found me in. Once I was left alone, I walked the length of the beautifully polished table, took out the note, which I had placed for safekeeping in my bodice, and laying it down at the far end of the table, smoothed it out with the back of my still-gloved hand. I hardly had time to consider what I would say to Soeur Madeleine before she appeared. I took it as a sign of tact on the abbess's part that the nun had been sent alone. She curtseyed from the doorway, although the look she gave me was hardly deferential; indeed, it was full of insolence. No doubt my reputation had proceeded me, and the young sister clearly believed that she had every right not only to judge me on what she may have heard, but to make that judgement plainly apparent. So it was that I felt myself blushing deeply as we walked towards each other.

'Good afternoon, Sister. I fear I may have misled Mère Agathe and have had you sent for under false pretences.'

'You mean, you do not wish to see me about a translation?'

'No, it isn't that. You see, it is a translation from Latin, not Italian. I suppose I could have asked anyone – even the abbess.' I saw the young nun's eyes light upon the slip of paper. I stretched over, picked it up and handed it to her. 'It is very short.' I am not sure what happened next. Or rather, as very little happened – perhaps it would be truer to say that I don't know how to describe what happened. Soeur Madeleine snatched the note from me and – how do I put this? – she seemed to read the words without even looking at them: '*Perdendo vobis Rosam do*'. She intoned the words in such a way that it didn't sound like Latin at all. And as she spoke she took a step backwards, away from me, clutching the note as though she were afraid I would snatch it back from her.

'What is it? What does it mean?'

Soeur Madeleine was pacing backwards towards the door: 'I – do – not – know,' she said, delivering a word with each step she took, and her every action making it clear that she did. I was quite at a loss to understand her behaviour. Then, as she reached behind her for the handle, she added, 'This is something that Mère Agathe must see at once.'

She slipped out of the dining room and pulled the door to, silently. Then I heard her turn the key. She had locked me in. For a second I could not believe what I had heard. I rushed to the door and tried the handle. It refused to turn. At first I thought that it was the young nun's spite. Did she so dislike me? Was this

242

not a very wicked jest? I went to the windows, but they too required a key to unlock them. I sat, too dazed to understand what was happening. Then, however, I heard footsteps on the stair. Voices. Soeur Madeleine was talking to the abbess. The conversation was held in a whisper; they were outside the door. They spoke in French, but I could catch none of it. Clearly, though, this was more than just the whim of that spiteful, insolent nun. It had something to do with the note. But what? I forced myself to concentrate, but couldn't. *Perdendo vobis Rosam do* – what did it mean? Losing, I give you the Rose. What was it that Hannah Hawke had said? It was about that ship. Plumley had betrayed the ship to the excise. This was Plumley's house. Somewhere, I knew, there had to be a connection. But where? How? I could make no sense of it.

And what did they mean to do with me? Locking me up, keeping me captive in a nunnery? It was ludicrous – it was positively medieval, like a scene from a gothic novel! I swear, it must have been more than half-an-hour that I was in that room. Locked in. I am sure, too, that I did not feel afraid. I was confused, generally perplexed. But above all, angry, angry at the very impudence of it.

It was only when I saw you pass the window that I realised how afraid I really was. What if you did not hear me? Or were a party to their mischief? Whatever did you think, seeing my contorted face at the window, hollering and banging with my fists against the casement? And yet to me it seemed an eternity before that door was opened.

There, Mr Penworthy – I have told you all I know. Perhaps you may make some sense of this tale, where I have failed to. I believe that you are an honest – nay – a righteous man. I would ask you to look to Mrs Tredennick, for after my experience, I too am convinced that there is sinister work afoot at

Porthcado, and that if she feels that the convent will offer her a safe refuge from whatever evils she may be exposed to, I believe that she is sorely mistaken. I leave it to your judgement, as to how much of what I have written you will reveal to her, Mr Penworthy, but please, do what you can to protect her. Tell her, too, that whatever wrongs she may imagine that she has done me have been forgiven. I am her friend – as I know that you are mine.

* * *

Revd. Penworthy to Isobel, November

Dear Mrs Wattling,

Your letter has given me much to think over, but as for your expressions of gratitude, believe me when I tell you that they are misplaced. I did nothing to effect your rescue. It is Providence that you have to thank for that. Indeed, at the time, your predicament scarcely registered with me, and though I noticed that you were highly fraught, I had little idea of what lay behind our meeting at Fretton Hall.

Undoubtedly, you have done the right thing in unburdening yourself to me as you have done: it is always best to follow the dictates of one's conscience.

When sudden tragedy overcomes a loved one, it is only natural that we blame ourselves. But do not, I beg you, judge yourself too harshly. Even if your surmises concerning your uncle's departure are true, then the more are you to be pitied, for this tragedy has been added to the monstrous crime committed against you. My dearest child, I have lived long enough in the world to know how easily and how often innocent young women are taken advantage of by unscrupulous men.

Moreover, I would advice you to think long and hard before you talk of these matters with your husband, for I can only see a great deal of suffering resulting therefrom. You have, I understand, a daughter to think of: what might be the consequences of your confession on her? And lest this advice seem to contradict what I have just written with regard to following your conscience, may I remind you that you have already offered to make your husband a full confession, when you wrote to him from Lancaradoc. If he does not press the matter, then neither should you. Take up the twenty-second chapter of Genesis, and reflect that you too have been tested: once the Lord's angel saw that Abram was prepared to offer up his own son, Isaac, the Lord, in His mercy, did not require him to make such a sacrifice. I believe your predicament is similar to that of the prophet: when the small voice urged you to make a full confession, you were willing to obey it; you are not, it would seem, given your husband's reluctance to broach the issue, now called upon to sacrifice your family, and neither their, nor your own, happiness.

As for your treatment at the hands of the nuns, at first I was mystified, and I must confess that initially I was inclined to believe that the story of them locking you up was surely a figment of your imagination, and the result of the considerable stress that you must have been under, following your uncle's disappearance.

Nevertheless, armed with what you have told me, I made it my resolve to talk with Mrs Tredennick. And as a prelude to that, I went over the details of your letter again and again, until I came to a very different interpretation of the events that you describe. To begin with, I believe that you are quite wrong to think that the note is some form of smuggler's pact – for I cannot give credence to the idea of the Roman Sisters meddling in such activities. Indeed, I will go further: I suspect that Plumley's note has nothing to do with the impounded ship at all, and that Provis, rogue though he may be, is, in this, an innocent victim. Hannah Hawke's obsession with Amos Provis borders on madness. You yourself suggest that not even Mrs Tredennick was convinced by her cousin's accusations.

And that, indeed, was a point on which I questioned her at great length when we met. I had only to elude to her cousin to see that she wishes to distance herself from Mrs Hawke, and that the debauchery which led to her behaviour at last month's wedding has caused her an embarrassment from which she still smarts. I cannot say that I learnt much from our interview. As you have remarked, she has been living in great fear since her husband fled, and is reluctant to discuss him. And like yourself, I felt that she had very little understanding of the events surrounding his departure. However, one piece of news I did manage to obtain: Mrs T is about to leave us. She is to sail to Liverpool and from there to Canada, where she is to join her husband. He has sent her the money for her passage, and would appear to be prospering.

What the note may be, and why it is of such importance to the nuns, are questions which can only be answered by the apothecary. This being the case, I have taken the liberty of giving Mrs Tredennick a letter to take to her husband. If he deigns to answer it then perhaps the mystery will out. However, if my suspicion are correct, then I fear that this tale involves more wretchedness and depravity than has heretofore been suspected. Moreover, were the whole story to come to light, I dare say it would effect the entailments of Plumley's estate, which would explain why Mère Agathe has such a stake in silencing the truth. She stands to lose her beautiful Cornish convent, else.

Isobel, I implore you, endeavour to find peace of mind. Resign yourself to the duties and pleasures of family life. If you must dwell on the past, then look again at the verses I have drawn to your attention. Take comfort from the story of the Almighty's compassionate treatment of Abraham. As to events in Porthcado,

I shall carry on your investigations surrounding the mysteries of Plumley's note, and try to ascertain whether any crimes may lie behind them. And needless to say, should there be any news regarding you uncle, I shall write at once.

John Penworthy

*   *   *

Isobel to the Revd Penworthy, November

Dear Mr Penworthy,

Your letter, so full of concern, well-meant counsel and wise homilies, touched me deeply. Yet if I have once again assumed the role of a prosperous draper's wife and a devoted mother, it is as much through my own torpidity than as a consequence of your advice. In truth, I am exhausted. I move through my days in a pantomime, every gesture and expression performing their accustomed function, while my feelings are quite dead. Were I a more histrionic woman, or born to an earlier age, no doubt I would count myself among the damned. How else to explain the harm I have brought upon my own family? I am to blame for abandoning my son, for my uncle's disappearance, for ruining my step-father's peace of mind, and – were it not for your intervention – for destroying my husband and daughter's happiness, too. And yet I keep house, and sometimes even manage to smile.

However, on one point I must disabuse you. I am far from being the innocent victim of Mr Kennington's advances. He certainly intended to do me no harm. Let me set the whole story down, in part to clear his name, and in part to make the confession which I no longer dare to make to my husband.

Have you ever been in love, Mr Penworthy? Known the one person who completes you as surely as a key fits its lock? I have. It is an awesome experience, when the casket of true love springs open, to reveal not just the treasures of the heart, but the

247

discovery that these are made from the gemstones of our very destiny. Such a love can transfigure a life – as it should have transfigured mine.

It was Mother's meddling that ruined everything. For I was in love with a dashing young cavalry officer, and he was in love with me. He was high born – I dare say, in the eyes of the world, too high born for the likes of a girl such as myself – yet in spirit we knew we were equals. He was prepared to put his feelings for me before all consideration of his own status; and, young though I was, I was not afraid to give a woman's love to the man whom my heart recognised as its own. His should have been the child I was carrying when I first came to Lancaradoc.

However, Mother could see only the humiliation that such an alliance might bring to our name. For hers is a fearful and suspicious nature, and she was convinced that nothing but scandal could come of such an attachment. So she wrote to the boy's father imploring him to intervene, and when that proved ineffective, she wrote to a certain officer in my father's old regiment to hasten his posting abroad.

A fine example she has been! Her own marriage was the product of the nicest calculation. Arthur Kennington is a kind and cultured man, but more to the point, he is a moderately wealthy one. How Mother managed to snare him is quite beyond me. I can only suppose that Kennington thought no further than his basest needs, for she knows how to keep house, and, despite her years, has a trim figure, which she takes pains to dress. Are men really so fatuous? Did he not take the time to read her character? Could he not see how shallow and stupid and grasping she is? Or did he simply not care?

When I was younger, Mr Penworthy, I would shudder at the thought of being the child of such a woman. And yet life has shown me that I am worse. Mother may have a soul of pinchbeck, but at least by clinging to convention she has passed through the world as a respectable woman. Whereas my supposed talents and superiority have wrought havoc. Moreover, my foulest deed was the product of pure malice.

When Edward was offered a secondment to the ambassadorial guard in Lisbon I urged him to go; young love believes itself capable of such selfless sacrifice! It seemed a perfect opportunity for him: he would travel, it was an honourable promotion, and though he would hardly be likely to see active service in the villas and orange-groves of Portugal, yet, secretly, I rejoiced at the thought. The week before he left, he rode all the way from Winchester to Frome and took a suite at The George. It was the most blissful week of my life.

Nor, after he had sailed out of Portsmouth, to take up his duties in the southern sun, did our feelings for one another diminish one iota. We wrote every week. After the initial excitement of his posting had worn off, I could see Edward was becoming bored and despondent. His duties were minimal; he found the company of his fellow officers gross and boorish. For my part, I fretted the days away. Mother was to marry on New Year's Eve, and although it was a very quiet affair, the preparations for the event dominated Mother's conversation and our activities throughout that autumn and winter. At Christmas, Kennington came to Frome, accompanied by his three sisters. On my mother's side, there was only myself, and Major Pelham, my father's friend.

The wedding breakfast was held at The George – in that very dining room whose door I had tiptoed past on my assignations with Edward two months previously. And although there were but two men present, it was a very gay party, largely because the Major was so keen to see that the bride and groom were liberally toasted. It must be his fondness for gin which makes the Major such a fierce soldier, for, in our circle at least, he has always held the reputation of a formidable warrior, even though there is little in his sad eyes and pot–belly to suggest such martial qualities. But then his feats of prowess were performed at the Siege of Bilbao, and for the last twenty years he has worked at a desk in Sandhurst.

Mother sent the Major out into the passageway when he insisted on lighting that foul calabash of his, for she cannot abide the smell of it, and it was there – for I had need to powder my nose – that we were able to exchange those few words in intimacy which were to have such terrible repercussions. Or rather, it was Pelham's question to me, for I believe I made no reply.

He was leaning against the banister at the bottom of the stair. His scarlet tunic was open and revealed a linen shirt, which I remember thinking was in need of a laundress. His small face was almost the colour of his coat, and somewhat sweaty. In short, he was looking quite dishevelled and though I am fond of the Major, for he is Father's one surviving friend, and almost an uncle to me, I was rather vexed with him for overindulging himself to such an extent on what should have been a decorous family occasion.

'Well, my dear, how is your gallant captain enjoying Portugal?'

At the time, his question to me seemed innocent enough and although it unnerved me, it did so for reasons that were very different from those which came to obsess me later. You see, Mr Penworthy, in that hotel and on that occasion, it was Edward's memory, more than my mother's matrimony, that filled my head and my heart. But these were very private thoughts: I had not expected to hear his name mentioned by anybody else, and least of all by the inebriated Major Pelham. So when I heard this question, it was as if my lover's shade had suddenly walked down the passageway before me. Do you wonder that I had not the wit to reply? I may have smiled at the Major, but that, in my confusion, was all he had from me.

The nuptial celebrations finished without incident. Afterwards, we walked up Butts Hill in all our finery and keeping to the middle of the road, for it was the one day when we had a right to be noticed by the town; my mother and I, who had always led such a retired and modest existence at Frome, we were to have our one day as grandees.

A cab had been called for 4 o'clock, to take Mother and Mr Kennington to meet the Bath coach. I was to spend the week alone, or rather, with only Dottie for company, for she had agreed to move to Robins Lane for the duration of their honeymoon.

I cannot remember which day of that otherwise pleasant holiday it was, but one morning while I was at my dressing table, a suspicion crept into my head, which, the no sooner had it lodged there, at once became a conviction: why should Major Pelham have asked about Edward, unless Mother had mentioned him to the Major, and if she had mentioned him, might it not have been in connection with Edward's secondment to the Portuguese embassy? For Major Pelham works in the Commissions Office, and if anybody could, he would have been in a position to put Edward's name forward for such a tempting post as the one in Lisbon. Had Mother written to Pelham proposing such a plan? Knowing her as I do, the answer seemed obvious: of course she had.

You cannot imagine how I passed the rest of that week. I was so enraged I could scarcely sit down. I would not stay in the house. I must have walked the path to Mells half a dozen times, yet even that quaint excursion could bring me no relief. Dottie hid in her kitchen.

On the afternoon of their return, which was a Thursday, I took the first possible occasion to confront Mother. It was the hour between tea and dinner, and she was upstairs, unpacking. Kennington had been banished from the house with his cheroot. I walked in, without knocking – a discourtesy designed to provoke Mother – and asked her, straight out, why she had written to Major Pelham.

'I was only taking steps to protect you,' or some such nonsense – that was all her answer.

'You have a right to a husband and I do not, is that it?'

'His type would never marry the likes of you.'

'His type, Mother? You've never even spoken to him. He's too good for me, is that what you're saying? By which you mean, he is too rich. Wealth is the greatest good, isn't it Mother?'

'Child of mine, you have to learn some common sense. You can't live on dreams, you know – dreams only lead to destitution. And no daughter of mine is going to play the minx and the trollop.'

'You had no right to interfere! How could you deprive me of the one thing I loved above all else? You're not a mother, you're a monster. A damnable, selfish, narrow–minded monster.'

'Isobel, I won't be spoken to in that way!'

'Then I won't speak to you in any way.'

'Be reasonable, child. Look to someone like Mr Wattling. He dotes on you. And he has the wherewithal to make you happy. Moreover, he's not a man to trifle with your sentiments for a few months, then dash off abroad.'

'Dash off? It seems that you were the cause of that.'

'One day you'll thank me for what I've done.'

'Thank you? No Mother, I curse you for it. And not one day, either. Now. Today.'

And that was only the beginning – so it went on, for

hour after hour. The same ground was covered again and again, with only the screaming getting shriller, and the insults more irreversibly reckless. It was 10 o'clock when I left her, both of us tearful, exhausted and still smouldering with rage. Kennington ate his supper alone that evening.

The following morning, when I woke, Mother was out. She had gone with Dottie to the fish stalls in Market Place, as she always did on a Friday morning, and I knew that she wouldn't be back until midday. After breakfasting alone, I returned to my room and I locked the door. Why, I know not, for that is something I never do. (Or perhaps it is true that a part of me knew just what it was doing, some demon perhaps: that whole day I seemed to have been in a subterranean dream, obeying the ice-cold demon that had taken possession of me.) I took off my beige, check morning dress, and tried on the new ball gown that mother had bought me: it was bottle green, laced with black, and though mother insisted that the whole purpose of a ball gown is to get one noticed, it really was somewhat ostentatious. Then I sat at the dressing table and pinned up my hair. When that was done, I opened the drawer and took out the silver locket which Edward had given me, and which is the one material record I have of him. I descended the stairs. Mr Kennington would be in the front parlour with *The Times* and his cigar, as he always was in the hour after breakfast. As I went down the stairs my teeth were chattering, although it was not cold at all.

'Papa, may I disturb you a moment?' I had taken to calling him Papa by way of a joke. You see, from the first we had fallen into an easy relationship, forged in part by a natural alliance before Mother's outbursts; anyone less the stern father than Arthur Kennington would be hard to imagine.

He looked at me over his paper, and over his reading spectacles too. 'Of course, Isobel. What would you have me do?'

I held out the locket on its delicate chain. 'My fingers are so clumsy – and it has such a tiny clasp...' Turning to face the window, I put a hand to the back of my hair, to push it up even further. As he manipulated the tiny mechanism with his broad, flat nails, I could feel the warmth of his fingers at the nape of my neck. Rather than thanking him, I reached over my shoulder when he had finished and squeezed his fingers. Then I turned to face him and pressed his hand against my cheek. 'You do have beautiful hands, Mr Kennington,' I murmured. All of this might be taken as no more than the fond attention of an affectionate step–daughter; but then I took the tip of his ring finger into my mouth and sucked it, though only for a second – which could not. Before Mr Kennington had time to express the surprise he must have felt, even in his eyes, I broke off, and scampered upstairs, to change back into my morning dress.

While we lunched on the halibut that Mother had chosen for us, and which Dottie had steamed to perfection, I could feel Mr Kennington's eyes upon me, and it was clear that his appraisal of me was a little more interested than usual. I am sure that had I looked demurely down, and communed with my dinner plate, as a young girl is taught to, by the time Dottie had brought in her *charlotte aux pommes* this interest would have waned. However, I was conscious of the fascination I held for him at that moment, and moreover – though I'm ashamed to admit it – of the power I consequently held over my mother. So I returned his glances. I only meant to tease him.

When Mother suddenly announced, over coffee, that she intended to return to town for a pair of kidskin gloves she had noticed on Catherine Hill, and that she required Dottie to go with her, it was a quite unexpected departure from her usual routine. Nor could I say why, when they left the house, I did not retire to my room, as I usually do in the afternoon. Instead, I accompanied Mr Kennington back into the parlour.

What passed between us happened only the once. Mr Kennington was filled with remorse.

I believe I realised almost immediately that I was with child; or perhaps it was just that I knew I deserved to be punished for what I had done, and such a punishment was the worst, most fitting outcome I could conceive of. I and my step–father never exchanged another word. If Mother noticed how Kennington and I suddenly began to shun one another's company, she gave no sign of it. Or perhaps she put it down to my moodiness, the cause of which was to have a satisfactory explanation when, in early March, I confessed my condition.

The rest of the story you know, Mr Penworthy. Except that just before I left for Lancaradoc Edward wrote to me. He had resigned his post in Lisbon and was set on rejoining his regiment to see some active service against the Kaffirs. Of course he wanted to meet me before he left. I refused. What else could I do? I was in Cornwall and carrying another man's child. It broke my heart.

And in case you may be wondering how Mother squares her calculations, I wonder too. The creature came early. Yet even so, a full ten months had elapsed since Edward left for Lisbon. Perhaps she imagines he came back at Christmas for another clandestine tryst. Or perhaps she permits herself to think the unthinkable – that it could never have been Edward's child. I know that she will have calculated the dates a thousand times, for that is her nature. I also believe that her nature lacks the honesty to query whatever suspicions she must have stumbled on. Yet surely at night she tosses in a stew of misgivings as thick and noxious as my own. Or were her plans to marry me off to a well-healed clod like Wattling enough to satisfy her that all had worked out for the best?

255

1853

Dear Mr Penworthy,

Your letter gave me great pleasure as well as coming as summat of a surprise. I had not thought to hear from anyone in the old country. Porthcado seems another world away.

And yes, your letter finds me tolerable well and flourishing.

After nigh on a year on the St Lawrence, where I found employment clerking for a glue factory, I came on out to Canada West last spring, in the hope of returning to my own calling, and hearing that there is more opportunity to start up where the settlements are still raw. I have reached the town of Hamilton – a considerable place, though it is all wood houses and mud streets for the present. There is a new neighbourhood going up with the railway, and now that I have a license from the governor's department, it is my hope and prayer that I shall be able to open a chemist's shop here this coming year.

Tis considerable fair, this land of Canada, but the winters are shocking. How Mrs T will cope with her rheumatics I dread to think, but with my prospects now established, and on the upturn, it is my fervent hope that I can make her snug, and that we shall prosper in the few years that are left to us, for there is more opportunity here than in the old country, for all its being a wild and unpredictable place. There are plenty of Injuns and Frenchies, the one savage and the other uncivil, but there be many good Cornish folk here too, so that it be not nearly so far away from what we knew as I had feared.

As to your inquiries, why I marvel at how much you have

understood from that little slip of paper, though you may not be right on all particulars.

At first I thought I would not reply, seeing as how no good can come of raking over the embers of such a story. Yet, I found I could not leave it alone. So I have decided to set down what I know. But heed my advice, Mr Penworthy: no good will come of rekindling a flame from such black ashes. Nothing will bring back poor Roslyn, nor console her family – should there be any left to console – nor bring justice to those who have gained benefit from evildoing. Meddling in the affair has cost me dear, and I would not have a similar price exacted from a gentleman such as yourself. So I beg you to read what I have to tell you and to bury it in your heart.

You are right in believing that the 'rose' that the note refers to was not the ship at all, but the Cridden girl. Like yourself, I had occasion to rue the squalid end of such a comely maid, all the more so as I was with her the night she died. She were little other than a corpse when I was called for, and I could do no more than give her a draft o' laudanum to ease her pains, and even that she could hardly swallow, poor mite. Doctor Killigrew had botched his operation something dreadful, but there was nothing the likes of I could do but keep my mouth shut. Besides, it wouldn't be the first time a squire has used a servant girl this way. Leastways, that's what I thought when she died. If I'd known the whole story then, I like to think I'd of done different.

The truth came out when I tended Arnie for the cholera. When old Cridden told me, I could scarce credit it – I thought it was just the ranting of high fever. Besides, it was a tale of such shocking villainy, even for old Plumley. Apparently, when the squire had gone through his money, yet still addicted to the gaming table, he offered the maid as his stake, on the understanding that his debts were to be cancelled should he win. Poor Roslyn was a silly goose, and forward, and no doubt too young to know the danger she were in. Moreover, the wager was repeated on a number of nights, and several of the players took advantage of the squire's offer – with the cards always going against him. So Roslyn was reduced to harlotry, and Plumley no better than a pander.

As I say, when her father told me I was disinclined to believe him; a man'll speak no end of nonsense when the delirium of chronic fever is raging through his brain-pan. But he sent me over to his sideboard and made me open the bottom drawer, where the stewin' pots were kept. There, under a lining of broadsheets, I felt around as he asked me to and fished out the note. Once I'd seen it I believed him alright. It was just like Plumley to scribble his wager in Latin. Anyways, Cridden croaked up and asked me, should anything happen to him, to take that note to the nuns, to show 'em how they came by that fancy house they were livin' in. It was clear to the both of us that he were dyin', but he still had the strength to spit upon the flags and curse them, and curse their religion too. I didn't make my promise lightly, either, for I realised that I'd have to do what I swore to, for I knew he wouldn't of seen the morning. And nor did he. Yet I accepted drekkly, not because I shared his detestation of popery, but because he were a good sort at heart, and did not deserve to of had his life blighted the way it had been. What I never expected was that my attempts to carry out Cridden's last wishes would have landed me in such deep water, or I would of thought twice before I gave my word.

But then he died, and I had the note, and I were in a right quandary. I mean, I could hardly just walk into Fretton Hall, fling down the note, then say, 'Well ladies, this here doesn't exactly do you credit – neither you, nor your religion,' though that seems to have been about the extent of Arnie Cridden's intentions.

So I did what I always did when I find myself in a tight corner: I went off to talk it over with my good wife. Only when I caught up with her, she were out to Hannah's place, and I hardly could get a word in before that daft old biddy started up with how the note were proof that Plumley sold out to the excise men, and how Provis hanged 'im for it. When she starts off on one of her tirades against Provis, there's never no stoppin'er. So I thought again and decided to keep my mouth shut. Just as well I did, as it turned out, for there's some affairs that men shouldn't burden their womenfolk with, and this turned out to be one of 'em.

I decided in the end that all I could do was go and speak to their Mother Superior, tell her everything I knew, and leave it at that. Leastways, that's what Arnie had asked of me, and though I couldn't see that anything would come of it, neither for better nor for worse, that would be the end of it. Just shows how wrong you can be! That Mother Agatha listened to what I had to tell her alright. I'd even of said, she were genteel and understanding. To my eyes, she were remarkably unruffled, though not exactly unconcerned: the first time she spoke, after she'd heard me out, it was to ask after Roslyn's family. I told her that to my mind there weren't no Criddens remaining. So she thanked me and concluded with much sighing and remarks about how the Good Lord manages to bring forth good out of evil, and such like, and I thought it were all genuine. As at times I still do.

I still can't fathom out how much Parson Finch was acting alone, or how much he and those nuns were acting in cahoots. But the fact is, that same evening, when I were on the road between Fretton and Porthcado, somewhere up on that bald hill above Winnard's Mill, I hear an almighty braying of hounds.

Twas a funny time to be out huntin, I thought to myself. Then I realise that they were only a couple of fields away and heading drekkly towards me. So I scurried up the hedge bank to let them pass. Only they don't. They come pouring in around me like the hounds of hell. For a moment I even thought it was the barghest, sent to rip out my soul. Only then I see Parson Finch coming through the far gate on that grey mare of his, with a whip in his left hand, and I realise that this is trouble alright, but it bain't no supernatural trouble. The old crock rides out into the lane, looks me coolly up and down then flicks his whip at me. It goes off like a gunshot right up against my ear – so close I can feel the wind of it.

'I want that note,' is what he says, looking me coolly in the eye.

'I ain't got it on me,' was how I answered him, even though it were in my breast pocket right enough. I don't know what made me lie, only there's some men so bent that you know they're never to be trusted with the truth – and Finch were one of 'em.

So he gives a whistle and three of his curs leap up the hedge at me. Thank God I'm armed with a stick, because I manage to fend two of 'em off. But the third gets a grip of my ankle. I'm wearing stout boots so he draws no blood, but even so, he's a big brute and I'm petrified of being dragged down from the hedge and falling among the pack of em. I let out a scream. After Finch has watched me struggle he calls him off with another whistle. 'I'll be by for it tomorrow, Mr Tredennick. Think on: there wouldn't be much left of you if you should have an accident with the hounds. Though I dare say it would a quick enough way for you to join the Lord.' And so saying, he gives a tug of the reins, the horse turns, and he's away, the hounds yelping and scurrying along behind him.

260

It's dark long before I reach home. And though I'm in a funk alright, I'm not so shaken as I can't reason. Indeed, on that long night walk back to town I get to thinking as I've never had to think before. Lucid. First off, I need to get away: I've no doubt at all that Finch would carry out his threat. I could see it in his eyes. Second, even if I give him the note, I'm just as like to meet with his accident. Because it occurs to me just what this is all in aid of: suppose the truth about Roslyn were to come to light? Plumley and Killigrew could still be found guilty of her murder. And if they were, then Plumley's will would be revoked and his estate fall forfeit to the Crown. The note is the one piece of material evidence the case would rest on. And moreover, having seen poor Roslyn on her deathbed, I'd be the prosecution's key witness. I have the power to wrest Fretton Hall from the nuns. Moreover, by turning up at the convent like that, it must of looked as though I were out to threaten 'em. Then I realise that that's the way Arnie had meant it to look.

Is it any wonder I fled for my life, Mr Penworthy? I'd been taken for a fool, and now I had to pay the price. Well, now was the time to wise up. First thing I had to do was put the evidence somewhere safe, and second, I had to scarper pretty darn quick. There'd be time to think what to do after I'd saved me own skin.

I got away, alright. Only when I get a letter from Mrs T three month later, I'm blowed if she hadn't gone to the one place I should of warned her off – straight out to Fretton! By telling my wife nothing, and letting her believe whatever her cousin could concoct, I had only thought to protect her. I tell you, I've been so worried all these months, my stomach's turned rotten beyond all physic that I know of. So if I'd ever of thought of telling what I knew before now, thinking on how Mrs T were out to Fretton were enough to make me keep my trap shut.

261

And now we're together again on the other side o' the world, it's like we were together in heaven, though I hope when we do get there, if ever we do, it'll not be half so cold as Canada, nor half so hot as that other place, neither.

So there you have it, Mr Penworthy: Fretton Hall's a tainted place, and the Roman Church's entitlement to it is based on a monstrous crime. But as I said, you'd be best to leave all well alone, especially now the note has been given up to those who have best cause to keep it hid.

*　　*　　*

Revd. Penworthy to Isobel, March

Dear Isobel,

Peace be with you, my child!

Forgive me for taking so long to make a reply. To tell you the truth, I was at a loss as to how to answer your letter. Remember, however, that time is the salve with which the Lord heals most wounds, even the deepest. For the rest, you must follow the promptings of your conscience.

I have today received an answer from Mr Tredennick, and have copied it out in full, so that you should know as much of the events you helped to uncover as there is to know. However, the apothecary is right: nothing can now be done to redress this dismal story, especially as you unwittingly gave up the only material evidence on which the case for justice could be made.

I have one other item of news for you, Isobel. It may prove to be significant, but I would caution against allowing it to raise false hopes.

On Friday last I was going over the month's accounts with Eliza Purvey; we were in the gallery at the back of the chapel, which, during the week, serves me as my office. Suddenly Sam Shepherd burst in, in a state of high excitement. 'Mr Penworthy, sir, you'm to come at once. They've come back. I see'd em. I see'd

262

em myself. Out to Cadoc's Zawn.' He was fair dancing around between the pews with excitement. I went downstairs to the boy and tried to calm him: more to the point, I tried to get some sense out of him, but as there's precious little sense in the lad to begin with, I soon gave up on a task that was hopeless. And though I was vexed by this interruption, I had little alternative but to fetch my cape and follow him. Outside it was a glorious day, such as our county is occasionally blessed with even in winter, with scudding clouds and choppy waves slapping against the hulls of those fishing boats that were left in the harbour. I hardly had time to appreciate the Lord's gift of such a fine morning, when Sam dashed off up the cliff path at a trot that would have taxed a man half my age. But the idiot boy had no pity, and we were soon round the point and down and up again to the lip of the zawn. When we reached the cliff–top, he flung himself onto the ground with such energetic abandon, that for one dreadful instant I thought he meant to throw himself headlong over that awful chasm. But no! It was but his excitement, and the lack of any understanding of the risk he was exposing himself to, in cavorting on the cliff edge in such a reckless fashion. For my part I sank down on my knees a good six feet behind him, and slithered forward on my elbows, the most cautious creature that ever crawled upon its belly.

I looked down: below, the cove lay half in shadow, half in brilliant sunlight. The curling breakers beat upon the yellow sands, throwing up plumes of spray from the grey rocks at the point. It was a magnificent sight, I grant you, but no different from the eternal drama to be found upon a thousand Cornish beaches.

As I stared down, I became aware that Sam, beside me, was making strange little gobbling sounds, which at first I took for some uncontrollable animal sobbing, until I realised that they were, instead, a weird species of laughter. He was chortling with excitement. 'What is it, Sam?'

For an answer, Sam sprang up and rushed back from the cliff edge. When he reached the footpath, which was about a dozen yards behind us, he began scrabbling around for stones. When he had gathered a dozen or so, he came back and knelt down, his knees now so close to the cliff edge that I was even more fearful for his safety than before. He hurled the first of his stones down into the chasm below. As it ricocheted off the cliff walls, a flock of choughs flew out in a ruckus of aggrieved squawks. With the second, four or five herring gulls took off from the sands to glide out over the breakers. But peering down at the beach, I could still see nothing. I was just considering what I should say, by way of a reproach which would nonetheless not upset the simpleton unduly, when suddenly his arm shot out, and Sam pointed to the far side of the beach. There at the entrance to Bartlett's cave, in a section of the cove that was wreathed in the deepest shadow, something moved. I could make out two pale and ghostly bundles.

'See,' said Sam, a few seconds later, as the two white peacocks crossed the divide between shade and sun: 'They'm come back. Looks like Rector's phoenixes have flown back to Porthcado.'

So there you have it, Isobel. Your uncle's birds have returned to us. Whether this means that your uncle is still alive, I cannot say. But to see those two magnificent peacocks strut out into the sunlight and watch them spread their magnificent tail fans, like the white sails with which Tristan's helmsman was supposed to announce Isolde's return, well, my lady, then and there, my breast was filled with hope and joy.